P9-DFF-427

THE REAVERS

ASHLAND PUBLIC LIBRARY
66 FRONT STREET
ASHLAND, MA 01721

THE REAVERS

George MacDonald Fraser

ALFRED A. KNOPF   NEW YORK   2008

THIS IS A BORZOI BOOK
PUBLISHED BY ALFRED A. KNOPF

Copyright © 2007 by the Estate of George MacDonald Fraser

All rights reserved. Published in the United States by Alfred A. Knopf,
a division of Random House, Inc., New York.

www.aaknopf.com

Originally published in Great Britain
by HarperCollins Publishers Ltd., London, in 2007.

Knopf, Borzoi Books, and the colophon are registered
trademarks of Random House, Inc.

Library of Congress Cataloging-in-Publication Data
Fraser, George MacDonald, [date]
The reavers / by George MacDonald Fraser.—1st U.S. ed.
p.   cm.
ISBN: 978-0-307-26810-5
1. Nobility—Fiction. 2. Great Britain—History—Elizabeth, 1558–1603—
Fiction. 3. Scottish Borders (England and Scotland)—Fiction.
4. Border reivers—Scottish Borders (England and Scotland)—Fiction.
5. Triangles (Interpersonal relations)—Fiction. I. Title.
PR6056 R287R43 2008   2007050904

This is a work of fiction. Names, characters, places, and incidents
either are the product of the author's imagination or are used fictitiously.
Any resemblance to actual persons, living or dead, events,
or locales is entirely coincidental.

Manufactured in the United States of America

First United States Edition

In remembrance of the law officers
"expert borderers"
John Forster, Lance and Thomas Carleton, Robin and John Carey,
Eure, the Scroops, Buccleuch, Carmichael, Hunsdon

and their equally expert adversaries
Ill-Drowned Geordie, Nebless Clem, Curst Eckie, Fingerless Will,
Evilwillit Sandie, Crackspear, Buggerback, Bangtail, Sweetmilk,
Gib Alangsyde, Auld Wat, Cleave-the-Crune, Sore John,
Wynkyng Will, Dand the Man, Hob the King, Unhappy Anthone,
David-no-gude-priest, Wantoun Sym, Dog-pyntle, Out-with-the-
Sword, Willie Kang Irvine, Jock of the Side, Black Ormiston,
Ower-the-Moss, Gav-yt-hem, Jock of the Peartree, Skinabake,
Mouse, Bull, Lamb, Shag, Richie Graham, Thomas the Merchant,
Sandie's Bairns, Red Rowan, and many others, because
it would be a shame to forget them

FOREWORD

This book is nonsense. It's meant to be. If I were a "serious" writer, which I'm not (I have the word of an eminent critic for this, and I know he meant it as a compliment, because he put the word in quotes) I might describe it as an octogenarian's rebuke to a generation which seems to have forgotten fun and become obsessed with misery, disaster, illness, operations, violence, climate change, guilt, obesity, cookery, football, racism, politics, and a general sense of doom. But not being serious as the literary world understands the term, I can offer no such pretentious excuse. *The Reavers* is simply G.M.F. taking off on what a learned judge would call a frolic of his own.

It began with a novel I wrote fourteen years ago, *The Candlemass Road*, an Elizabethan swashbuckler set on the Anglo-Scottish border. That in turn had its origin in a play written much earlier; it was never produced, so I used its plot for *Candlemass*, which was kindly received by readers and critics, being full of bloodshed, brutality, treachery, and betrayal. By one of those ironies of the writing business, I was then able to turn it back into a play, for BBC Radio.

So much for *Candlemass*, a plain enough tale, but since I can never resist comic experiment, and the wilder the better, I found myself considering a different approach, first imagining and then inevitably writing *The Reavers* as a fantasy in the style of another book of mine, *The Pyrates*. Both are eccentric, as advertised by the fanciful archaic spelling of their titles; both are completely over the top, written for the fun of it. In that spirit I offer *The Reavers*, with gratitude to the happy band of *Pyrates*-lovers and any others of like mind, now that sufficient time has elapsed for the original *Candlemass Road* to slip quietly into the shadows of bygone fiction.

G.M.F.

THE REAVERS

It was a dark and stormy night in Elizabethan England, a night of driving rain and howling wind, God save the mark! when even the stately oaks bowed their great heads and giant ash trees clawed with spidery fingers at the tempest, duck ponds and horse-troughs were lashed into foam, chimbley pots toppled on the heads of honest citizens, staring owls clung to their perches with difficulty, and broom-riding witches circled crazily over blasted heaths, stacked and waiting in vain for clearance to land, Steeple Bumpstead was whirled away leaving a gaping hole in the middle of Essex, cows and domestic animals were overturned, slates and washing flew every which way, and stout constables, their lanthorns awash, kept out of the way of sturdy beggars and thanked God they were rid of a knave, leaded casements rattled in stately Tudor homes, causing the noble inhabitants to give thanks for roaring fires and bumpers of mulled posset what time they brooded darkly about sunspots, global warming, and the false forecasts of Master Michael Fishe, he o' the isobars, who had predicted only light airs gentle as zephyrs blowing below the violets, would you believe it, while out yonder, in lonely hamlet and disintegrating hovel, the peasantry scratched their fleas and gnawed lumps of turnip and blamed it on the Almighty (poor churls, what did they know of warm fronts and depressions o'er Iceland?) or on the hag next door, her wi' the Evil Eye and black familiar Grimalkin and devilish spells, curse her, and wagged their unkempt heads as haystacks and livestock crashed through their thatches, and asked each other in fearful whispers whether such raging fury of the elements portended the end of the world, or the Second Coming, or another bloody wet week, and agreed that it was alle happenynge, gossip, and where would it end?

Well, that takes care of the weather, and before meteorologists start hunting through their almanacks for the date of this monumental tempest, we shall tell them that it befell on a certain February 2—but make no mention of the year, save that it was sometime between the foundation of Kiev University and the discovery of Spitzbergen, and they can make what they will of that, my masters. Why such reticence? Because the moment a romantic story-teller starts committing himself to actual years, and similar pretensions to strict historical fact, his character is gone, being at the mercy of nit-picking critics who will take gloating delight in pointing out (for example) that Attila the Hun couldn't possibly have studied Monteverdi's second madrigal book, because it hadn't been published in his day, see? Nor were pretzels available in the '45 Rebellion. Out upon them, pedants.

Another reason is that many of the principal characters in our little moral social fantasy wouldn't have known what year it was anyway, they being carefree primitives chiefly concerned with sheer survival, clobbering their neighbours, armed robbery, animal (other people's animals) husbandry, protection racketeering, arson, kidnapping, irregular warfare, and general mischief, all of which, being natural poets, they described as "shifting for a living." Now and then they pondered about which religion they ought to belong to, inevitably deciding that on the whole they'd let the hereafter take care of itself, thus freeing themselves for any amount of boozing, guzzling, dicing, hunting, racing, and swiving, this last being a popular pastime of the period, and still carried on today under a variety of names.

Indeed, they were a stark and ignorant lot, and if you'd asked them what day it was, it wouldn't have occurred to them to reply "February the second, good neighbour"; they would more probably have responded with "Candlemass, ye iggerant booger," because that is how they talked, and they were used to reckoning by their old Christian festivals in that happy, far-off time when there were no desk diaries or wall-planners (though even then the precocious Flemish schoolboy, P. P. Rubens, may well have been making furtive sketches of sporty nudes in his exercise books, in anticipation of the *Playboy* and Pirelli calendars).

Not that everyone was backward and unlettered in Good Queen Bess's day, mind you. Sir John Harington, for one, was a man of much learning and science, but since at the time our story opens he had just installed the world's first flush toilets in Her Majesty's palace of Richmond, and the royal apartments were ankle-deep in water, with little Tudor plumbers going hairless, hammering pipes and crying "Good lack!" and "Where's the stopcock, missus?," he had more to do than worry about what year it was. He plays no part in our tale, by the way, but has been introduced merely to provide a little period colour, like the scenes and characters in the next couple of pages. Irrelevant they may be, but they are familiar and therefore may be useful in evoking the spirit of the Elizabethan Age and letting the audience know what is going on behind the scenes of our tale.

So . . . on that tempestuous night of February 2, 15—, when Merrie Englande was being sore buffeted by storm, and the plumbers were warning a distraught Sir John that he was flying in the face of nature and the union wouldn't let them mop up . . .

In the Mermaid smoker, two playwrights were engaged in a game of envious one-upmanship, with Marlowe snidely advising his rival to get out of drama and into poetry ("because your Saturday-morning serials are a real dead end, I mean, three parts of *Henry VI*, for God's sake, people are beginning to ask what next, *Kemp and Somers Meet Henry VI?*") and Shakespeare was countering with back-handed compliments about *Dr. Faustus* ("loved the costumes, Chris") while wondering if he dared hi-jack the character of the grizzled old fatso at the next table, who was being extremely coarse and funny, and didn't look like the kind who would sue . . .

and at Richmond, Gloriana herself was standing for her portrait to Marcus Gheeraerts the Younger, in a raging temper and a tent-like gown of cloth of gold with enormous winged sleeves which she was convinced would make her look like a vulture about to take flight,* wherefore she would crop his ears, by God, and that went for that knock-kneed rascal Harington, too, him and his gang of splashing tatterdemalions wi' their honeyed promises and leave it to us, your grace, shalt have no need o' chamber-pots hereafter, forsooth! And that reminded her, that pack of upstarts in her Parliament needed instruction "not to speak every one what he listeth—your privilege is *Aye* or *Noe*." And it had better be Aye, or there would be a few by-elections pending . . .

while in his cabinet her minister, Lord Burleigh, was wrapping cold towels round his head as he struggled to make sense of a list of "those malefactoures of the name of Graham who doo infeste oure Skottische border," and finding it no easier because his agents' reports spelled the name variously Graeme, Grime, Grim, Gremme, Groom, and even Greene, godamercy, and wishing he had a computer . . .

a convenience which had not yet been invented, although had Burleigh but known it, the next best thing was in the office across the way, functioning smoothly between the ears of Sir Francis Walsingham, the original "M" who ran Elizabeth's espionage and dirty tricks operations, and was so secretive that if he wanted a new feather for his hat, he would buy three separate pieces at three different shops and sew them together in the dark. It cost him a fortune in sticking-plaster, and his bedraggled headgear cracked up the mocking gallants in Paul's Walk, but as Sir Francis dryly observed, you don't need to be in *Esquire* to combat the devildoms of Spain . . .

which at that very moment were preoccupying King

* See the National Portrait Gallery, and sympathise with Her Majesty.

Philip II in the Escurial, where he was scoffing pastry (as was his wont) and planning that second forgotten Armada which came to grief in 1597 in an unforeseen hurricane (loyal Master Fishe strikes again!) and wondering if it might not be a better idea to build holiday villas on the Costa del Sol and bankrupt the heretics by luring them into time-share deals . . .

while in Edinburgh another monarch, James VI (shortly to be James Numero Uno), was hugging himself with glee as he conned the proofs of his new sure-fire best-seller, *Daemonologie, or Alle Ye Ever Wantit Tae Ken Aboot Witchcraft But Were Feart Tae Speer,* a natural for the MacBooker—a confidence not shared by Master Napier down the street, who was wondering gloomily if his projected treatise on logarithms would even be noticed by the reviewers . . .

but at least he knew they would work, which was more than could be said for his fellow-savant in distant Pisa of Italy, where Galileo wasn't sure whether he'd invented the thermometer or not (that at least is how we interpret a cryptic entry in a learned work which states that sometime in the 1590s "Galileo invented thermometer [uncertain]") . . .

and in the far-off Caribbean a splendid old pirate was being laid to rest in his hammock by grieving shipmates who could not guess, as the deep sea swallowed him off Nombre de Dios, that far from being dead he would live for ever . . .

And while all these important things were happening, give or take a year or two, elsewhere an ingenious cobbler was creating the first stiletto heels, Henri Quatre was deciding that Paris was worth a Mass, an English eccentric named Fitch was removing his boots after *walking* much of the way home from Malaya, the game of cricket was receiving its first mention in print, an excited alchemist was identifying a new element and dreaming of Nobel prizes as he christened it "zink" (all unaware that Paracelsus had beaten him to it by half a century), Sir Walter Raleigh was encountering poisoned arrows on the Orinoco, a French physician diagnosed whooping-cough, an absent-minded Italian composed the first opera and promptly lost the score, religious persecution reached a point where *autos da fe* were causing industrial pollution and Jesuits were being wait-listed for priests' holes, Japan banned missionaries and invaded Korea, and English vagrants were making a bee-line for the new parish workhouses in the ill-founded hope that these would offer a relaxing change from delving, spinning, swinking, and being turfed out by brutal landlords.

None of which really matters to our story, except as a brief erratic survey of the distant background, and to set our narrative tone, which may already have convinced the reader that he has not stumbled on a supplement to the Cambridge Modern History. Far from it: this is just a tale, and if it takes occasional liberties of style and speech, who cares? If Shakespeare can have clocks striking in Caesar's Rome, and give his plebs the street-smart backchat of Tudor London, a poor romantick can surely have similar licence. If we seem to treat history lightly in this regard, that is not to say we are false to it; mad fancy may go hand in hand with sober fact so long as the two remain distinct. So, in confidence that you'll spot the difference, we return to that wild Candlemass night and our story, which is at last getting under way in a desolate waste on the Anglo-Scottish frontier, that blood-red Borderland where the laws of shrewd Queen Bess and canny King Jamy do not run, except for cover, and the motto of the wild frontier tribes (those carefree primitives to whom we referred earlier) is "Thou shalt want ere I want"—a widely held philosophy in any age and clime, recently imputed to the Thatcher and Blair governments, and to trade unions by employers (and vice versa), but only the old borderers were honest and dumb enough to inscribe it on their coats of arms, holler it aloud in their cups, and scribble it on the Roman Wall when the Wardens weren't looking.

A shocking place, the border, and for those unfamiliar with the works of Sir Walter Scott, a brief word of explanation may be in order. As any schoolboy and football supporter knows, England and Scotland beat the bejeezus out of each other during the Middle Ages (Bannockburn, Flodden, and all that), and those unfortunates caught in the middle (i.e., the borderers) were ravaged, savaged, and put upon to such an extent that, when peace finally broke out around the 1550s, they found it uncongenial, and continued to practise the techniques they had learned over three centuries (murder, armed robbery, cattle rustling, extortion, rape, ravagery, savagery, etc.). Well, it was the only trade they knew, and better fun than farming, and if in consequence the border country made our modern inner cities look like eighteenth-century drawing-rooms, the borderers didn't mind, because anarchy was what they were used to.

The English and Scottish governments, of course, denounced this state of affairs as "totallie unacceptable"—which meant, as it still does, that they accepted it wholesale, and made only a few futile gestures, like confirming (under a sort of Anglo-Scottische Agreement) a special code of laws for the area, which didn't work, and setting up international commissions which drank deep and stuffed their guts at a safe distance in places like Kendal and Peebles Hydro, surfacing occasionally to issue joint communiqués and assure broadsheet conferences that "thaire wolde bee noe surrender to terrorisme."

Now and then the March Wardens, sorely tried and underpaid officials with inadequate forces, got exasperated and visited the worst offenders with fyre and the sworde, but since the borderers had forgotten more about both than Genghiz Khan ever knew, and were expert at fading into the hills or defying the Wardens from rather impregnable stone peel towers, Authority could only burn a few villages, pose for pictures by the smoking ruins while the reporters took notes for Ballads and Laments (later collected by W. Scott in "Border Minstrelsie"), and withdraw, followed by raspberries and even coarser noises from the peels. Of course they rounded up the usual suspects, whose convictions were invariably held to be unsound because of sloppy forensic evidence—after all, if your worst enemy turns blue and explodes at your dinner table, the traces of ratsbane on your hands *may* have come from chessmen used by warlocks at the Necromancers' Social Club, which you visited a couple of months back. One result of this was that the Wardens' officers took to hanging suspects on the spot (known as "Jeddart justice," from the town of Jedburgh, where the authorities were unusually liverish), but only if they weren't important people with dangerous friends.

All this was water off a duck's back to the borderers, who carried on killing and robbing each other as before, and since they never bothered anyone more than fifty miles from the frontier (except on the notable occasion when some of them raided Edinburgh and surprised a Very Important Person in the lavatory, much to his embarrassment*) the two governments were inclined to take a why-the-hell-should-we-care-it's-a-long-way-off-thank-God attitude, and recommend another Publicke Inquirie.

* True, really.

So that's the border for you, and we apologise for the brief history lesson. Actually, we haven't told you the half of it—for example, that in addition to the reivers and robbers, the place was crawling with agents, spies, messengers, plotters, double-o triggermen, moles and other assorted Smyllii Personae, as they were called, intriguing away like anything between London and Edinburgh. Secret diplomacy was in a fair old state, the question being: would James collect the royal English franchise when Elizabeth fell off her twig, as might happen any day? Rumours abounded that His Majesty was already being fitted out with tropical kit, Scottish courtiers were practising drawls and trying to stop saying "whilk" and "umquhile," the Scottish National Party were preparing banners reading "Home Rule *in* England" and "It's Scotland's Cheddar!," London merchants were taking options on supplies of Japanese haggis, and Home Counties landowners were preparing to turn their estates into golf courses. But alle was uncertayne, and remayned to be seene.

Like our story, which is coming up at last, honestly, without further discursions; any more need-to-know history will be sprinkled in lightly as we pursue our headlong tale of adventure, romance, knavery, ambush, disguise, escape, abduction, seduction, and Kindred Mischiefs, deploying an all-star cast of steely-eyed heroes, noble ladies, unspeakable villains, gorgeous wantons, corrupt creeps, maniacs, freebooters, freeloaders, and hordes of colourful extras, in a variety of Great Locations, including lonely fortresses, mysterious mansions, hide-outs, dungeons, boudoirs, bawdy houses, wizard's caves, dens, kens, and the occasional shed and hovel—for while there will be ample cut-and-thrust, passion tender and blazing, splendid costumes, Technicolored set decoration, and four-page menus, we'll not neglect the squalid social material for those in search of a Ph.D.

But now we cry "Quiet, everybody, let's try to get it right first time, action! camera! QUIET!!"—for Scene One, a desperate encounter between one of our Principals and a Supporting Heavy, is opening up with a long shot of that desolate waste which we mentioned several pages ago. Since then the storm has blown itself out, farther south the last witch has taxied thankfully to a standstill ("Talk about fog and filthy air—never been so glad to get off a bloody broom in my life!"), and we pan slowly across dripping bushes wreathed in clinging mist with icy patches which should clear towards dawn, pale moonlight gleams cold on the gullies and moss-hags, and no sound is heard save the plaintive wail of a sodden rabbit and the muffled crackling and swearing of someone trying to get to sleep in a patch of wet bracken, and making nothing of it.

Peering through the fronds we can see that he is a scarecrow figure, ragged and besmirched, hair unkempt, boots leaking, shirt and breeches sadly out of crease, and hasn't shaved for a fortnight. A pathetic sight, as he writhes vainly to snuggle down on his couch of wet heather, rocks, and mud, but make the most of him, for this bedraggled bum is one of our heroes—yes, he is. Never, you exclaim, not in those trousers! Relax, peer more closely, and note that while he is one who has clearly fallen on evil days (and a couple of dunghills en passant), yet is he modelled on the lines of Gary Cooper crossed with Steve McQueen, six feet two of lean, muscular modesty; the matted stubble cannot conceal the resolute manliness of firm chin and interesting nostrils, nor the caked muck the steady brilliance of grey eyes ready to dance with gentle mirth or harden in stern resolve, whichever is appropriate. Quiet humour sits relaxed on his mobile lips, integrity keeps his ears at a proper angle, humanity will shine in every strand of his fair hair once it's been blow-waved, and wit, intelligence, and responsibility are evenly distributed over the rest of his active frame. All right?

But at the moment he looks awful, having been pinched for vagrancy in Northumberland two weeks ago, set in the stocks, and then confined in Haddock's Hole, the most verminous chokey in all the wide border. Paroled a couple of days since, flea-ridden and friendless, he has nowhere to go but up. He is English, goes by the name of Archie Noble, and is a broken man—which doesn't mean he is a spent force, but is the local term for one who has no chief or protector to vouch for him or sign his passport application, no allegiance, no home, no visible means of support. A wanderer on the Marches, a denizen of Cardboard Hamlet, of no account, but don't worry, he's literate and normally quite couth, well-spoken when he wants to be, and once he's had a bath and a shave and his rags pressed, you won't know him.

For the nonce he wriggles in damp discomfort, munching a tuft of grass to allay his hunger, and trying to sing himself to sleep with one of those lovely, sentimental old border ballads which were to cast their spell over Wordsworth and the Grasmere Gang two centuries later:

> *We hangit twa cows on the gallows tree,*
> *We hangit them high, wi' screech and shudder,*
> *They twisted and turned in the wild, wild wind,*
> *And ye couldnae tell one frae the udder*

quite unaware that in the neighbouring gully Destiny is approaching . . .

. . . in the unlikely and repulsive shape of Black Dod Pringle, a fell Scotch thief of Teviotdale, returning with his thuggish associates from a raid into Cumberland; he is a squat, ugly, villainous figure clad all in steel and leather, has bad breath, bites his nails, and is commonly called Bangtail—all reivers had weird nicknames, usually based on appearance or behaviour, and Bangtail's signifies that he is not immune to the allurement of the female form. His gang are called Fire-the-Sheep, Blacklugs, Grunt, Slackarse, and Wandered Tom, and all are members of the Pringle family except the last, who thinks he's a Turnbull but can't be sure because he has lost his birth certificate (he says). Like the Mafia, borderers operated in family groups, with close friends and allies to make up the numbers; the big tribes, like the Armstrongs, Elliots, Johnstones, and Maxwells (of Scotland), and the Fenwicks, Grahams, and Forsters (of England) could sally forth hundreds strong, but the Pringles, although under the protection of the powerful Kerr family, were second division players, and Bangtail's was a typical small raid.

It was also a disgruntled one, because they'd had no luck. Bangtail had got them all excited with big talk of descending like a thunderbolt on the Foulbogsyke Women's Institute during its annual meeting, raping the committee, and making off with their prize entries of crochet and home-made jam, but the ladies had word of his coming and defied the raiders from the W.I. tower, hurling down missiles of potted meat, jellies, raffia-work, and blazing handbags. Foiled, Bangtail had to be content with running off the livestock, which consisted not of cattle and sheep, but of half a dozen hens and a couple of cats. So it is a sorry band of ruffians that we see riding through the murk, herding their clucking plunder before them, while Bangtail rides well ahead, gritting his teeth in frustration at the memory of the plump and roguish Institute treasurer flaunting her curves on the battlements as she blew him jeering kisses and invited him to climb up and show her his muscles.

Archie Noble came out of his doze at the sound of the reiver's hoof-beats, starting up from his bed among the bracken. Bangtail saw the bedraggled figure not ten paces away, concluded that here was some lonely wanderer on whom to vent his ill-temper, and with a "Har-har!" of wicked glee clapped in his spurs, couched his lance, and charged, intending to open him up just for laughs. But it wasn't a good night for Pringles, for the victim leaped smartly aside, whipped a poniard from the back of his waist, and with a tricky underarm throw planted it neatly in Bangtail's neck, causing him to crash to the turf, his sensibilities outraged and his throat cut. After which there was nothing for Bangtail to do but thrash about a bit, go limp, gasp the word "Rosebud" (which was the name of the plump W.I. treasurer, actually), and expire.

And that's Bangtail out of the story, and Archie Noble nicely into it. Moving with cat-like agility he retrieved his poniard, glanced keenly about him in alarm (for even heroes don't expect to find themselves committing manslaughter before they're properly awake), congratulated himself on his reflexes—and then his eye fell on the dead face glaring irritably up at the pale moon, and a startled wince caused the clotted debris to fall from his unwashed brow.

"Black Dod Pringle, alias Bangtail!" he exclaimed. "Dead by my hand, all unintentional! Now, harrow and alas, but here was dire mischance, and as for mouth-to-mouth resuscitation, forget it! Nay, he's past mending, and I in jeopardy o' my life, for those hoof-beats I hear betoken not th'arrival o' the Salvation Army, I warrant!"

It was customary, you see, for Elizabethan performers to speak their thoughts aloud, for the benefit of the groundlings. But having got his dismay off his chest, our hero moved like a well-oiled ferret (belying his nickname of Waitabout, from his habit of philosophic loafing). Trained frontiersman that he was, his senses told him that five riders, driving hens and cats, were just over the hill (Slackarse's shout of "Keep them bloody poultry away from the moggies, you four, or the boogers'll stampede!" merely confirmed his deduction), and with Teviotdale's top gun going into rigor mortis at his feet, and a bloody poniard in his hand, Archie could see awkward questions being asked by the deceased's buddies if he lingered. On foot he was coffin-bait, for those expert trackers would read his trail like motorway signs, wheresoe'er he turned and doubled. On the other hand, Pringle's horse was hanging about, looking bored . . . yet our hero, hard man though he was, hesitated to take away a vehicle without the owner's consent, and that was now unobtainable. Anyway, broken men got hung for horse-rustling, didn't they? Decisions, decisions . . . and then as a frantic cat came rocketing out of the mist, with an enraged chicken in hot pursuit, and Slackarse's cry of "What did I tell ye—the bastard hen's run amok!" reached his ears, Archie Waitabout waited no longer. With one bound he was in the saddle, accelerating smoothly from nought to twenty-five in four seconds flat, and by the time the Famous Five had come on their defunct leader and were speculating about suicide, divine retribution, or (Wandered Tom's theory) whether Bangtail had stopped to shave and ballsed it up, our hero was a mile away and going like the clappers o'er the misty moor, muttering "Land's End or bust!" as he counted the cost of his fatal encounter.

Why, what's to worry, you may wonder—no witnesses, no incriminating broken cuff-links or cigar ash left behind . . . file the serial number off the poniard, ditch it, and he's well away, surely? Oh, yeah—what about the horse? In these parts, where everyone knows everyone else, including their livestock, he might as well carry a full confession in Day-Glo on his chest. But dammit, you point out, he's on the moral high ground (self-defence), and no previous record, your honour . . . But unfortunately, there is: Archie's past is not entirely unspotted; necessity has driven him to hire out now and then to heavy mobs like the Charltons and the Maxwells; he has lent a hand, and reluctantly committed G.B.H., in those just-lawful pursuits picturesquely called "hot trods," he has no references or paid-up insurance, and being a broken man and therefore heavily suspicioned of *everything,* he is ripe to be put in the frame for *anything.* Like killing, however innocently, the local equivalent of a Chicago *capo,* whose family have been known to pursue a feud as far as York, and Batley even.

Our boy, in fact, is now without a future. Either the Pringle hit-men will sign him off, or the Wardens will give him a suspended sentence eight feet up in the air—for while a well-connected reiver may get off with a fine plus interest and a promise to behave, broken men can expect only the gallows, decapitation, or the drowning-pit in which offenders were economically dunked to death.

Either way, a parlous plight, and Archie's brow is furrowed with care beneath the grime, and even the horse is shaking its head and shooting him glances of concern as he leads it through the wreathing mist a couple of hours before dawn. They are

cold, wet, fed up with tripping over rocks and falling in bogs;
Archie's stomach is starting to rumble—that last clump of grass
had definitely been off—and the horse is burping with fatigue;
sustenance they must have, and that right speedily. And just as
they are starting to eye each other cannibal-wise, the mist thins
suddenly, and in the distance a light gleams in the gloom. The
mist thins a bit more, and the outline of a large building comes
into view, and then with a final ghostly whiffle the mist packs up
entirely, and lo! it's a great fortified mansion, with crenellations
and mullions and a massy stone wall all around with a frowning
gateway flanked by a sullen sally-port and a mildly annoyed
tradesmen's entrance above which is a battered notice board
reading:

THRASHBATTER TOWER PLC.
SCOTS KEEPE OUTTE!
FORAYS BY APPOINTMENT ONLIE.
NOBILITIE, GENTRIE, WARDENS FAIRLIE WELCOME.
BROKEN MENNE ARE YOU KIDDING?

The whole place looks as though it's been built in a bad
temper, bats squeak round its dark central tower, bloodhounds
growl in its outhouses, and in its cellar the very mice are bickering in their straw.

Archie is still too far off to hear them, or to read the notice,
but even if he could it wouldn't matter; his eye is fixed on that
one small lighted window, which his reiver's instinct tells him is
a pantry containing a half-finished game pie, a mortress of
brawn, savoury pasties, toothsome pizzas, sundry kickshaws,
and enough booze to raise the *Titanic*. Slavering slightly, he
mounts his steed, murmuring "Hi-yo, Silver!," and is hurled

headlong as the beast rears obediently on its hind legs, whinny-ing. Picking himself up, and with the William Tell overture whispering gently o'er the moss, he steals forward like a ragged ghost, ears pricked, eyes gleaming like grey fog-lamps, gastric juices fermenting, while the horse takes a dyspeptic glance at the gloomy mansion, obeys its animal instinct, and leans despondently against a convenient tree reflecting that it's not *that* hungry . . .

Well, it's probably not the Inn on the Park, but it should furnish our hero a quick snack and a packed lunch for later. Unless . . . who knows what lurks within this estate agent's nightmare—phantasms, man-traps, burglar alarms, a police stake-out? Does he realise he isn't dressed for dining out? But let's wish him Bon Appetit anyway, and move on to the rest of the cast, wherever they are . . . a Mad Villain, perhaps? A spy? A corrupt plumber? No, we've had enough of Heavies in Chapter One, and it's time for a touch of glamour, the rustle of silk and whiff of perfume, as we bring on the girls . . .

It's quite a commentary on our so-called scientific progress that while we can send men to the moon (well, possibly you can, even if this correspondent can't), getting stuck on the high fell road between Scotch Corner and Carlisle is just as liable to happen now as it was in the sixteenth century. In some ways it's worse nowadays, when your carburetter's flooded, not a callbox in sight, and nothing for it but a ten-mile walk; in the 1590s you could always huddle up in a corner of your satin-lined luxury coach, swathed in silks and furs, beguiling your impatience with peach brandy and sweetmeats o' Peru, while outside in the raging blizzard your lackeys heaved and whimpered to get the show on the road, and Coachman Samkin clumphed around giving futile instructions to the grooms, like "Keep them nags in low gear, the chestnut's over-revving!"—assuming, of course, that you weren't just any old wayfarer, but the pampered and wealthy Lady Godiva Dacre, proud flower of the nobility, owner of half East Anglia, and accustomed to having every whim, let alone crisis, attended to instanter by droves of head-knuckling servitors. There were a round dozen of these floundering knee-deep in slush as they strove to force the great gilded carriage ahead, and Coachman Samkin waved his lantern and vanished in a snowdrift.

Inside, her ladyship tapped dainty foot and drummed slender fingers in Krupa-like crescendo, signs which her companion, mischievous little Mistress Kylie, watched with covert amusement as she waited for Krakatoa to blow, and tried to think of some remark which would get the eruption going.

"Perchance," she ventured brightly, "the weather will clear ere long, or mayhap some travellers will fare this way, bringing timely succour. Or a road scout, wi' spanners and gadgets—"

"—and a team of oxen, and wainropes, and a fork-lift truck!" stormed Lady Godiva, finally giving vent. "God's light!" she seethed. "Was ever poor debutante so sorrily served? Twelve reeking fat knaves that have gorged and swilled enough for a regiment since we left London, and cannot shift me a featherweight coach through a pinch of snow! Yeomen of England, yet! How we beat the Spaniards I'll never know! Can nothing stir them, jelly-muscled churls?"

"Have 'em lashed with horse-whips," suggested sweet Kylie. "Mind you, they're probably too numb to feel it by now, but it's worth a try."

"And have 'em run whining to an industrial tribunal!" The fine eyes of scornful Lady Godiva flashed like violet detonators.

"With my fair name bandied in the gutter press as merciless employer! Thank you, Mistress Thinktank! Who are you working for, me or the *Sunday Sport*?"

"Marry, 'tis a thought," admitted Kylie. "Certes, the tabloids would eat it. 'My Flogging Frolic i' the snow with Gorgeous Goddy,' by Postillion Tim . . . And 'twould be just like them to use that kinky picture of you in Ben Jonson's last masque—remember, Diana chastising the fauns? All right, all right," she added hastily as her mistress began to gnash pearly teeth, "just speculating. I always said amateur court theatricals were a lousy idea, but you would fancy yourself in tights . . . Here, have another snifter."

And while tactful Kylie sets the decanter merrily a-glug, and Lady Godiva extends smouldering goblet, let us cast an eye over these two ladies fair—or rather, in Godiva's case, let us gaze in stricken admiration, for they're not making them like that any more. Superbly tall, with the flawless ivory beauty of some Nordic ice queen, and a shape whose curvature could not be concealed even by the voluminous finery of the day, our heroine (yes, it is she) was a breathtaking mixture of Marlene above the neck and Jane Russell below. Her white brow was lofty, her eyes of deepest midnight blue, her nose classically sculpted, her lips an imperious rosebud, and her ears shell-like gems peeping from beneath magnificent fiery tresses which cascaded like glossy red curtains to shoulders of alabaster smoothness. Her chin and teeth were all right, too. Add to this assemblage a mien before whose frigid disdain accountants trembled and barristers fairly grovelled, clothe her in cloth of silver (by Balmain), and let Van Cleef (or Arpels) loose wi' gewgaws of price wherewith to deck her slim hands and snowy bazoom, and you have a picture of feminine perfection that would take the paper off the wall. Rumour had it that she had been Master Spenser's original model for the Faerie Queene before wiser counsels led him to ascribe his inspiration to Her Majesty's person, and that Shakespeare himself had her in mind when he penned that immortal line in *Much Ado* which begins "Here's a dishe . . ."

In short, Lady Godiva Dacre was the ultimate Elizabethan knock-out, and if among the sonnets, songs, wolf-whistles and cries of "Gaw!" with which courtiers paid tribute to her peerless oomph, there were occasional murmurs of "Haughty piece," "Stuck-up icicle," and "Payne i' the butte," this was no matter for wonder.

For, as our description and the foregoing snatch of small talk suggest, our leading lady's temper was wilful, headstrong, passionate, and proud to busting. Spoiled from infancy by a doting grandsire and squads of devoted nurses, grooms, and hangers-on, our orphaned heiress had realised at the age of about three that beauty, money, and blue blood had placed in her tiny hand the throttle of a steamroller on Life's highway, and she had been winding it on ever since. Sent to court as a child, she had modelled herself on the Queen's Grace, to whom she had been maid-in-waiting for several years; hence those outbursts of tantrum when any inconvenience (like having to sit in a coach moving at one mile an hour through a snowstorm) came to disturb the rose-strewn progress of her existence. We see her now aged twenty-two, journeying north to visit the distant estate of her late grandfather, old Lord Waldo Dacre, recently succumbed to a surfeit of reivers. She wouldn't have come—too far, too rude, and oh, sweet coz, the *people!*—had she not been commanded away by the Queen, who, it was rumoured, had been itching for an excuse to get shot of an attendant who gave herself impossible airs and whose naturally flame-coloured coiffure was a maddening reproach to Her Majesty's weekly gallon of henna.

So there's Lady Godiva . . . sorry? Lovers, you ask? Well, none of your business, really. Yes, granted, a lady with her equipment and ardent spirit, when aroused by Cupid, might well make the Maneaters of the Kumaon look like stuffed mice . . . and, indeed, there has been talk, but that's the court for you. Suffice to say that while she has had legions of open admirers with whom she has dallied coolly before giving them the old-sock treatment, we are not prepared to speculate about anything steamier. Don't worry, her passionate nature will take off before we're finished . . . but mum.

Now, if you can tear your eyes away from our heroine, we turn to little Kylie, her attendant, a perfect complement to Lady G. Kylie is petite, blonde, pert, and chocolate-box pretty, with those generous contours common among saucy milkmaids and well described by the modern expression "stacked." Inseparable since they won the two-woman bob-sleigh title at their Swiss finishing school, they spar almost continuously, for Kylie couldn't care less about her imperious employer's outbursts, and needles her freely, a familiarity which Lady Godiva secretly enjoys because she feels such tolerance becomes her aristocracy. Just let anyone but Kylie try it.

Having brimmed her companion's goblet with the electric soup, Kylie remarked that it would keep out the cold, and got her head in her hands for her pains.

"Cold, quotha!" withered haughty Godiva. "What shouldst thou know of cold, overweight and padded wi' blubber as thou art! Nay, had I thy surplus tissue I might sit me starkers on an ice floe and be warm as toast, I'll warrant!"

"Pleasingly plump and eight stone in my pantyhose, I," murmured Kylie, no whit abashed. "And who tipped the scale at nine stone two last Twelfth Night? Do I hear the name Dacre?"

"But then I'm not a midget, am I?" riposted Godiva with acid sweetness. "I don't roll for miles when I fall over, like some butterballs I could mention. Sure, nine-two is nought to one o' my stately inches; 'tis but sweet proportion. Oh, come on, top me up again, and if it makes me car-sick, what the hell, it's better than freezing."

"Aye, let's get loaded," sighed Kylie, dispensing joy-juice. "'Twill make our present plight seem the less woeful, and banish fond regrets that we might ha' been snug at Greenwich, simpering at Her Grace, dancing corantos, and sizing up the Yeoman Warders . . . if only someone had had the sense to wear a black wig . . ."

Lady Godiva's lovely eyes glinted like dangerous sapphires. "If you're trying to wind me up, dear heart," she purred, "you're getting perilously warm. Well ye know that I am up to here, repining this unlooked-for voyage to my Cumbrian estate—but what could I do, with Her Grace insistent and Grandpops handing in his bucket untimely?" Moodily she plucked seed pearls from her ruff and flicked them at the decanter, her bosom quivering in a sigh that would have had strip-club patrons clambering over the seats. "Aye, me, I suppose someone's got to mind the store, and who but the old goat's heiress? 'Tis the penalty of uncountable riches and social status that they bring Care and Duty in their wake. Ah, sweet Kylie, sometimes I wish I had been born a poor beggar maid, with no cares but ducks and manure. Or whatever," she added vaguely.

"'Tis hell in the trenches," sniffed cynical Kylie. "But when her ancestors collar the monosodium glutamate monopoly from Henry the Seventh, what can a girl do but wallow lamenting in the dividends? Heart-breaking, I call it."

"It keeps you in tights and Chanel," flashed Godiva, "so knock it not. Skip off the gravy train an ye list, but remember, baby, it's cold outside. Aye," she resumed in pensive mood, "this same wild wind will be sighing its plaintive dirge through the battlements of Thrashbatter Tower, where I was born, 'neath the grim shadow of the lonely fells. We'll be seeing it shortly, assuming these layabouts get us moving before Easter—a stark and lonely hold, gentle Kylie, fronting the grim border. And yet . . ." Godiva's marble beauty seemed to soften in creamy-dreamy reminiscence ". . . and yet 'twas there I played, as tender little child, by rippling beck and oozing bog, and harkened me to the murmuring of butterflies and badgers in the greenwood, all carpeted with daisies . . . And what the hell do you want, clodpole?" she concluded as the coach window flew open to admit a rush of freezing air and the empurpled face of Coachman Samkin under a thin sheet of ice.

"'Tis of no avail, my lady!" he quavered through chattering teeth. "My big end's gone!"

A dozen crisp rejoinders jostled for priority on the red lips of quick-witted Kylie, but Lady Godiva ignored the opportunity, so great was her fury.

"Have ye not tried kick-starting, fool?" she railed.

"Aye, mistress, but 'tis vain! Boot their buttocks as I may, they stagger like men stoned! The wheels slip, wi'out purchase, and us wi' no chains nor grit—"

"Then find something else!" stormed her ladyship. "Where are your wits, looby? Lay two o' the smaller lackeys 'neath the wheels, so shall ye find purchase enough! Stay, dolt—cover them with blankets lest their liveries be soiled. Jesu, must I think of everything! And close the dam' window!"

"Oh, kindly mistress! Oh, sweet consideration!" grovelled Samkin. " 'Tis done in a moment, wi' all despatch! I go, see how I . . . aaargh!"

His fawning protestations ended in a sudden yowl as tender Kylie closed the window on his fingers, and while he is bathing them in snow and calling for volunteers to prostrate themselves beneath the wheels, we pan and zoom dramatically to the night skyline far above the road. You know the shot—usually it reveals Comanches or Riffs gazing down on the unsuspecting wagon train or Legion column, but this is something more sinister by far: a dozen steel-capped border riders sitting their hobblers like black phantoms in the swirling snow, motionless save for the play of their cloaks in the wind and the fidgeting of the man on the end whose chilblains are killing him. A fearsome sight, and worse when you get close and see the gaunt profiles of the long horse-like faces—and the riders are nothing to write home about either, grim and bony villains with wolfish expressions and hungry sunken eyes, for these are Charltons and Milburns of Tynedale, the hardest of hard men on the English side. Plagued by a power cut in their valley, they have been raiding their own countrymen (nothing unusual on the frontier, believe us) for firelighters and primus stoves; now, on their homeward road, heavy with plundered matches and kindling and a-reek with paraffin, they have spotted the stranded coach, and are arguing not about the practicality but—would you believe?—the morality of attacking it.

You see, if we haven't already mentioned it, the border reivers had eccentric notions of what was fair game. Livestock of any kind and the contents (what they called the "insight," a definition probably unknown to C. P. Snow) of farms, crofts, churches, and other people's peel towers were legitimate loot, and murder, arson, kidnapping, extortion, and terrorism were simply part of their business—*and none of these things did they consider criminal.* But there was a line which no respectable reiver would cross, if he could help it: mugging, pocket-picking, fraud, embezzlement, highway robbery, or oath-breaking—these things were out, as the State Papers testify, and if you think the borderers were crazy, well, that was their code. The line got a bit blurred sometimes, admittedly—which was why the Charltons and Milburns were getting all het up as they eyed the great gilded coach with hungry doubt and their extremities froze. They were talking, or rather growling, in Northumbrian, a form of English incomprehensible to outsiders, chiefly because it features a deep guttural noise as of a motor starting up, in place of the consonant "r." In translation:

"Ye cannut tooch it, man!" The leading Charlton, a gaunt cadaver known as Wor Jackie, was adamant. "The bloody thing hez wheels, sista! Rob that, an' yer a flamin' highwayman!"

"If it's got a roof, an' isn't moovin', it's a hoose!" objected a Milburn, producing his dog-eared *Reiver's Year-book*. "Haud up the lantern, Sandie! Aye, theer y'are . . . 'Any immobile dwellin' or sim'lar accommodation may be visited, ploondered, th'inhabitants assaulted, the thatch boorned—' "

"An' wheer's the thatch on that friggin' thing?" demanded Oor Kid Charlton, who always supported his big brother.

"Haud on a minnit," demurred an awkward Robson. "Peel towers hezn't got thatches, an' we boorn *them*."

"Peel towers hezn't got wheels, ye daft git! A coach isna an immobile dwellin', neether!"

"It wad be, tho' if 'twas in a caravan park or trailer camp."

The Milburn shop steward was consulting his index. "Wheer is't? 'Pyped watter . . . refuse disposal . . . landlord-bashin' . . .' Aye, here it's! 'Trailers, albeit wheeled, shall be deemed crofts, cots, or steadings, so they be stationary . . .' Weel, that booger's stationary, so Ah say we're in business!"

"Naw, we's not," snarled Wor Jackie. "Bastard thing's moovin'. An Ah doobt if that's a caravan park."

"Aw, coom on, man! Hoo d'ye ken, wid a' the snaw?"

"'Ey, we could run-off th' hosses! They're livestock, so we're entitled—an' *then* it wadn't be moovin'! Warraboot that, Wor Jackie?"

A further moment's debate followed in which a Milburn was unhorsed and two Charltons received flesh wounds, and then Wor Jackie sheathed his broadsword and gave his casting vote.

"We tek th' hosses, awreet—but if them fellas that's pushin' the coach can keep it moovin' . . . hands off! An' they're not to be strucken, nor tripped neether, thou base football players! But the minnit they stop shovin', an' it stops, it ceases tae be a ve-hickle, an' we can git stoock in! Awoy, Tynedale! Up the Magpies!"

Like a black avalanche the scrupulous freebooters swept down the snow-clad slope, flourishing swords and supporters' club scarves, lances couched and rattles a-clatter, and before the bewildered grooms knew what had hit them they had been pinioned and dropped in wayside drifts, and the coach horses had been neatly whipped from the shafts and labelled "Spoyle." But alas for the reivers' hopes: the coach kept rolling slowly, because the lackeys behind, all unaware of what was happening up ahead, were packed down in three-two-three and putting in a splendid shove, with Coachman Samkin hovering at their heels yelling: "Keep it tight, back row!" The two loose lackeys who'd been under the wheels were receiving attention from the trainer, but soon they too piled into the ruck, and the coach crunched merrily o'er the snow, to the disgust of the reivers, who could only mooch along behind, foiled but still hopeful.

"This lot'll be weel knackered afore they're halfway to Alston," opined Wor Jackie, wi' vulpine grin. "An' then—away the lads!"

Meanwhile, within the coach, its evident progress had restored Lady Godiva to her normal petulance, and she was reduced to complaining about the Peruvian sweetmeats (no soft centres), when Kylie, peeping out of the back window, let out a girlish whoop.

"Gosh, Goddy! Clock this lot! Great hairy chaps in black leather and spurs! Wow! Eat your heart out, Schwarzenegger—it's goose-pimple time! Oh, good mistress, shall we not bid a couple of them in, for refreshments and the like?"

Lady Godiva cast a languid eye astern, and wrinkled aristocratic nostril. "'Tis but the local rough trade, or itinerant bikers, and far 'neath the notice o' gentlewomen such as we. Stop smirking, wench, you're not a groupie!"

"I could be," sighed wanton Kylie. "Regard me those bulging biceps on the gorilla wi' the tin vest—and talk about designer stubble! Flutter, my maiden heart!"

"Maiden, my foot!" snapped Godiva. "Why, thou randy minx, hast no shame—Godamercy!" she exclaimed. "We're stopping!"

It had been bound to happen, of course. One of the back-row lackeys, pausing for breath, had glanced behind, and noticed that he was being shadowed by what looked like a dyspeptic Jack Palance, who stropped glittering blade on horse's flank and inquired wi' gloating leer: "Gittin' tired, son?" Three seconds later a dozen lackeys were in screaming flight across the snow, Coachman Samkin had fainted, the carriage was at a standstill, the Charltons and Milburns were pillaging the rear luggage-rack with cries of "We're in, Meredith!," and Lady Godiva and Kylie were exchanging wondering glances (not unmingled with excitement in Kylie's case) and asking each other what this might portend.

Well, we know, don't we? Here's beauty unprotected, and a gang of licentious bandits, not one of them in need of vitamins, working up a head of steam on the spare bottles of peach brandy in the boot—and now they tear open suit-cases and goggle in lustful amaze at piles of frilly undergarments and fishnet hose which even their untutored imaginations have no difficulty in filling. In an instant they have put two and two together, and are climbing over each other to get to the coach door, flinging it wide and feasting lewdly bugging eyes on their gorgeous prey, one of whom sinks back all silkenly a-flutter while the other sits bolt upright, ba-boom! in voluptuous indignation. For one stricken instant the principals regard each other, Wor Jackie licking gaunt chops as he lamps Godiva's vibrating fury, while Oor Kid leers drooling on buxom Kylie. Then, as often happens in unexpected social encounters, everyone speaks at once:

"Aaarrnghhh!" growls Wor Jackie, pawing with his feet. "Broomphh!"

"Are ye doin' anythin' the neet, hinny?" inquires Oor Kid.

"Alack, we are undone!" twitters Kylie hopefully.

"Doesn't anyone north of the Humber *knock*!" demands Lady Godiva, bosom flashing and eyes heaving. "Mannerless rabble, shalt lose thine ears, and other bits as well, for this rash intrusion! This is a private compartment! Back, I say, and on your bikes! Dost know who I am?"

"The answer to a randy reiver's prayer!" squeaked a small Milburn at the back, leaping and ogling. At which the whole sweaty mob, beards a-bristle and visors misting up with unholy desire, surged forward with gloating yells of "Gang bang!" "Bags I the redhead!" "Ah'll bet the little 'un doesn't half bounce!" and "Keep th' hosses, who needs them?," only to be flung back by Wor Jackie's iron arm.

"Haud oop!" he thundered. "Are ye men or beasts? Two defenceless gentlewomen, ladies o' birth an' beauty, an' ye'd be at 'em like rootin' stags gone crackers! For shame! Is there nae decency or order among ye?" His dreadful eye rolled from the lovely twain to his panting followers struggling with their buttons, and back again, what time he doffed steel cap, bared snaggle teeth in a hideous grin, and ran a small comb through his beard. "Them as fancies Blondie, line oop behind Oor Kid! All them for Carrot-top, follow me!" He seized Godiva's horrified wrist in a paw like a hairy shovel. "Your place or mine, duchess? Coach or snowdrift—choose! Har-har!"

His grating laugh ended in a strangled croak as a dainty satin slipper, scientifically driven, smote him in his tenderest spot; not for nothing had Lady Godiva captained the Benenden karate team. And back with him reeled Oor Kid, neatly headbutted by resourceful Kylie, who had repented her wanton flirtatiousness in the face of brutal assault. As the reivers collapsed in a tangle, their two leaders clutching themselves and making statements, the coach door slammed, Lady Godiva's crisp command of "Drive on, Samkin!" rang clear—little did she realise that Samkin was three fields away, crouched in a ditch with his eyes shut, whimpering: "Take the credit cards, mister, but please don't hit me!," and that the coach was without means of propulsion. Our gallant girls have won themselves but a brief respite, the reivers are staggering afoot again, full of rage and frustrated libido, and if we are to avoid the kind of explicit X-Certificate stuff which no romantic adventure can afford (not as early as Chapter Two, anyway), drastic intervention is called for, preferably in the shape of virtuous muscle—which, thank heaven, is e'en now thundering down the highway, snow flying beneath its charger's hooves, moonlight glinting on drawn broadsword and gleaming teeth, the latter bared in a reckless fighting smile between a pencil-slim moustache and a rakish little chin-beard. Like a thunderbolt he speeds to the rescue, awakening the echoes with his laughing slogan: "Teckle low, Eccies!," a cry which consternates the startled reivers and brings hope and joy to beleaguered beauty. For only heroes and idiots make that kind of noise when faced with odds of ten to one, and this character's got hero written all over him.

No, it isn't Archie Noble, who at this moment is miles away trying to jimmy a larder window. Archie was in rags, remember, whereas this new chap isn't dressed, he's positively Attired, in the latest romantic gear of boots, cloak, Mechlin at wrists and throat, gems o' price in his baldric, and a plumed hat that would make Sir Francis Walsingham gnash and turn green. He spurs among the astonished heavies, scattering them with plunging hooves and darting blade. In the time it takes to leap nimbly from the saddle and cry "Sa-ha, muckrakes! Hev et thee!" he had his back to the carriage door, rapped on the panels, cried: "Knock-knock—who's thair?—Hatcher—Hatcher who—Hatcher survice, ladies!," pinked Wor Jackie in the shoulder and Oor Kid in the leg, and was fronting the dismayed remnants of Tynedale Athletic, perfectly poised, point snaking in and out, clean-cut features reflecting the moonlight, ruby earring fairly dancing with glee of combat, and joyous laughter bubbling on his lips and bursting on his moustache.

A rotten prospect for the remaining reivers, who could read the signs as well as we can—six feet plus, immaculately clad, foppish finery belying steely wrist and sinewy speed, handsome, dashing, merry to the point of hysteria, and obviously slated to get the girl in the last reel: the kind of super-gallant for whom they, being expendable extras, were so much rapierfodder. But they did their best, flinging themselves on him with despairing cries of "Pantywaist!" and "Snob!," and falling back, gashed and cursing, before a dazzling point which was everywhere at once or, if you prefer it, simultaneously ubiquitous.

You've seen Tyrone Power do it often enough—engaging three blades at a time from opponents who stand obligingly frozen in the lunge position while he cries a cheery reassurance over his shoulder to Maureen O'Hara, carves his call-sign on their linen, stoops to let an attacker fall over him, and finally leaps forward with stamp and sweep to drive them off in panic-stricken rout. And not even breaking sweat.

Our boy was like that, only better: within a minute there was a pile of reivers on the deck, bleeding and going "Aarrgh!," and only the squeaking little Milburn was left, hacking away gamely at that impenetrable guard.

"Kiss my steel!" cried the gallant gaily, and the little Milburn, seeing the chance to deliver the best riposte in the whole encounter, cried: "Kiss my arse!" and died happy.

Frantic stuff, and watched with finger-twisting admiration by our beauteous duo in the coach, respectively gasping with apprehension and emitting squeals of "Wow! Gotcha!" Now, as their saviour wiped his blade on a lace kerchief and louted low, plumed hat in hand, they let down the window, Kylie fairly gushing with girlish congratulation and even Lady Godiva warming the knight-errant with her most queenly smile. Indeed, a hint of blush undercoat appeared 'neath the ivory satin finish of her cheek, and her ruby lips parted with a soft splooch, for if this was not Master Errol Flynn in Elizabethan costume, she'd never seen him. Kylie, less mistress of her emotions, gaped starry-eyed and gasped: "Golly, quel hunk!" The newcomer shot them a brilliant smile and spoke.

"Oll raight, gurls? Ai hope these belly reskals didn't hurrt you. Ai'd hev hasted to yur aid even fester, but the road's in a helluva state, simply fraightful. You shoor yur okay?"

Being unprepared for the accent of Glasgow W2 from this Apollo, Lady Godiva was momentarily taken aback, but came off the ropes with speedy aplomb.

"We are much beholden to you, sir," said she, all peerless dignity, and extended a white hand over which he bowed reverent curly head, the bristles of his lip-cosy sending electric tingles up her arm to her smooth shoulder, whence they dispersed delightfully through the rest of her, a sensation which would have caused her to go "Eek!" had she not been schooled to hide girlish emotion.

Little Kylie knew no such reticence. Proffering eager mitt in turn, and feeling her knuckles nibbled (this gallant can obviously tell top quality from mere talent, and responds accordingly) she exclaimed: "Yikes! Much beholden nothing! 'Tis miracle that sends such dashing champion to our aid—oh, sir, your footwork was brill, and how may we repay you?" As if I didn't know, thought the wanton hussy, lowering coy lashes o'er worshipping orbs.

"Och, don't menshn'it—no bother, reelly," was the modest reply. "Pleez, just sit taight while Ai round up those varlets of yurs, whurrever they've got to. Going laike the cleppers when Ai saw them lest. Heff a jiffy, end Ai'll be beck!"

And with another graceful bow and flash of gum-gear, he sprang lightly on his horse, and with the command "Come on, Garscadden—away!" cleared the roadside hedge from a standing start and was off across the snowy fields shouting: "Ho there, leckeys! Get yurselves follen in! Where urr you, desh it? Yur mistress ken't stay heer oll naight!"

A faint furrow did its stuff 'twixt Lady Godiva's delicately pencilled brows. "Methinks," said she, "this gentleman should be a Scot, by his tongue."

"Who cares about his tongue?" enthused glowing Kylie. "Regard me rather those super shoulders, chiselled clock, sexy legs, and the Mephisto-gleam in his tawny eyes! And what a mover—nay, 'a went through those nasties like a dose of Dr. Lopez his salts!" She sighed. "Bit of a waste of beefcake, if you ask me, but that's the way the farl fractures. What makes you think he's Scotch, Goddy?"

"His speech, dum-dum!" quoth impatient Godiva. "Had ye but marked the dialogue in *Macbeth*,* 'stead of ogling the husky who played the Bleeding Sergeant, you'd ha' noted that the nobles of Scotland—you know, Angus, Lennox, McHaggis, whoever—spoke exactly as doth our rescuer. A quaint affected dialect, which they do term 'toffee-nosed,' for that it apes

---

* Alert readers may think they have spotted an anachronism in this paragraph, since the first public performance of *Macbeth* did not take place until 1610. In fact, Godiva and Kylie had attended the sneak preview held in the 1590s, after which the play was shelved for more than a decade because Burbage refused to appear in a kilt.

gentility—sex are what they keep coal in, and a crèche is two carts colliding on Byres Road," she explained, but with a musing, dreamy look that suggested preoccupations other than nutty slack and vehicle pile-ups. Aware of Kylie's slantendicular smirk, her ladyship feigned a yawn. "Thus talks he—aye, and plies pretty rapier enough. For the rest"—she shrugged indifferent shoulders—"I marked him not."

"Get her!" scoffed Kylie. "You marked him ten out o' ten! Going to offer him a lift, are we?"

Disdain tilted the exquisite nose and squiggled the delectable mouth of the Thrashbatter heiress. "And if I so condescend," she snooted, "to one that hath done me service, why, what's it to thee, sauce-pot? He may be mere gentry and talk as if he had a mouse up his nose, yet is he the most presentable thing I've seen this side of Watford Gap."

"Does that mean I have to ride on the roof?" sniffed Kylie. "Or don't you mind the competition?"

"That," quoth Godiva, patting complacent coiffure, "will be the day. Bear us company an ye list, sweet child—but try playing footsie with him and I'll break your leg."

Thus it was that when the stranger had scooped in Samkin and the perspiring lackeys, with brisk halloo and cries of "C'mon, churrls, move it! Run laike stegs, you aidle shower!" and they had put to the horses and tidied the fallen reivers into the ditch, he found himself bidden to a seat in the carriage, his horse being anchored astern. Kylie, with pretty becks and flutters, proffered a brimmer of peach brandy, which he accepted with a courtly "Gosh, thenks, offly kaind of you, cheers!" while Godiva appraised him 'neath interested lids and concluded that, eccentric accent or no, this gorgeous specimen had the message for the Soroptomists, in spades. And vanity demanding that she exercise her charm on such male perfection, she thought, mm-m, right, we'll give him the Languid Glow for openers . . .

"We are deeply in your debt, fair sir," she drawled, "and agog to know the name and quality of our gallant preserver. I am the Lady Godiva Dacre"—she inclined her regal scone to give him the full colour contrast of flame-tinted hair, creamy complexion, and violet pools—"and this my small companion, Mistress Kylie Delishe."

"Is thet a fect?" The cavalier paused courteously in mid-swig, and eyed her with a warmth that sent a tremor through her shapely knees. "Whay, you must be the grend-dotter of the old chep who popped his clogs et Threshbetter Tower lest Martinmess—offly sed, mai hurtfelt condolences." And if you want a stalwart shoulder to cry on, dive right in, was the message in his smoky eyes, at which the love-gremlins let out her knees another couple of notches. Pity he couldn't talk like a human being, but it could be a gas teaching him received pronunciation . . .

"You knew my Lord Waldo?" she murmured, all decorative attention.

"Och, heer end there," was the airy reply. "Ai hendled a few property trensfurs for him . . . But enough of thet—let's tock about yew!" Without warning he leaned towards her, masterful elbow on ardent knee, his classic profile cleaving the astonished air and coming to a stop inches from her own. "Mai God, but yur gorgeous! Who gives a tosser for business and ex-grendfethers in the presence of beauty that out-marvels th'exotics o' the Orient, end would put Fair Helen hurself to the beck of the stove!" He raised his glass in passionate salute. "Ai pledge yur metchless loveliness, Godaiva—nay, Godess-aiva, I should say!" And he took a saturnine shlurp while her senses did the splits, one half bridling at his presumption, the other rendered momentarily legless by his worshipping regard.

Of course, blast-furnace wooing was nothing new to one of her endowments, physical and financial. Raised at a court where they couldn't even say hello without vowing undying devotion, she'd heard it all, and knew how to cope with supercharged acceleration of the love-god's chariot. But now, ere her glance could refrigerate in reproof, he had flipped his glass to Kylie, crying "Ketch!," done a lightning kneel, 'prisoned Godiva's hand, and locked his eyes with hers, azure amaze tangling with amber yearn.

"Ye spoke of being in mai debt!" he baritoned. "Ah, the gentlest touch of thet sweet mouth on maine, divaine creechur, the teensiest sook of those juicy wee lips, end that'll take care of thet! For a furst instollment, anyway."

It needed not Kylie's exclamation of "Strewth, talk about Speedy Gonzales!" to summon proud outrage to Godiva's breast—and then, she knew not how, as the hypnotic spell of mischievous dark eyes and tang-fresh dentifrice enveloped her, some reckless imp of mad desire booted proud outrage aside, crying "Go on, why not?," and yielding to that wild impulse she lowered tremulous lids and submitted parted lips (was it those outlandish words "juicy" and "wee," so barbarously sensual, that had defrosted her?) to his smouldering munch. And in that moment she was lost, dignity and modesty joining proud outrage in the corner pocket; no longer noble lady but some abandoned jungle groupie in the embrace of her caveman lover, thrilled and helpless as he swung her with muscular expertise from tree to tree while the *Match of the Day* music rang in her ears, and Kylie's distracted cry of "Break, break, a God's name, or you'll suffocate!" was as the distant mewing of sea-birds o'er the beach of some tropic paradise . . .

Their mouths parted with a long, lingering squelch, and through a cinnamon mist in which dark eyes and lambent moustache still glowed, Lady Godiva came to herself and saw, in dishevelled bewilderment, that her erstwhile lip-ravisher was back in his seat with a jeweller's glass screwed in his eye, examining—nay, it could not be!—her priceless necklace (yes, it's the Dacre Diamonds, that fabulous collar nicked by Sir Acre Dacre from the harem of Suleiman the Improbable in the Third Crusade), her emerald earrings, sapphire fillet, pearl brooch, gold rings, and even her platinum zip-fastener, dammit! Dumbstruck Kylie was giving a creditable impersonation of a Black Hole—and now the gorgeous swine was slipping the lot in his pocket and regarding his victim with heavy-breathing admiration.

"Not bed et oll—and Ai don't mean the spurklers, eether," he added, wi' sexy significance. "Bai jove, yur ladyship hesn't spent oll her taime on embroidery. What a smecker! Fur a moment there Ai was too kerried away to concentrate on mai wurk." He phewed respectfully. "But, please, don't be alurrmed. 'Twas just technique, to save oll thet 'Hends up!' end 'Stend end deliver!' nonsense. Quaite offen," he added modestly, "the patient pesses out, end doesn't come round till Ai'm heff-way down the stair—or 'oot the windae,' as they say in Paisley."

Rage, wounded pride, and a savage desire to see the colour of this unspeakable cad's insides boiled up in Godiva like vengeful molasses and found furious utterance.

"Dastard! Rotter! Oh, miscreant and toad!" Blue hatred

lasered from her eyes, and her Titian tresses cracked like shampooed whips. "To dare—to have the immortal crust to lay polluting lips on mine, and snitch my rocks all surreptitious!" Her dainty manicures were poised to chain-saw him, but ere she could strike he was snogging again, with gentle mastery, and at that magic touch her fury drained away in bubbles of rapture, tingling her from fiery head to gilded toe-nail, the sea-birds did an encore . . . and heavens to murgatroyd, she was kissing him back! As he desisted, swaying and looking slightly baffled, Godiva sank back all giddy and misty, as one punch-drunk or ensorcelled.

"Ah, me!" she whispered. "Oh, brother! What . . . who . . . what art thou? Do I dream, or is it the peach brandy?" She stirred feebly, like a landed salmon trying to think straight. "Why . . . thou robber, to steal away my senses, my code of conduct—my jewellery yet!" she yipped, as the last effects of his embrace wore off. "Give it back, base handbag artist—"

"Take it easy!" he implored. "Let me get a wurrd in, or Ai'll hev to smooch you again, end we'll be here oll naight—you want to get home, shurrly? You esk who Ai em?" He rose to commanding height, hand on swaggering hip, and chuckled à la Fairbanks. "Know then, proud Godaiva, thet Ai—wait for it—em Gilderoy!"

If he'd said "Ichabod Schmultz" it couldn't have meant less to Godiva, but Kylie, who kept up with the tabloid broadsheets, went a whiter shade of pale and squeaked like a goosed budgie.

"Gilderoy!" she quavered, her eyes terrified gob-stoppers. "Not . . . not *Bonny* Gilderoy! Cripes! Goddy, we are undone! 'Tis the Claude Duval of Newton Mearns, the notorious highwayman and terror o' the roundabouts, known and feared from Tyne to' Solway as the Tartan Raffles—"*

"Och, away, ye've been listening to the bellad-singers—"

"What!" decibelled Godiva, now fully recovered. "Oh, direst shame! I, of my gentility, to be embraced by common criminal—"

"No, heer, heng it oll! Criminal, Ai grent you, but not common—"

"—drugged by his loathsome kisses—aye, for I warrant me his ghastly 'tash is steeped wi' LSD to space out defenceless ladies—"

"No sich thing!" he protested. "Look, ken Ai help it if mai lip-wurk robs wimmen of their reason? It's a gift—quaite hendy professionally, but it makes it deshed difficult to esteblish any meaningful relationship, Ai ken tell you!" And his voice was so full of wist that Kylie could not repress a studio-audience "Aw-w-w . . . ," and even distraught Godiva felt a sympathetic pang. Not for long, though.

"Set it to music, cut-purse! Of all the sneaky snakes—"

"Wait! Nay, hear—and pity me!" He did another swift genuflect and raised entreating eyes, nobly anguished with a touch of spaniel. "For et lest Ai em hoist with mai own petard! Aye, this naight hev Ai found me a she who doth turn me on as Ai do she!" He paused, frowning. "Or her? Or me? Ach, who cares,

---

* For the record, Gilderoy, alias Patrick Macgregor, was a dashing Scottish highwayman whose victims included Oliver Cromwell and Cardinal Richelieu (yes, he operated in France, too). He was famously handsome and well-dressed, and the lethal quality of his kisses is suggested by the ballad in Percy's *Reliques* which refers to his "breath as sweet as rose" and describes him as "sae trim a boy" with "two charming een" and "costly silken clothes." No wonder Kylie was impressed.

the point is thet Ai em shettered end fettered bai yur kisses—it
was thet lest smecker that did it! Efter years of osculatory
immunity, Ai em keptive of thet little bestard Cupid." He
heaved a sigh that lurched the speeding coach. "Peerless
Godaiva, mai heart is et yur feet!"

The impulse to tell him to pick it up and stick it trembled on
her tongue, but dived off unuttered. Fury told her to kick him
in the slats, yet her emotions were cartwheeling before his adoration, and the memory of his embrace sent fire whooshing
through her veins. Torn by conflicting passions, she hesitated—
and then remembered that she was the scion of one who had
conned a monopoly out of Henry the Seventh.

"Fair words!" she sneered. "Enslaved wi' love o' me,
quotha—that's a laugh! Prove it, then! Lay me those looted
goodies where you say your heart is—at my feet! That'll do for
starters!"

Shock, amaze, reproach, and angst scampered after each
other o'er his flawless features, and he fingered dubious beard.
"Oh, here! Thet's a bit much, desh it! Ai mean, what a prece-
dent! Gilderoy restoring plunder on request—whay, Ai'd be the
leffing-stock of every thieves' ken in the country! End Ai'm not
sure," he added solemnly, "thet yur ladyship couldn't be done
for receiving stolen goods. Ai couldn't hev thet. Nay," he clarioned winningly, "take mai love, end forget these trumpery toys,
et least until Ai can get legal advaice, end you've hurd from the
insurers—"

"Oh, base!" cried Godiva. "Oh, false insinuating crumb!
Hand them over, you . . . you kissing bandit, you, and void my
sight!"

"You ken't mean it!"

"Why not give them back in return for another kiss and a waltz by the roadside?" ventured Kylie. "Highwaymen do, all the time."

"Not this skunk! 'Tis how he gets the stuff, the viper!"

"Rensoming valuables by necking end dencing is raight out these days," said Gilderoy, shaking his head. "Honestly, it got so that every coach you stopped, some gruesome old beg would be sitting there with her lips purrsed and a consort of viols in the beck seat." He continued his imploring kneel, arms wide. "Murciless enchentress, Ai appeal to—"

What would have ensued none can say—a right to his jaw from raging Godiva, another dumb suggestion from Kylie?— for at that moment there rang out a distant challenge on the frosty air: "Hold! In the Queen's name!" and Gilderoy reacted like an electrified lizard.

"The polis, demmit!" he exclaimed, and with one bound had a leg over the window-sill, wincing sharply as he came down on the frame. "Hither to me, faithful Garscadden!" An instant only he paused, and searing passion flame-throwered from his eyes to envelop her ladyship.

"To our next joyous meeting, sweet Godaiva! Thay beauty shell draw me laike a megnet, end we'll get everything sorted out, you'll see! For the nonce, the tall timber bids me away!"

"My jewels!" screamed Godiva. "Help! Aid, ho! He's taking off with my ice . . . the gorgeous brigand," she faltered, eyes misting.

"How about one for the road?" pleaded Kylie hopefully, puckering up with her eyes closed, but Gilderoy was gone with a last "Adjoo, mai love!" and a rattle of coconut shells as he thundered away. Constabulary voices were raised afar, crying: "'Tis Gilderoy, the Peebles Predator! After him! Tally-ho!"

while our girls clung to each other, bosoms a-flutter and ankles jellified, like partners in a dance marathon. Then:

"Well, that was fun," mused Kylie. "Can't complain about boring old travelling, can we? Nay, but Goddy—oh, sweet gossip, what's amiss?" For Lady Godiva's damask cheek was flushed like strawberry puree, e'en as she gnashed pearly incisors, and two great tears welled up, teetering on beauteous lids ere they blooped over to burst on her angelic chin.

"Oh, dear Kylie, I am distraught, my senses riven every which way!" she lamented. "To be so cruelly deceived—my tender heart so wrung, my treasures ta'en . . . Gosh, but he'll pay for it, the two-timing rat! What, trifle wi' me, will he?" And she punched the upholstery with mortified yowls, only to prostrate herself on it a moment later, sobbing and whimpering "Sorry, cushions!" in remorse.

"Nay, mistress, what gives?" cried Kylie, all anxiety. "You rage, yet heave great sighs! Grind teeth, yet flutter maidenlike! Your mascara's a mess, incidentally, and you need a hairdresser, pronto—"

"Ah, fond child, I'm in a state!" Godiva raised her lovely tear-streaked face, oomping piteously. "I hate the smooth Scotch crud . . . and yet . . . oh, when he kisses, 'tis like being eaten by a pagan god! In his arms I am molten Jell-O! What am I to do? The softer, weaker, wanton, love-happy me yearns for him e'en now . . . the low-down rock-snatching renegade!" She sat up, dabbing herself, and sighed dolorously. "And yet . . . my better, sweeter, gentler self is consumed wi' such longing . . . to see him dragged to the gibbet, half-hung and disembowelled, his quarters sent by parcel post, and what's left swinging in chains for the crows' elevenses . . . the adorable sexy big beast!" She did another gnash and sigh, her eyes shining like soft acetylene. "He hath rendered me schizo quite. Ah, faithful Kylie, of your charity, advise me. What am I to do?"

"Abate these fancies, you'll get over it," counselled Kylie, setting a compassionate arm round Godiva's shoulders. "Sure, this Gilderoy is Superman on wheels, but the woods are full of them. Thy timely need is for a nice warm bath, a flask of peach brandy on the bedside table, and a good, long sleep . . ." The sound of hoof-beats and stern voices was heard outside the coach. "In the meantime, the marines have landed, so let us e'en compose ourselves—who knows, there may come now some gallant young officer whom you'll want to bowl over, and 'tis not meet that the proud Godiva D. should be seen looking like a lovelorn bag lady."

"Ah, little Kylie, so wise beyond thy years," murmured Godiva, kissing her companion's cheek. "Thy comfort is vain, I fear, yet would I requite thee for it."

"No problem," said Kylie promptly. "Lend me some of your spare jewellery, buy me a runabout coach ticket, and wish me luck."

On which tender note we end Chapter Two, with our Heroine in bittersweet turmoil, Gilderoy off with her bijouterie, and Kylie wondering hopefully if he's got a younger brother, maybe. Elsewhere the surviving Charltons are emerging from the ditch, demanding Band-Aids and revenge, and as for Archie Noble's supper . . . but let's not talk about food just yet, for in a cave under the dreaded Eildon Hills things are happening which would ruin the keenest appetite . . .

The Eildons are those three peculiar eminences, rather like green slagheaps, which you see on crossing the border at Carter Bar. They're just hills, but there's something not quite canny about them in that regular landscape, and you're not surprised to learn that legend links them with sorcery and black magic, for it was here that a celebrated medieval necromancer, mathematician, and Scotsman-on-the-make, Michael Scott, known locally as Mike the Magic, cast some of his best spells, when he wasn't blinding the experts with legitimate science at the universities of Bologna, Toledo, Paris, and Oxford. He must have been pistol-hot, academically, but however sound he was on Aristotle, astronomy, and long division, his forte was wizardry, and long after his day the Eildons continued to be a sort of social centre for alchemists, witches, thaumaturges, Satanists, and enough supporting fiends and goblins to stock a Dennis Wheatley novel. Especially in the sixteenth century, which is why we now approach the fearsome triple hills with wary tread, chewing garlic and muttering "Tripsaricopsem" to ward off evil spirits, for it is still dead o' night, and bitter cold wi' sleet and wind, and as we stumble through the gullies, leaping three feet whenever a bat squeaks or a sheep rumbles, and Fearsome Shapes seem to come and go in the murk, frankly we'd rather be in Philadelphia. But this is where the plot is happening, down there in a dank and dismal cave at the very roots of the Eildons, where five sinister figures are seated about a boardroom table of polished black basalt, in the centre of which a cauldron has been sunk; it bubbles fitfully, and green steam wreathes along its rim—but this, like the ultra-violet fog carpeting the floor, and the spark-shimmering red glow visible in the arches 'neath the Exit and Toilets signs, is really no more than set-dressing to terrify the tourists. Likewise, the five s.fs. round the table may be eccentric, but they're not supernatural, being perfectly ordinary Villains hatching the usual diabolic scheme of fiendish normality—mind you, it's a pip, if we do say so, but there's nothing necromantic about it, just political skulduggery on an earth-shattering scale which, if it succeeds, will play havoc with the history of our tight little island. Let's look them over.

First, at the table head, looking like an emaciated Gandalf, is the Wizard—silver hair to his waist, a face that would split kindling, glittering eyes, long bony black gloves, gown of cobra fur covered with cabalistic signs, etc. But if his appearance is outlandish, there's nothing other-worldly about the framed diplomas and group pictures hung on the nitre-streaked walls of his lair: honorary degrees from St. Andrews and Tarzana, autographed likenesses of Ibn Khaldun, Cagliostro, and Roger Bacon, a pennant inscribed "Hold 'em, Yale," and a colour print of the All Souls *Come Dancing* team with the young Wizard in a sequined jacket in the front row.

On his right at the table sits a paunchy, oily, utterly repulsive specimen in Gaudy Finery, hairy fingers a-glitter with gems, yellow jowls quivering and piggy eyes disappearing in folds of flesh as he munches candies from a silver comfit-box and washes them down with copious draughts of Malaga. Robert Redford he's not, but the Spanish Ambassador to Scotland, Don Collapso Regardo Baluna del Lobby y Corridor, scion of one of the noblest houses of Castile and ancestor of at least one memorable Viceroy of the Indies in the next century.* He is perspiring freely, conscious that as an accredited envoy he's got no business to be here, but orders are orders, so he has snuck down privily from Edinburgh, disguised as a prop forward for the Escurial Inquisitors who are due to compete in the Langholm seven-a-sides (a rotten pretext in his opinion, but it was King Philip's personal brainwave, so who's arguing?). Dropping off the team bus at Hawick, disguised in domino and snow-covered boots, he has made his way across country to this summit of evil.

Opposite him sits the reigning Scottish Traitor of the Year, Lord Anguish. Left to ourself, we would have dressed him in normal garb of the period, but since this is an American co-production he has got to wear a full outfit of the MacDali tartan, with a soft-watch sporran, red whiskers, golfing stockings, and a three-foot feather in his tam-o'-shanter. A ghastly sight, but wait till he starts talking, hoots awa' wi' ye and whigmaleeries

* See *The Pyrates*, and shudder.

being the least of it. He is half-drunk, and lolls och-ing and aye-ing in his chair, dunking a haggis sandwich in his goblet of Chivas Regal.

Fourth man up is an inscrutable monk, cowled, habited, and betasselled, whose marzipan features and beady currant eyes betray no emotion save when fanaticism grips him—at *autos da fe*, Inquisitorial interrogations, and Real Madrid home games—and his mask-like face hardens into cruelly ascetic lines, his currants glitter with a baleful light, and his lips contract into steel-trap implacability. Yes, Mr. Pickwick one minute, Peter Cushing the next, that's Frey Bentos, and you won't be surprised to learn that he isn't really a cleric at all, but an operative of the Spanish secret service, former head of their New World bureau (hence his Deep South accent), and now the Escurial's top banana in charge of Operation Heretic, as the new super-plot is officially called. For several years Frey Bentos has been a mole, under cover as chaplain to old Lord Waldo Dacre at Thrashbatter Tower, where he ministers to the peasants, organises garden fetes, emcees concerts, and trains the pensioners' bowling club, while secretly furthering King Philip's vile machinations and waiting for *Der Tag*, or rather, *La Dia*. Lord Waldo had no idea what a tarantula was running his Sunday School; nor will Lady Godiva when she moves in. A worrying thought, but that's the devildom of Spain for you.

Fifth—well, fourth-and-a-half really, since he's an Amazon pygmy—is Clnzh, a squat, misshapen mannikin complete with blowpipe, poisoned darts, and designer loincloth. Frey Bentos found him on top of a motel wardrobe while on leave in Acapulco, and if a South American savage seems a bit over the top for the border country, well, Clnzh adds a bit of colour, and you'd have been pretty let down if we'd made him an Etterick and Lauderdale district councillor. But isn't he a bit conspicuous, you ask, tooling about Tudor Britain in war-paint and feathers? Not at all; being small, hairy, and ugly enough to break mirrors, he is perfect casting as a local brownie or goblin, with which the frontier was infested in those days (see W. Scott, *The Black Dwarf*). Clnzh sticks to Frey Bentos like plaster, but seldom speaks, letting his blowpipe do his talking for him; he is barely house-trained, and has just had to be restrained from drinking the cauldron.

So there they are, and before anyone notes that two of them are Hispanic and a third ethnic minority, we must point out that this is the sixteenth century, when the heavies were invariably Spaniards devoted to the overthrow of Anglo-Saxon culture, religion, institutions, and everything True Blue, so we simply cannot give our villains a balanced racial mix. Anyway, come on, one of them's Scotch. God knows what the Wizard is, but he's a British resident, and you can bet that'll be enough for the Inland Revenue.

And now things are happening: the steamy surface of the cauldron is clearing, developing snowy lines, crackling with static (some damned goblin using a hairdryer close by), and finally settling in a sharply defined picture of two people crouched over a roulette wheel, their eyes intent on the spinning goolie. One is a nondescript male in a feather bonnet, doublet, and trunk hose, with a straggling beard, goggle eyes, and slobbery lips; as the ball rattles into its slot he gives a cackling cry of "Bingo, new shoes for the bairn!" But none of the five viewers minds him; their eyes are focused on his companion, a voluptuous brunette of sultry mien whose gold lamé halter and jeans are visibly creaking under the strain of her steatopygous charms. Her crimson lips twist in a contemptuous smile as her grotesque companion rakes in the chips. The Wizard adjusts the fine-tune on the cauldron and speaks.

"The Isle of Man casino. Note the three-legged croupier in the background, and, if I turn up the volume, the roar of 750 cc Hondas and Yamahas." He fiddles the controls and the picture freezes on a close-up of the gloating punter in the feather bonnet. "How say you, senors—is't a true likeness?"

Don Collapso pursed doubtful lips. "He dozzn't look mooch like the Kinga Scotland to me."

"No?" purred the Wizard. "And what says our Scots friend?"

Lord Anguish belched, stirred, and peered blearily at the cauldron. "Nivver saw the man before in ma life!" he declared.

"You are certain?" said the Wizard dangerously. "Look again, drunkard! Look well."

Lord Anguish paled beneath his ginger whiskers, blinked, took a quick shlurp of Chivas Regal, and changed his mind.

"It's him!" he cried. "Hullaw rerr, Jimmy, hoo's it gaun, son? I mean, God bless Your Majesty! Hey, but, whit's he daein' in the Isle o' Man? It's no' Gleska Fair Week yet, surely?"

The Wizard smiled cynically and turned to the monk. "Frey Bentos?"

"Ah seen worse lookalikes," conceded the master spy, shrugging beady eyes. "Sho'nuff, he might impersonate His Scottish Majesty indifferent well, if he kin do th'accent an' slobber convincin'ly. The way Ah heerd it, no one's bustin' a gut to git close to King James anyhow, so Ah guess this impostuh could git by."

"Eez he revolting enough?" wondered Don Collapso. "I

mean, onteel you've eaten weeth the Scotteesh monarch, you ain't seen-a nothin'! I sat nex' heem at a Holyrood banquet . . . boy, talk about Friday night at the abattoir! Deez-gusteeng!"

The Wizard stabbed a talon-like finger at the cauldron image. "He has been trained for years, coached to perfection in Parliamo Glasgow and all aspects of Scottish culture. Our leading experts in drooling, stammering, and eye-rolling have tutored him to a point where I am sure he will nauseate even such an outstanding slob as yourself, Don Collapso." He glanced at the ambassador, who was cramming a fistful of sweetmeats between liver lips, and shuddered. "And his Latin pronunciation is perfect—wayni, weedy, weeky, and so forth."

Lord Anguish surfaced, waving a doubtful haggis sandwich. "Aye, but is he bent? Gay, ye ken—ambisextrous. A'body kens Jamie the Saxt is the original chocolate moose. Whit aboot that?"

The Wizard frowned. "In that respect, I admit, our impostor has proved a disappointment. He showed not the slightest interest in a screaming pansy introduced to him during training—an agent known, incidentally, as the King's Quair."

"You mean King's Queer, surely?" objected Frey Bentos.

"No, Quair," said the Wizard. "He was an Irish pansy. However," he continued, "it boots not, since the real king is not averse to female company also. Mind you," he added, glancing at the cauldron-screen, which now showed the plume-hatted impostor slavering lustfully as he poured roulette chips down the cleavage of his statuesque companion, "'twere well if we fed that little blighter bromide before he reaches Scotland, or people may start wondering."

"Who's thee beembo?" asked Don Collapso, smacking eager lips.

"That, senors," said the Wizard significantly, "is none other than the Castilian hidalga whose skill and daring as a secret agent are known and feared from the Indies to Cathay, the Mata Hari of Manzanilla, mistress of disguise and intrigue, she who set up the fatal hit on Henri Quatre of France, filched the industrial secret of caviar from Ivan the Terrible, and brought the Paris ambulance service to a standstill on St. Bartholomew's Eve! Yes, senors," and his eyes shone with admiring glitter, "'tis she, none other, La Infamosa!"

There were startled gasps around the table, and even Clnzh stopped toying with his girdle of shrunken heads. "La Infamosa!" they whispered. "Wow! *Por los Entranos de Dios!* So that's what she looks like! How d'you disguise *those*, for Goad's sake? La Infamosa! An' I colled her a beembo! Well, if that doan't beat fried chicken!" etc. The Wizard switched off the cauldron and rapped sharply on the table.

"Enough, senors! It sufficeth that La Infamosa is bringing this impostor to our border country where," he leaned forward, glinting evilly, "the *real* King James is about to begin one of his periodic hunting and reiver-hanging trips. Thus the scene will be set for the first stage of our master-plan, Operation Heretic, which will consist of the secret substitution of our impostor for the Scottish monarch. Full details of how this switch, code-named Jimsnatch, is to be accomplished, are contained in dossiers which you will collect at the door on your way out; nothing has been overlooked. Aye, senors—only a few days hence, we shall have the authentic James the Sixth under wraps, while our impostor will be lording it in Edinburgh and occupying the royal box at Murrayfield, unsuspected by any!"

"And then?" Don Collapso gulped Malaga with wolfish eagerness.

"Then!" quo' the Wizard, rising to his full skeletal height, sparks flying from his silver coiffure, "then, when the bastard Queen of England turns up her toes—Ah, God, let it be soon!—our impostor will succeed to the English throne! Think of it, senors! Our man in Whitehall, wi' power unlimited! In no time flat under orders from the Madrid hotline, he will have the English state on the brink of collapse! First," he chuckled malevolently, "he will alter the county boundaries, then decimalise the currency, make them drink beer by the litre, introduce comprehensive education, bring in hordes of asylum-seekers, subvert the heretic Church of England with gospel singers, undermine the national diet with garlic and peppers, cause psychedelic music to be played in their pubs, dribble away their sovereignty to foreign powers, and even," his voice sank to a grating whisper, "install a baseball diamond at Lord's." A gasp of awe-struck amazement greeted this diabolic proposal. "The fibre of the English will be shredded to tatters! They won't know who they are, even! Aye, where the great Armada failed, thanks to the endemonised Drake and the abominable disinformation of those villains Fishe and McCaskill, our great Operation Heretic will be a stone-ginger shoo-in!"

"Hallelujah an' Opus Dei!" interposed Frey Bentos, getting all fanatical. "Yes, sirree, an' the way'll be paved for peaceful take-over by our good ole boy King Philip an' the True Faith! 'Fore yuh kin skin a cat, the red 'n' gold bannah of Castile will be a-wavin' an' a-flutterin' o'er the Tower o' London, they'll be standin' in line for bull-fights at Wembley, an' con-fused Anglo-Saxons will be drivin' on the right-hand side an' takin' wrong exits with the road-signs bein' in Spanish an' all! Yes, suh!"

Delighted exclamations sounded round the table, Don Collapso choked with glee on his Malaga, Clnzh gibbered in savage triumph, and only one cautionary belch marred the general jubilation.

"Haud on a meenit," cried Lord Anguish, looking owlish as he voiced the national pessimism. "Are we no' a wee thingy pree-mature? Ye'll substitute this impoaster fur Oor Jimmy, ye say—but suppose some o' oor guid Scots lords sees the difference an' blaws the whustle oan him—"

"You will see to it that they don't!" snapped the Wizard. "By judicious distribution of gold and unlimited Cutty Sark— why, half the Scottish nobility are crooked anyway, or crazy enough to sell their souls for a Partick Thistle season ticket, and the other half will go along just for laughs. They would, in their own parlance, boil their grannies down for soap!"

"Aye, a' right!" quavered Anguish. "But even if ye get oor nobility tae recognise the impoaster—or raither, no' tae recognise him," he added, sniggering, "are ye sure he's up tae the job? Does he ken the wurrds of 'Flower o' Scotland,' for instance?"

"He sings it in his bath!" snapped the Wizard. "Word perfect!"

"Aye, weel, naebuddy in Scotland is," sniffed Lord Anguish, "so ye'd better tell him tae forget them pronto." He inhaled another portion of dunked haggis and slipped comatose from his chair.

"La Infamosa shall be informed," said the Wizard. "Nay, senors, nought shall go amiss—our plan is silky smooth and lubricated to perfection. But should some unforeseen impediment occur, know that a secret mini-Armada, manned by Mediterranean football hooligans, is e'en now lying off the Solway coast disguised as peaceful shrimp-shooters, ready to invade at a given signal and spread fire, sword, and Continental diseases throughout the Borderland. But it won't come to that," he added confidently. "Any questions so far?"

At this Clnzh emitted a series of grunts and whistles which, being translated by Frey Bentos, meant: "How does first-stage Jimsnatch actually work?"

"Pertinently inquired, aborigine," the Wizard commended him. "As you saw, senors, the impostor and La Infamosa are at present masquerading as tourists in the Isle of Man—where, for tax purposes, we have based Operation Heretic plc. This very daybreak, disguised respectively as an accountant and an exotic dancer from one of the hotel cabarets, they will make—"

"La Eenfamosa deezguised as a streeper?" gloated Don Collapso. "Fabuloose casting, Weezard! I can't wait, hubba-hubba!"

"She will impersonate the accountant," said the Wizard coldly, leaving the obese Iberian bewildered. "They will travel by smugglers' sloop to the Cumbrian coast, journey overland by express hay-wain to Carlisle, and there lie secure in a safe house, a bordello-cum-library known as the Thynkynge Man's Strumpet—"

"Eet sounds kind-a public," Don Collapso was beginning.

"Prithee, peace, Excellency! 'Tis an ill-frequented ken, since lusty gallants care little for books, while serious readers take no joy in slap and tickle. There, I say, they will lie safe, in the Priest's Hole Suite, 'twixt the sauna and the reference section—and there Frey Bentos will rendezvous with them tomorrow night, convey them hither, and thereafter to a secret spot marked X—see map reference in dossier—which lieth i' the forest nigh Peebles Hydro, where King James lodges with his hunting party. Ye will all three keep your heads down i' the forest until"—the Wizard's voice sank to a sinister hiss—

"King James's hunt shall happen by. You, Don Collapso, will be with the royal party on a Distinguished Foreign Visitors' ticket, and on some pretext of bird-watching or bug-hunting or being taken short or whatever, will lure away His unsuspecting Majesty from his attendants—"

"To thee seeclouded spot marked X!" yipped Don Collapso excitedly.

"—where he will be bushwhacked by seasoned local talent, a highly regarded Scottish combo known as Bangtail's Boys* whose services have already been booked by this drunken sot on the floor." The Wizard's lips writhed in a bloodless sneer. "Poor peasants, they know nought of our dark design, but think 'tis straight kidnap, and will turn his maj. over to us for a cut of the ransom and ten per cent of the residuals on the memoirs they fondly suppose he is going to flog to the tabloids when we release him—which, of course, we won't! Nay, senors, 'twill be the Big Sleep for Jacobus Rex! Our impostor, already on the spot, having changed into His Majesty's garments, will presently return to the hunt, accompanied by Don Collapso, the royal attendants will suspect nothing—and that, fellow-conspirators, will be Stage One (Jimsnatch) happily concluded! Thereafter, Operation Heretic's final consummation, the Enterprise of England, Mark II!"

Demonstrations of delight and congratulation broke out among the assembled baddies at the conclusion of the Wizard's diabolic briefing. Don Collapso hurled his plumed bonnet on

---

* Little does the Wizard suspect that Bangtail is even now clocking in to the Great Corral in the Sky, and that his leaderless band, wending home disconsolately with their plundered cats and poultry, are at this moment trying to coax a panic-stricken chicken down from a lamp-post in Galashiels. So they can be ruled out . . . or can they?

the floor and went into the Mexican Hat Dance, Clnzh dived into the cauldron and splashed with abandon, Frey Bentos resumed his imperturbable mask, and Lord Anguish rolled over, croaking: "Hey, barman, whaur's ma bluidy pint?" But we will not linger on this scene of Villainy Exultant; shuddering wi' dismay, we pull back and up to a long downward shot of the cavern, atmospherically bathed in eerie violet and crimson lighting, with green steam rising from the cauldron to envelop the conspirators in ghastly fog. With Don Collapso's triumphant "Olé's!," Clnzh's animal barks, and Lord Anguish's rendering of "I Belong tae Glasgow" sounding in our ears, we flee appalled from this nest of evil and zoom dramatically o'er the border wasteland, cleaving the thinning mist until we close on that lighted window in Thrashbatter Tower behind which, with any luck, Archie Noble must at last be stoking the inner man to some purpose . . .

Considering that the light in the Thrashbatter kitchen was supplied by one guttering rushlight, far too dim to make out sell-by dates, let alone lists of ingredients, our stalwart reiver hadn't done too badly. After pondering the great hams which hung in rows from the smoke-blackened rafters, the chines of beef, game pies, cold roasted fowls, and assorted joints littering the massive tables, and stroked his chin thoughtfully over the oven-ready trenchers of made dishes in the adjoining ice-house, he had chosen a carefully balanced snack consisting of a mortress of brawn for starters, pickled herrings for the fish course, a couple of sirloins removed with a brace of ducks, and a morsel of Stilton to clear the palate. A bowl of custard he had rejected as holding too much cholesterol, and now stood sipping a flagon of Diet Sack and nibbling a sugar-free comfit as he reflected that a kitchen so amply stocked with goodies argued an establishment doubtless furnished with other necessaries—like clean rags to replace those dropping in mouldering lumps from his athletic frame, and, if fortune smiled on him, washing facilities, bath gel, talc, and a hair-brush.

He listened, senses quivering, but the great house was silent save for the creaking of timbers, clankynge o' pypes, soughing of wind in the tall chimneys, grooms and wenches rioting in the staff quarters, a muffled voice upstairs groaning: "Come back to bed, woman, a God's name, 'tis after four and the jordan full!," and a piteous snuffling at the kitchen window to remind him of his famished horse without.

Being a Hero, and kind to animals, he placed a roast goose and a bowl of walnuts on the sill, and with a whisper of "Dig in, Red Rum," glided out into the passageway. Stepping carefully over the sleeping lackeys who littered the floor, he reached the main hall and, pausing only to soothe a wakeful bloodhound, tap the barometer out of sheer habit, and ignore the visitors' book, passed like a muscular ghost up the great oaken staircase bathed in moonlight to the upper floor. His uncanny reiver's instinct led him, after only two wrong turnings and mutters of "Oops, sorry, miss, wrong chamber!" to a huge draughty room full of arras, wardrobes, and chests-of-drawers. These, to his chagrin, were stocked entirely with monk's habits, chasubles, and other items of Clerical Attire, plus a puzzling assortment of tiny loincloths, each embroidered for a different day of the week; equally bewildering was the small hammock of woven twigs and tropical creepers slung between the bottom uprights of the huge four-poster bed, and, in the bathroom, the matching towels marked "His" and "Its." But most curious of all was the discovery, under a pair of ruby-studded dress thumbscrews in the bedside cabinet, of a first edition of Torquemada's *Inquisitting for Beginners*, signed "To my old amigo, Flash Bentos, from his room-mate Alexander (Big Sandie) Borgia," and a Spanish cypher book with a defaced fly-leaf label which read "Stolen from the library of Philip R., and may his royal curse go with it."

Archie pondered the volumes with a thoughtful frown, but since his search had produced nothing like a change of linen, he finally repaired to the bathroom for a quick shave and sluice, taking heavy toll of the shampoo and body splash. And he was just reluctantly resuming his sorry rags when his keen ear caught the sound of an indignant Mississippi voice raised on the battlements outside the bedroom window, apparently in altercation with a disgruntled taxi-driver.

This, you at once deduce, was Frey Bentos returning by hired mini-broom from the Wizard's conference, and having listened impatiently through the freezing aerial journey to the warlock-driver's views on capital punishment, torture, and them bleedin' sturdy beggars, he was now explaining that he was all out of bat's wool and newt's eyes, and could he please pay the fare in regular money? By the time he had settled up, and the warlock had whizzed away, bawling abuse, Archie was concealed behind the arras. Through a convenient hole he observed the entrance of an irritated monk with a frost-rimmed tonsure, muttering about goddam Limey socialists who didn't accept Vatican Express, and an Amazon pygmy fairly spitting with rage, for the warlock's censures had included non-white immigrants, and Clnzh was a sensitive savage.

It was obvious to Archie that evasion was impossible until this strange duo had got their heads down, so he continued to observe, trying not to sneeze, and witnessed two interesting events. The first was mere light relief, when Frey Bentos emerged grimly from the bathroom to accuse Clnzh of having drunk the body splash *again,* dragged the protesting pygmy from his hammock, and dropped him from the battlements with instructions to go haunt a peat-bog for the rest of the night and take his dam' blowpipe with him. But the second incident was drama of a hair-raising kind, for before retiring Frey Bentos went through the standard drill followed by all secret agents in the field, gumming a thread from one of his tassels across the door jamb, dusting the cords of his valise with talc, examining the candle-stick for bugging devices, looking under the bed, and thrashing the arras with a carpet-beater at hip level.

As a result of this last precaution, it was some five minutes before Archie, green-faced and weeping softly, was able to straighten up again, with his hands clamped between his thighs, and resume his survey through the convenient hole, and half-ruined though he was, what he saw and heard was bizarre enough to banish from his mind all thought of ice-packs and armoured underwear.

For now Frey Bentos was standing at his writing pulpit, clad in a Sea Island leisure chasuble and loafers, smoking a Hoya de Monterey and encoding his report of the Eildon Summit with the aid of his cypher book—and since this entailed much cross-checking and losing the place, he was muttering each word aloud as he encoded it. Muttering in *English,* too, thanks to his years in the New World and Cumberland. Careless, you think? Un-Bond-like? Right you are, but highly convenient, nay essential, for our story, for behind the arras our hero, whimpering inaudibly with his knees together and his ears flapping, was getting the ghastly outline of Operations Heretic and Jimsnatch, from "For His Catholic Majesty's Eyes Onlie" to the pathetic postscript: "Should your grace wish to honour your servant's poor efforts with some mark of favour, like the Order of St. Iago maybe, please note that the name is spelled B-e-n-t-o-s . . ."

Unaware that he had spilled the whole works to alien ears, the Spanish super-spy made ready for bed, slipped an arquebus under the pillow, flung wide the casement, cried "Buenos noches, birdies!.," poured a jugful of water on Clnzh, who was barking and whistling piteously beneath the window, climbed between the sheets, and was presently snoring like a tuba. At which point Archie Noble hobbled cat-footed to the door and out to the landing, his manly features furrowed with care—but who can say why? Is it that his one desire is to get out of this awful house with its manic carpet-beaters and immerse himself up to the waist in a freezing duck pond, or is he aghast at what he has just heard? Hard to say; after all, he is a mere broken man, not even on supplementary benefit, so why should he worry if King James is replaced by an impostor, or a cardboard replica, for that matter, and England falls 'neath the tyranny of Spain? But, hang it, he must have some patriotic feeling, surely . . . mustn't he? For the moment we just don't know, and can only dog his silent shuffle as he creeps wincing to the top of the stairs, and makes his stealthy way back to the kitchen unobserved. All is now deathly still; the grooms and wenches have stopped merry-making, the wind has dropped, the pypes clanke only occasionally, the effects of the carpet-beater have worn off, and it is with a debonair smile that Archie tips an acknowledging salute to the darkened kitchen, murmurs "Compliments to the chef," leaps nimbly to the window-sill, slips on the bowl of walnuts, and with a despairing cry takes the ultimate purler head over heels backwards onto a table which collapses beneath his weight and sends seventeen large copper vessels cascading on to the kitchen flags with a resounding series of *doiiiings*! reminiscent of the church bells of England on VE Day.

In an instant Thrashbatter Tower is ablaze with light, the occupants starting from their beds with cries of "Fire! Thieves! Popery! The Dagoes have landed!," wenches scream, grooms rush to the kitchen with clubs and find Archie helpless with his foot stuck in a bucket. "'Tis Edgar Kennedy! Down with him, seize him!" is the immediate diagnosis, followed by cries of "Nay, 'tis a broken man and runagate walnut-snatcher! Bind him, beat him, give him the message, bullies!"

Which they did, wi' many a buffet and sore stripe, before dropping him, trussed and sick as mud, into the cellar, to await judgment and punishment on the morrow, while outside in the frosty dawn his horse was leaning helplessly against an outbuilding, cracked up and neighing hysterically.

Well, it's been quite a night . . . highway robbery, swordplay, various raids (including one you haven't heard about yet); hens, cats, and a fortune in jewellery carried off; Bangtail deceased, Beauty robbed and beglamoured, our leading man in deep shtuck (but at least he's fed and redolent of after-shave). What else? Ah, yes, dastardly Spanish rogues a-plotting to o'erthrow our green and pleasant land. A tangled skein, gossips, but fret not, it's all under control . . . we hope.

"One thing at a time!" clarioned Lady Godiva, and smote her silver egg-spoon on the oaken table in imperious wrath. "Why, what a bedlam am I strayed into! After umpteen hours in a freezing coach, beset by brigands, my lingerie strewn o'er the snow, my best rocks reft from me, I arrive to find a house like a storm-tossed pigsty, wi' a bedchamber I'd not give to the chain-gang—who seem to have been using it, anyway—five minutes' sleep on a mattress apparently stuffed with logs, my coiffure in ruins and not a beautician nearer than Carlisle, wherever that is . . . and now! Now, when I sit me down to my noon-meat in this mouldy barn you call a banqueting hall, the posset's cold, the toast charred, and if this is a two-minute egg, fillip me with a shotten gurnet! Or a three-man herring!" Her teeth flashed and her eyes ground with regal rage. "And on top o' that, I am deafened by the unmannerly clack of unwashed proletarian employees who uproar my presence wi' whines and plaints ere I have seen a menu, even! I had been better served in a pot-house, aye, or Ye Little Cheffe!"

"She's always like this when she gets up," murmured Kylie to the trembling steward who stood ashen-faced behind my lady's chair.

"I heard that!" snapped Godiva. "What, simper and give me lip, will you, and before these churls? Nay, madam, ye were best button up—and that goes double for the rest of you," she added to the nervous servitors knuckling their brows and cowering before her dining table. "Just one peep before y'are spoken to, and the stocks and whipping-post shall have employ, and I kid ye not!"

Yes, our tempestuous heroine has finally checked in at Thrashbatter Tower (at 3 a.m., convoyed by the Warden patrol whose arrival, you remember, set Gilderoy in motion towards the tall timber) and after a few hours' troubled dozing in a master bedroom notable for bats and broken windows, has descended to partake of brunch and vent her temper on the amenities and staff. Can't blame her, really; her late grandsire, Lord Waldo, had been a fairly primitive peer who talked with his mouth full, slept (and pleasured the kitchen wenches) in his boots, and bathed by going out in heavy rain; his notions of *haute cuisine* stopped at roast-ox sandwiches and ale by the quart, and the furnishings reflected his homely taste, having remained unchanged since the Black Death (and they were sale-room rejects then). As to the personnel, this consisted of varlets, loons, and lurdens answering to names like Hob, Gob, Slob, etc., and bare-foot slatterns wi' unkempt hair and greasy aprons, supervised (if you could call it that) by a fat, flustered, and incompetent bailiff, Master Hodgson.

So it had never been the Savoy, and since Waldo's demise had degenerated even closer to Skid Row, hence my lady's displeasure—which, actually, was being soothed by the evident terror she was inspiring, plus the knowledge that in her gown of mulberry velvet with its puffed sleeves and lace collar sewn with pearls, her immaculate make-up and glossy hair-do confined in a diamond-studded gold net, she looked terrific, and was knocking Thrashbatter Tower and all therein for a collective loop.

As could be seen from the awe-struck expressions of the senior sluts and lackeys grovelling as she sat in state, criticising the bill of fare. Only Frey Bentos, watching narrowly in the background, failed to goggle; he had seen Sloanies before, and had other things on his mind. For while under the lax regime of old Waldo, who wouldn't have known religion if it fell on him, the Spanish agent's position as chaplain to the household had been secure, he couldn't be certain of retaining his firm base under this new C. of E. proprietress, whose disconcerting reply to his introductory greeting had been: "Out of my way, papist shaveling, and take your incense with you!" Plainly, with Operation Heretic coming to the boil (he's due to meet La Infamosa and the impostor in Carlisle this evening, remember), it behoved him to keep a low profile, so he lurked, trying to look benign, while my lady nibbled an angry oatcake and glared on the bailiff, who had been rash enough to clamour for her attention before she'd even got the top off her boiled egg.

"Well, sirrah, since I'm to starve I may as well listen while I'm doing it. Kylie, bid them give this sorry mess back to the piglets. Now, fellow Hodgson, what is this urgent matter that must take precedence o' my nourishment—and it had better be good!"

The bailiff tugged perspiring forelock and whimpered. "Nay, my lady, sweet mistress, an't please yer grace, 'tis a hell of a note, surely! Aye, 'tis the Nixons, d'ye see, fell thieves o' Scotland, that but last night rode on yer poor tenants o' Gungemyre, aye, to blackmail 'em, look'ee! An' if they don't pay up by midnight, the Nixons'll come back to raid, rob, ravage, rape, an' ride roughshod o'er the whole village! Prob'ly graffitti the place, an' all! Oh, my lady, yer worship, what's to be done, for us has no defence, belike, nor handy muscle to withstand the fearsome buggers, so shall we be undone—at least, Gungemyre will. An', kind mistress, beggin' yer pardon, 'tis up to you, bein' our lord an' protector to whom us poor agrarians look for succour, which is what us pays rates for, surely!"

[This speech should have been rendered in broad Cumbrian, but try telling that to a Burbank dialogue coach. Bound as we are by Hollywood convention, which recognises only three types of English accent—Oxford, Cockney, and Mummerset— we are obliged to make Hodgson and his fellow-rustics talk like Robert Newton playing Churdles Ash; sorry, but it's that or forget the Middle West.]

Amazement elbowed displeasure off the white brow of Lady Godiva as she turned bewildered glance on Kylie.

"Did he say 'blackmail'? Among this lot? I mean," she gestured helplessly, "'tis a mite sophisticated, is't not, for a populace who'd look more comfortable going on all fours? Doubtless they have beastly practices enow, but do they care who knows it? Marry, ye'd as well try to put the bite on cavedwellers!"

"Gungemyre may be the porn capital o' the borders, for all

we know," shrugged Kylie. "Some guilty secret they must have, that these Nixons hold the proof of. But what?"

"I don't think I want to know," mused Godiva, but steeled herself. "Speak, Hodgson—what vile shame doth Gungemyre harbour that these Scotch knaves would blow the whistle on? Wenches, cover your ears! Kylie, stop smirking!"

Master Hodgson looked puzzled. "Come again, my lady?"

"What has Gungemyre got to hide?" cried impatient Kylie. "Group sex? Nameless orgies? Are livestock involved? Are they all a.c./d.c., or what? Has somebody got pictures? Oh, disclose, fellow, we're all agog!"

But blank gape sat on the florid features of the bailiff until Frey Bentos, a-hemming diffidently, interposed. "By yore leave, mah lady," he nasalled smoothly, "we got a cross-wire sitooation heah, yessiree, ma'am. Yo' gracious grace is three centuries up front in supposin' that blackmail is a squeeze paid to prevent disclosure o' juicy scandal an' all. 'Mong these paysans 'tis a mere pro-tection racket . . . y'know, pay-up-or-we-torch-grandma's-toilet—or, in the case o' Gungemyre, flatten the whole dam' place wi' fire and sword, run-off the dogies, and gang-bang the broads." He bowed tonsured head, deprecating. "Sorry 'bout that, ma'am, but 'tis the name o' the game, yassuh."

"We are beholden to you, sir priest," said Godiva stiffly, and then did the grandpa of all double-takes. "WHAT?? You mean Scottish bandits are threatening one of *my* villages? Demanding money from my personal vassals, wi' menaces? God's light! Thou jestest? Thou dostn't? God's light! That did it!" And she shot from her chair, foot stamping, eyes aflame, and coiffure bursting its net and swirling like a conditioner advertisement, while the assembled servitors bent like saplings before the tempest of her wrath as she told Frey Bentos to say that again; refused to believe it; swept the crockery from the table; bade them send for the police, militia, and Securicor; boxed the steward's ears; screamed at Kylie to bring the peach brandy; and, finally, having run out of breath, demanded venomously who the hell were these Nixon people, anyway?

Master Hodgson emerged from beneath the table to tell her, in blood-chilling detail, with Frey Bentos filling in background as required, but we will not give a blow-by-blow account for two reasons: one, it's difficult to describe a three-sided conversation in which one of the participants sounds like an eagle with its tail in the mangle, and two, you know the essentials, having read them in Chapter One, which Lady Godiva hadn't. Being a novice in border affairs, she didn't realise that blackmail by powerful reiving families on small communities was everyday stuff; it came as an even greater shock to learn that the Warden authorities wouldn't do a thing about it, regarding it as trivial (and also because they didn't care to offend the blackmailers), and that the usual procedure was to pay up and look pleasant— which the Gungemyre villagers couldn't do, being overdrawn, and knowing from bitter experience that blackmailers didn't take payment in turnips, grass, or bits of stick, their only movable property.

It took about two hours' discussion, punctuated by outraged oaths, more broken crockery, and several jolts of peach brandy, to bring home to Lady Godiva that, at the end of the day, the buck was firmly in her court, and she had three choices:

1. subsidise Gungemyre to pay up;
2. allow the village to be done over by the Dirty Dozen;
3. fight.

Being not only Pride personified but as big a tight-wad as the next millionairess, she rejected the first course with a violence that broke a window. The second was unthinkable, and the third presented problems, since the armed men whom Lord Waldo had retained to guard his property had all picked up their cards at his death and gone their various ways, into crime, politics, and public relations, and the villagers themselves, like the Thrashbatter employees, were without exception Base Hinds and Sorry Caitiffs who would squeal and fall down at the mere mention of the name Nixon.

A parlous plight, you'll admit, for a tender maid (well, not all that tender, really, but quite untrained in crime-busting) on her first day in residence, and 'twas a distracted Lady Godiva who presently paced up and down before the hall's great fireplace, fingering luscious lip and kicking passing menials, while placid Kylie sat by embroidering an Armada 88 T-shirt which she intended to send to Sir Walter Raleigh with her picture and address pinned inside.

"The Queen shall hear o' this!" raged Godiva, for perhaps the eighth time. "What, Scotch robbers come in, cool as dammit, and put the frighteners on my peasantry—and where's the law, wi' a wannion? Harassing honest chapmen, moving on Sturdy Beggars, and chasing horses wi'out lights, I warrant me, while these thieving haggis-bashers set me—*me*, Lady Godiva Dacre, Young Noblewoman o' the Year, at defiance!" She clenched white fists and shook them to heaven. "Nay, but I'll fix their wagon—aye, but how, how? Oh, stop fiddling with that dam' vest, girl! Raleigh was nowhere near the Armada, and it'll just finish up in a puddle with Her Majesty jumping up and down on it! Counsel me, Kylie, how I may meet this hazard and maintain mine honour!"

"What you need," suggested Kylie, "is a red-hot trouble-shooter, like Gilderoy." She sighed, and her mistress quivered, glooped, and ground passionate molars.

"What you'll get," she retorted, "is a red-hot ear, if you mention that kiss-snatching cut-purse again! Ah, my knees melt and my blood boils to think on him!"

"All's one for that," said pert Kylie. "He signed off those stark skinheads last night, and they a score to his poor one. But what a one, heigh-ho!"

Lady Godiva let out a sarcastic whoof. "And he'll be i' the Yellow Pages, to be sure! Well, if he was, I'd none o' him! He robbed me of more than wealth and modesty, the smooth skunk! My good name rests on the recovery of that valuta— never mind why," she added, as Kylie registered surprise. "Have ye writ to the insurers yet?"

Kylie's answer remained unspoken, for at that moment there was without the sound of a broken man being dragged bound from a cellar and calling for his lawyer. Lady Godiva's angry demand to know what in God's name was happening was answered by Master Hodgson's crimson face appearing round the door jamb.

"Beg pardon, yer grace, an' that," quavered he, "'tis sneakin' runagate knave as bust into the kitchen last night, afore you came, an' gutsed yer ladyship's private grub, to wit, pickled herrin', beef, ducks, an' a bowl o' walnuts, an' made a hell of a mess, an' all." He scratched grizzled head. "Summat else—oh, aye, he's a fugitive murderer an' 'oss-thief, likely. So, I'll have him to Carlisle, that the law may mete out condign justice on pilferin' pest, aye, up i' the air an' swing on his ankles! An't please yer 'ighness," he concluded hopefully.

"That's all it needed!" exploded Godiva. "I'm not here five

minutes, and already 'Take Dacre, she's loaded' is the county's new motto! Vile reivers despoil my luggage, highwaymen glom my jewellery, blackmailers descend on my village, and some second-storey man cleans out the pantry! Great!" She rounded on Hodgson, glaring. "And ye'd send him to Carlisle to hang? Don't make me laugh! From all I've heard so far, they couldn't hang curtains! Hale him before me, bailiff! I'll bid him welcome to the club myself!"

"Are you sure you feel up to it, Goddy?" asked solicitous Kylie. "Certes, it hath been a trying time—"

"And I'm just in the mood!" seethed my lady. "You, fellow— ye ha' horsewhips and branding-irons to hand? And buckets o' hot tar? Splendid, bring him in!"

Now, her voice had carried beyond the door, and a keen observer would have noted that Archie Noble, bound between lackeys, reacted strangely at the point where she referred to the theft of her jewels. Cleansed now of its crust of mud, his alert, clean-cut map was clearly visible, and a flicker of surprise had crossed it, accompanied by a gleaming of his bright grey eyes, a tautening of his ankles, and a barely suppressed cry of "Stone me!" from his chiselled lips. In an instant he had schooled himself to imperturbability—a waste of time, actually, for when a moment later he found himself confronting a gorgeous redhead whose mulberry velvet was undulating with emotion, all his symptoms of astonishment broke out again, and had to be re-schooled. But inwardly he thought, well, they don't build them like that at the Townswomen's Guild, and eyed her keenly.

Lady Godiva did a bit of eyeing herself, for this handsome husky was not the cringing wretch she had expected. His rags did nothing for him, of course, but she had to admit that the fill-ing was impressive, being stalwart, shapely, and topped by features whose steady gaze, manly chin, tousled fair hair, sensitive teeth, etc., betokened breeding and undoubted sex appeal. Her hauteur blipped momentarily, and Kylie set aside her embroidery with a murmured "We-ell, hell-o!," at which Godiva stiffened back to icy disdain, her full lips hardening in ominous sneer.

"So, fellow," quo' she, "hast hoovered thy way through my comestibles, aye, and wouldst ha' left without paying, I doubt not. Well, shalt pay in full, and chance it." And she sat down leisurely, giving him time to sweat. "Thy name, sirrah?"

Now, we know our hero is not quite what he seems, being a man of parts, and at the moment he is wondering which one to play with this oomph-laden number whose flaming tresses and blue-steel regard betoken a dangerously short fuse. Subtly (he hopes) he opts for his Innocent Comic routine, smiling with just a smidgen of wist as he answers playfully:

"Noble lady, Noble's my name, tho' simple my nature, and simply noble was my appetite yestre'en, and nobly simple my means to satisfy it. That, noble lady, is simple Noble's simple tale, who trusts his poor simplicity to the mercy o' thy gracious nobility." He checked an impulse to add "Ba-boom!," since he was in no position to cap it with a quick chorus of "That's Entertainment" and dance off beaming.

Not quite alternative comedy, perhaps, but he knew it would have laid them in the aisles of any Elizabethan playhouse, and indeed it brought Kylie to her feet clapping and crying "More!" Not so Godiva, who had been a head prefect and sat on the bench down south. Her perfect features set like bored marble.

"Guilty," she said, and stifled a yawn. "Fifty lashes and two weeks i' the stocks, eating only what they throw at him. Wheel him out, Master Bailiff."

But as they laid hands on him, Archie quickly changed gear. "But, madam!" he cried. "You haven't even read me my rights yet! Is this Soviet Tartary? What o' my lawyers, my defence, my appeal, my suit for lackey brutality 'gainst these thy hirelings—"

"Nay, Goddy, hear him!" cried compassionate Kylie. "'Tis o'er the top and beyond the guidelines! Ye cannot whip him—well, not publicly, anyway, and sure," she stooped to whisper "'twould be wanton waste o' manpower, I mean, regard him—'tis likely hunk, and would look super in swim-trunks. Tell you what," she murmured innocently, "why not bind him over, metaphorically speaking, and make me his probation officer? Ah, sweet mistress, 'twould be such a challenge, and I've always fancied social work . . . and counselling . . . you know . . ."

Lady Godiva waved her to silence, for Master Hodgson was claiming her attention with more frantic brow-knuckling and pointing a grubby finger at a saddle borne in by a staggering lackey, which carried on the maker's label the legend "Property of B. D. Pringle, Smailholm Tower."

"Please yer ladyship, but ye're forgettin' the best bit, beggin' yer pardon! This be off the 'oss this villain rode hither, an' this"—he produced a wicked-looking dagger crusted wi' rusty yuggh-stains—"be his flick-poniard, yugghed as ye see wi' suspicious deposit which, by'r lady, the Warden's forensic boys will doubtless prove to be bloody blood matchin' the deceased Pringle's group, wi' a murrain, an' that! For 'tis my belief that the accused hath given Black Dod Pringle the long goodbye, an' nicked his 'oss to boot, oh gracious mistress!"

At which Godiva's chill beauty froze another two degrees, and Kylie's eyes bugged in proportion.

"So whiles I say good on yer ladyship for the floggin' an' stockin', an' that," continued the bailiff, fawning greasily, "murder's summat else—though how the hell he peeped the gas o' Black Dod, that was the roughest, toughest, rootin'est, tootin'est varmint south o' the Picketwire, I mean the Teviot, God alone knows." Grudgingly he scratched admiring poll. "Whatever, 'a must to Carlisle for the Harraby hornpipe, once we've done the floggin' bit to yer sweet gentility's likin', an' serve him right."

"And you wanted to put him on probation, Mistress Hotpants!" withered Lady Godiva. "A homicidal horse-thief, go to! For 'tis plain, as our worthy and keen-witted bailiff hath shown, that this simple Noble is up to the armpits in murderous guilt!" Her violet orbs narrowed as she regarded the prisoner, and you know why, don't you?—that brief aside about the character and abilities of the late B. D. Pringle had sparked a sudden wild idea in her shapely mind, an answer to her Gungemyre problem, and as it jelled, her delectable mouth writhed Medusa-like, her tawny locks sneered, and she almost gave a mocking laugh. (Over-acting? Well . . .)

"Indeed, good Hodgson, ye say sooth," she purred. "'Tis gallows for one, surely—but why in Carlisle, at cost to the ratepayers, when private enterprise can see him off cheaply, efficiently, and wi' minimum o' bureaucratic pother? Let's scrag him now, on some convenient tree!" She clapped her hands in delight. "I know—give the staff a half-day, picnic lunch for all in the barnekin, kiddies' sports, a prize draw for who gets the rope, and a dance in the evening!"

Gasps of amaze, horror, and approval greeted this proposal, and if they didn't come from Archie it was because he was rethinking his position. Comedy and protest had failed him so far . . . what remained? He thought furiously . . . ah, he had it! Play it by the book, blind her wi' science, no more messing about. He drew himself up to his stalwart height, held his head high, adjusted his manly profile, and spoke wi' crisp authority.

"Sorry, nought doing. Can't have it. Alleged crime committed in Scottish jurisdiction. Present court incompetent. Nothing further to say till I've seen my lawyer—and the Warden. Yes, I want to go before the C.O., so march me out, sarn't major! That's all, folks."

It sounded good, and Kylie gave a cry of relief, for hers had been the horror gasp noted above. Hodgson, who had done the approval bit, looked baffled, but Godiva didn't bat a scornful eyelid.

"Aye, sirrah, is that so?" said she, all silky menace. "Right, scrub the murder charge for the nonce—and return we to the ducks purloined in my kitchen. Poaching is a capital offence, I ween—"

"You can't poach dead ducks!" cried Kylie wildly.

"Since when are you an authority?" snapped Godiva. "What odds whether they're dead or crash-diving the marshes?"

"But you were just going to flog him for that! Nay, Goddy, leave it out, you can't just up his sentence—"

"Peace, hoyden! Who says I can't?" Lady Godiva tossed petulant head. "Oh, very well—but I can still bust him for breaking and entering! True, Master Hodgson? Are not hanging, drawing, and quartering the penalty for—"

"Ears, stop thy vents, for I believe it not!" shrilled Kylie. "Oh, sweet schoolmate, what's got into thee? See, on my knees I plead! You cannot be serious! Spare him, and . . . and I'll give thee my Philip Sydney autograph, honest Injun, and my William Byrd Live at Wembley souvenir programme—"

"Silence!" Lady Godiva rose imperiously. "My will is fixed, and his duff with it. What, have I not the right of pit and gallows on mine own patch? You bet I have! And if I repent my leniency of a moment since, and doom him to dangle, who shall say me nay?" Her eyes swept the room like phasers on stun, and her slender finger indicated the prisoner with fatal precision. "Have him hence, bailiff! No prayers, no chicken dinner, no last words, just up in the air, you flying cadets, and that's final!"

"She's gone barmy!" sobbed Kylie. "'Tis all that peach brandy and red meat! Oh, sirs, she isn't usually like this, not even when I double-faulted at match point 'gainst Cheltenham Ladies—"

"Madam, ye wot not what ye do!" Archie Noble's voice was spirit-level steady, his gaze erect, his head fearless, and if his stomach was right off the Richter Scale, you'd never have known it. "I demand to see the Warden!"

"To cop a plea, rascal? To blame it on your parents?" scoffed merciless Godiva. "Fat chance! Bailiff, set him dancing!"

"Madam, I insist! What I would impart is bigger than both of us! Nay, if not the Warden, thyself shall hear me—just two minutes alone, and then you can hang me all you want to, honestly!" His resolute gaze commanded her, seeming to plead "Come on, come on, you implacable cow, be reasonable, it matters, dammit!" But Lady Godiva's classic features remained utterly glacial.

"Not a hope, sirrah. You hang this instant . . . unless . . ."— and here she paused dramatically—"unless you agree to do a little job for me."

A renewed outburst of gasping greeted this thundering anti-climax, but now it was of bewilderment, hope (in Kylie's case), and speculation. Only Noble remained unmoved, save for an almost imperceptible frown, a woof of relief, and a prolonged gurgle as his internal economy readjusted itself.

"Ye would make a deal, madam?" he asked. "Why, what's your will?"

"Nay, first, your word!" insisted subtle Godiva. "To serve me, whatso'er the caper?"

He answered with the age-old pledge of the border. "You name it, duchess, you got it."

With a triumphant smirk at Kylie, Lady Godiva seated herself and invited the bailiff to explain the Gungemyre situation, and her urgent need for a proven hit-man to organise resistance, put spirit into her villagers, and generally give the blackmailers their lumps and pin them up to dry. To which Archie listened intently, chewed his lip, asked to be unbound so that he could scratch his chin, eyed my lady slantendicular, smiled a grim fighting smile, and remained unperturbed as Hodgson listed the opposition:

"'Tis the band of old Sir Prising Nixon, curse him, and wi' him Dicky Nixon, an' Tricky Nixon, an' Dicky's Tricky, an' Tricky's Dicky, an' Dicky's Tricky's Dicky, an' Hairless Will, an' Gormless Will, an' Fingerless Will, an' Trouserless Will, an'—"

Archie cut him short. "Race not thy motor, bailiff, 'tis all one how many they be, they are crow's bait." He turned to my lady, and wondering Kylie marked how, despite his sorry rags and wrinkled boots, he-man confidence shone from his comely features, assurance rippled his biceps, and (unless she mistook) an ardent light glowed in his grey eyes as he once-overed the beauteous tyrant who but a moment since had been scheduling him for the Tyburn tango. Blow me, thought jealous Kylie, talk about a hundred ways to get a man.

"Your grace shall not repent her clemency," he cried. "And I have thy pledge to free me afterwards—win, lose, or draw?"

Suspicion hauled Godiva's slim brows together. "What's this, sirrah? Ye purpose not to take a dive, I trust?"

"Dive, madam? I? Nay, Archie Waitabout goes i' the tank for no one." He gave a light laugh, hand on gallant hip. "Nixons, Schmixons, I'll lay them at thy dainty feet." And he cast an admiring glance at her ankles. "Yet first," he stepped closer, confidentially, "I would entreat a private conference wi' your gracious grace. 'Tis o' vital import, truly, and will save a hell of a lot of trouble to boot."

Disdain and surprise looked down my lady's classic nose as she wondered, is this a pass? Surely not, from one who had just escaped a manila cravat, yet she had known them come at odd times and from all angles. There was an eager urgency in his regard, an impatience as of a wrestler hot to come to grips, which she associated with love-seats, secluded arbours, and the backs of taxis . . . well, six feet and sexy though he was, he could forget it, a mere broken man to eyebrow a lady of her quality, and in those ghastly rags, too!

"Ye presume, fellow!" quo' she icily. "And as to the Nixons, ye talk a good game. When ye ha' put your muscle where your mouth is, it may be thou shalt have leave to join the queue for private audience." She accompanied this with the enigmatic half-smoulder and careless shrug which had sent countless admirers off to duels and jousts under the impression that they were on to a good thing if they played well; after all, he wasn't bad, in a dishevelled way, and there was no harm in kidding the poor boob along.

"As my lady pleases," said he tersely, and his look added "Stuck-up bitch" as he bit vexed lip and louted low, making that strained suppressed noise that betokens bursting impatience or an ill-digested prawn. "Yet 'twere best ye gave me privy speech instanter, for this is top priority—"

"Enough!" hauteured Godiva, and rose. "You have your orders. Bailiff, let all my able-bodied vassals know that this person is Numero Uno Honcho, see him furnished wi' all requisite arms and equipment, and in the morning I expect to see Gungemyre clean, bright, slightly oiled, and not a hair out of place— or else." She waved imperious dismissal. "Come, Kylie, I would have ye read me a sonnet and bathe my temples in rose-water, and my toe-nails need re-gilding, too."

She swept out, leaving a bewildered bailiff reflecting that whoever accompanied this ragged headcase to Gungemyre, it wasn't going to be him, and a broken man knitting frustrated brows and gritting irritated teeth as he muttered: "Why the hell can't she *listen*, dash it!" And as she mounted the staircase, Godiva was congratulating herself on one problem on its way to solution, thanks to her ruthless will, and enjoying the admiring prattle of her blonde companion, whose relief at Archie's escape was matched by awe of her mistress's iron maiden behaviour.

"You don't half wind people up, Lady G!" she exclaimed, as she sluiced rose-water on Godiva's milk-white brow with one hand, and stretched to paint her toe-nails with the other (not easy when you're only five feet two). "You had me going, I can tell you. But wouldst ha' hanged him, truly? Nay, Goddy, thou wouldstn't, thou couldstn't—not wi' those tumbled curls and Muscle Beach physique!"

"Who can say?" murmured languid Godiva, closing flawless lids. "I might. I mightn't. Depends on my whim o' the moment. 'Tis froward rogue, but all right if you go for the *Boys' Own Paper* type. So he protects my peasants, he will have served my turn."

"He'd ha' served more than that, given the chance," sniffed Kylie, gilding and sluicing moodily. "Couldn't wait to get you alone, could he? Mind you," she went on, speaking as distinctly as she could with a hair-brush held between her teeth, "I read somewhere that reprieves make men randy, so 'tis well you denied him private audience, or who can say what might have befallen?" Anyway, she thought, why should you have all the fun?

Because she's the heroine, that's why, and attracts men like a magnet. Tho' we suspect that Archie's desire to get her all to himself has some deeper purpose than mere canoodle. What can it be? Let's slip out of grim Thrashbatter Tower unseen, and wend our way through the gathering dusk to Gungemyre village, where all sorts of action will be hotting up shortly, and we may just learn the answer . . .

Here we go, here we go, here we go!
Liddesdale are the best team we know!
On booty and plunder we're bent,
And we all give two hundred per cent!

The blood-chilling strains of the ancient border war song echoed o'er the night-dark hills, reverberated across the waste, and bounced off the surrounding forest as the marauding Nixons, a hundred strong, swept out of their lonely mountain glen and galloped full tilt for England, their sights set on distant Gungemyre. A hellish, murderous crew, unshaven, unbuttoned, and reeking of strong drink, their string vests plainly visible beneath their mail jacks, grimy headbands under the visors of their steel caps, rolled-up copies of the *Daily Record* wrapped about their lance-butts, they presented a sight to unman the boldest and render the nervous totally paralytic.

At their head, looking like a bare-legged Darth Vadar, rode the notorious Trouserless Will, so called because he had vowed not to wear breeches until he had settled his deadly feud with the Dumfries Dry-Cleaning Company (a painful story which we won't go into here), and behind him surged Dicky and Tricky and all the rest of his ghastly foray. Over the heath they flew with an uncanny instinct guiding them clear of marsh and quicksand, except for those who blundered into bogs and peat-cuttings and sank bubbling without trace; through moonlit glades they thundered, swerving neatly between gnarled trunks, clearing fallen logs and picnic benches, and only occasionally being swept from the saddle by low branches; out on to the plain they drummed, addressing each other as "Jimmy" and shouting their marrow-freezing war-cries: "Gungemyre ya bass!" and "We're impartial, we don't care who beats England!" as they bore down on their quarry, save for those who veered off in search of licensed premises, or fell asleep in the saddle, or simply got fed up and went home—for a capricious, undisciplined shower were the Nixons, which was why shrewd old Sir Prising, their chief, had sent out a hundred on this petty blackmail, knowing well that quicksands, low branches, pubs, lethargy, and ennui would have reduced their strength to the requisite half-dozen by the time they reached the target area.

So into England they rampaged, a vocal but dwindling band, and at their doom-laden passing even the rabbits shuddered in their burrows, night-jars had hysterics in the foliage, and tramps cowering 'neath their old newspapers exchanged fearful whispers: "The Nixons are abroad" and "They are? Then who's out there galloping—their travel agent?" And now, on the last lap of the fell errand, their yells took on an even more menacing note, with "We're the wee boys!" "Go on yersel', Jock!" and "Thistle for the Cup!" piercing the night air and quivering the moonbeams . . .

Masterfully poised on the village dunghill at Gungemyre, Archie Noble caught the echo as it floated down the night wind, and smiled again his grim fighting smile—which was getting a trifle strained after two hours spent trying to put mettle and patriotic spirit into the reluctant villagers, and getting no takers. He had started with the Crispin's Day speech, which was greeted by full-blown raspberries and a hail of vegetables, and progressed through Drake's Prayer, selections from Magna Carta, and a couple of verses of "Onward, Christian Soldiers," to a naked threat to have their social security stopped if they didn't rally round and avail themselves of the assorted weaponry he had brought from the Thrashbatter armoury. All was in vain: the churls and wenches stood in vacant apathy, scratching their rags and only occasionally raising two derisory fingers in his direction. Archie, his manly features desperately glowing with derring-do and his boots sinking ever deeper in the sludge, made a last impassioned appeal.

"Men of Gungemyre! What, are ye men indeed, or cattle?"

"Moo!" bellowed the crowd.

"Moo yourselves, idle rotters!" cried Archie. "Why, have ye no thought for your wives and sweethearts, maids and tender virgins, assuming you have any, and the fate that awaits them from these hairy musclebound merciless Scotch ravishers?" Ignoring the hopeful murmurs and preenings of the wenches, he swept on. "An ye get not fell in and arm yourselves, how will ye save them from shame and ill-usage, and yourselves from ruin and slaughter?"

"We'll bugger off an' hide in ditches!" roared a large lurden at the back, and the mob bayed approval. "We've done it afore, we can do it again," they chorused. "'Tis the Gungemyre Deterrent, an' works every time!"

"And your homes?" Archie flung out a passionate hand at the row of mouldering shacks and pre-fabs, accidentally hitting one, which promptly fell down. "When your thatches are aflame, your wallpaper peeling in fiery strips, your rugs and duvets charred and reeking beyond repair, what then?"

"Council property, who the hell cares?" chanted the crowd, and our hero, viewing those scowling peasant faces, unmoved save for those who were waggling their fingers in their ears at him, played his last card. Proudly erect, his fair curls undulating in the night breeze, the moon-glow highlighting his flawless ear-lobes, he squelched to a surer footing and voiced with soft yet resonant vibrancy that age-old call to action which never yet failed to touch the sturdy Saxon heart.

"Then hear my final plea," quo' he, and his words dropped like syrup-coated steel. "Since nought else avails, I put it to ye, as yeomen of England, sprung from her soily bosom, proud heirs of Crecy and Poitiers and Colombes Stadium, victors o'er Frogs and Jocks and Dagoes on bloody fields innumerable . . ." He paused, and his listeners, moved despite themselves, craned unwashed heads as he spoke, a wistful smile on his proud lips. "A shilling an hour, and threepence overtime after midnight! How say ye, bulldogs? Death before dishonour, and a five-bob bonus to the man who nails Trouserless Will!"

An ear-splitting cheer rang out from the villagers, damaging the welkin and bringing two more hovels down in crumbling ruin. They surged about Archie, horny hands clapping his back, eager faces giving him the benefit of their halitosis as they shouted amain those inspiring slogans which had sounded across the dewy plain at Agincourt and rung round the sun-baked cliffs of Roncesvalles: "Double time after 3 a.m.!" "What about third-party cover?" "Can we keep their horses?" "Half a dollar up front!" until our hero was like to choke, though whether with emotion or the noxious airs released from the dunghill by their enthusiastic trampling, who could say?

"Right, get fell in and number off!" he commanded briskly. "This is how we do it! Stunt men—up in the trees, ready to swing down on creeper ropes and boot them from the saddle! Feet close together, mind, and wait for the Korngold fanfare! Hedgerow Commando—into the brambles ready to spring out and drag them from their mounts—and I want to hear lots of 'Take that!' and 'Merry ho-ho-ho!' You men, there—your names? Warner, eh? Right, Warner brothers, start digging pits for them to ride into, and the rest of you make nets to drop on them from convenient buildings—oh, and ladies, we'll need you to reload and arrange refreshments and cut up the remains! To it, bullies, they'll be here any minute!"

He strode about heroically, humming the Warsong of Dinas Vawr, slapping shoulders, radiating encouragement, dragging shirkers from under the horse-trough, raising morale, and generally behaving like a born leader, or, if you prefer it, a first-class prat, his bright eye missing nothing as he disposed his forces, examined their weapons, ordered the more dishevelled to get hair-cuts, and picked out a nice safe line of retreat. "And give a rouse for Lady Dacre, wi' three times three, if you can count that high," he bade them cheerily. "She has a dinner engagement, but sends her good wishes, and I doubt not she'll be along in the morning with medals and cooked breakfasts for all—and then," he grated to himself, "she'll get a piece of my mind, the stubborn, stone-deaf hussy!"

But wait, hold on, you protest . . . what was that about "a nice safe line of retreat"? Our hero isn't going to slope off in the crunch, surely? Well, yes, he is—in fact, there he goes, fading like an intelligent phantom into the undergrowth while the sturdy Gungemyrians stand to arms, climb trees, crouch in ambush, and wonder uneasily if they shouldn't have got a written contract—but it's too late now, for out of the gloom comes the terrifying glottally stopped clamour of the approaching Nixons: Archie hears it too, and pauses in flight, spasms of heroic anguish ruffling his B.O.P. profile—for of course he isn't chickening out! He's answering the Call of Duty—and if you find that confusing, just imagine how the Gungemeronians will feel when they discover they're without a leader to shout "It's cutlasses now, men!" and cop the first bullet, with luck.

Cursing his necessary scram, and wi' many a reluctant backward glance, Archie sped unwillingly up a wooded slope from whose summit he should have a grandstand view of the action—and got the shock of his life as a mounted figure, black and spectral in the moonlight, reared up in his path. A headless horseman? A stray Nixon? A jockey out for a practice gallop? Whoever, it was someone on whom to vent his frustration, and without breaking stride he launched himself in a flying tackle, shouting "Geronimo!," misjudged the height, and brought the horse down with his arms wrapped round its fetlocks.

In an instant he was afoot, only to find the fallen rider poised in karate fashion, snarling "Ha!" So, he thought, a fellow Black Belt—and after that it was all too fast for the eye to follow, as feet flashed, hands chopped, nerve centres were probed, insteps were locked round necks, somersaults and rolls were performed, drop-kicks delivered and avoided, and boot-sole met boot-sole as each tried that rather awkward savate kick where you stand on one leg and lash out sideways—risking a hernia, by the looks of it, but that's martial arts for you. At which point Archie, silently acknowledging his opponent's skill, had recourse to that deadly ploy known only to the ninja masters—hobbling suddenly with a cry of "Ouch! My blasted knee's gone again!" It took the other off guard, and with a cunning clutch and heave our hero bore him to the earth and was preparing to butt him stupid when the rider's hood fell back to reveal—did you guess?—features of marble beauty gleaming in the moonlight, flashing violet eyes, auburn tresses cascading o'er the dew-pearled sward, and parted red lips only inches from his own.

"You!" he cried.

"Thou!" exclaimed Lady Godiva, emphasising the social gulf between them.

Yes, recognition was mutual, and you know what happens when a hero finds himself unexpectedly prone on a supine heroine (especially when they've got off to a bad start) and her p.r.l. are only inches from his. A moment's breathless pause as their eyes meet, and then he's locked on to her like a hydraulic pump, apparently trying to eat his way through to the back of her head, and the only question before you go for pop-corn is: will her limp hand a) clamp passionately round his neck, or b) ball into a fist as she lands him a big one?

In this case, neither. Godiva was too stunned to resist (or was she secretly enjoying it, the wanton?), and when he unplugged presently for lack of breath, and she too had taken in life-giving oxygen, they stared bug-eyed on each other for a space, snogging forgotten in simultaneous astonishment. Then:

"What are you doing here?" in unison, Godiva forgetting the second person singular in her confusion. Shades of pink, denoting bewilderment, outrage, and finally fury mantled her ivory cheek as she surged to a sitting position, pointing downhill to mist-wreathed Gungemyre, whence came din o' combat: clash of steel, bodies falling in pits and leaping from bramble bushes, creepers snapping under the weight of swinging stuntmen, and shrill appeals for paramedics.

"Deserter! Base recreant scarperer!" flamed Godiva. "Ah, what o' my village that thou wert sworn to succour? Dastard, to leg it in coward flight at the first onfall——"

"Madam, belt up!" Before his curt command her violet pools widened to startled ponds, for this was a new Archie Noble, harsh and tight o' lip, his eyes gleaming like fridge-fresh martinis. "Peace, dammit! Here is no time for lady airs or dumb misprisions!" His lips untightened in a sardonic smile. "'Twill save a deal o' hassle if I tell thee thou art looking at Head of Station B for Border—aye, a double-nought operative, licensed to slay and ignore traffic signals——"

"Thou?" Godiva's slim fingers flew to stricken lips. "An agent o' Sir Francis Walsingham?"

"We professionals call him W," snapped Archie. "Right, mistress—why are you stoodging around at this time of night, dressed like a principal boy?" For my lady was fetchingly attired in traditional panto gear of Robin Hood cap, shortie tunic, tights and high boots—convenient active service gear for an Elizabethan heroine, and guaranteed to draw two-tone whistles from pit and gallery.

So startled was she by his revelation that Godiva actually answered without even a preliminary "How dare you?," though there was much miff in the gesture with which she flicked a stray beetle from her hair, and her words were as proud icicles.

"Patrician concern for my dependents drew me from my scratcher—aye, noblesse oblige, a concept beyond the ken of mere cloak-and-dagger artist," she added, her wonted hauteur taking over again. "Dacres frowst not abed when their vassals are in peril, Master Spy—but when I fare forth to see how you and the Gungemyrers are doing, what do I find? Thyself impersonating a frantic rabbit, abandoning the poor souls to merciless rapine—"

"Rapine, my foot! Know, gormless aristocrat, that Gungemyre is secured, thanks to my dispositions, and I withdrew only because the info I carry is too precious to be perilled in such petty turn-up—in which your bone-headed whim had landed me, remember?"

"And whose fault was that? Why didst not disclose thyself for government hit-man this afternoon?"

"Fat chance had I! Was I to blow my cover before thy minions? Did I not sue for private audience, and drop code-words and secret signs like I was scattering confetti? But hoity-toity never noticed, did she? Too busy swanning around like Lady Muck lording it o'er the humble peasantry! So I must e'en play along, allowing myself to be dragooned into defending your ruddy yokels, and hoping I could put you i' the picture anon!" He snorted a contemptuous pshaw. "This is what comes of recruiting amateurs from Girton!"

"I wasn't at Girton! And Sir Fran—W, I mean—gave me ne'er a code-word!"

"Well, he picked a real dilly in you!" quo' merciless Archie.

"'Hang him, bailiff! Set him dancing! Up i' the air wi' him!'
What art thou, some kind of sadistic kook? By heaven, mistress,
ye came nigh to popping my cork, which matters little," he
added, shrugging nobly padded shoulders, "but thy prideful
folly might ha' sent England itself down the tube!"

"I was but kidding, to pressure thee!" retorted indignant
Godiva. "And how was I to know who you were? No one
warned me that Head o' Station B would look like an out-of-
work bin man who went around murdering stray reivers and
snitching steeds and scoffing other people's walnuts—"

"That," grated Archie, "was mere mischance! Could have
happened to anyone. It didn't entitle you to press-gang me into
Operation Gungemyre!"

"I was only doing my job as landed gentry!" stormed
Godiva. "'Tis fine for some, wi' nought to do but undercover
snoopage! Some of us are but part-time agents, with civilian
responsibilities . . . nay, but hold the phone!" She slapped a per-
plexed thigh. "How knew ye that *I* was a W agent?"

"Keep it down!" he hissed. "Know ye not there be bugs i'
the wood? Aye, Spanish bugs trained to listen and report to
Onionland! Earwigs—get it?" He chuckled, grimly, but getting
no ovation from Bemused Beauty, sighed, and became the steel-
cold agent again.

"I shall take it from the top, lest the readers get confused,"
said he crisply. "Know then that I, posing as a broken man, have
been on the look-out for Dago plotters hereabouts, and to
finance my operation, W was to send abundant lettuce in the
form of jewellery, by secret courier—"

"Me!" said Godiva, proud if ungrammatical. "*My* jewellery, too!"

"—who would deposit it at the Cart and Wain left luggage

in Carlisle, for collection by one Prometheus Progmore—an alias of mine, and I didn't choose it," he added curtly. "But when I heard thee this afternoon bewailing that thy rocks had been reft from thee, the old computer registered that thou must be the courier (that's a laugh!) and that anyone calling at left luggage asking 'Anything for Progmore?' was in for one hell of a wait." He drew breath, flexing denunciatory brows. "So prithee, Mistress Foulup, discourse—as to how ye lost that vital cargo, and why a God's name did W entrust it to a half-witted Sloane Ranger wi' no obvious qualifications save blue blood, red hair, and more curves than a scenic railway—which is probably why he took you on, the impressionable old snob," he added, this time with a disgusted tchah.

"Quite finished—sirrah?" inquired Godiva, whose peerless profile had clicked up another notch with every scathing word. She yearned to kick in the slats of this presumptuous Civil Servant, but schooled herself to reply with sub-zero composure.

"For starters, the jewels were mine own, gladly placed at the disposal o' cash-strapped State, to pay the wages of such as thou. Secondly, I was employed as courier because, half-witted Sloanie though an envious hireling may deem me, yet am I a Dacre, bottle-fed on loyalty, weaned on honour, nourished on patriotism, and (when need arises) slimming on self-sacrifice, aye, dedicated only to service o' this fair land of ours!" At this point a noble mist filmed her uplifted eyes, while the strains of "There'll Always Be an England" floated o'er the moonlit glade, and in the bushes even fugitive bunnies and pursuing ferrets stiffened to attention. "Nay, we o' the Upper Crust serve not for gold or guerdon, but only for our country's glory—oh, and for all those precious things, like honey on the lawn at evenfall, the scent of yeomen wending their way home from honest toil, the clonk of leather on willow, maypoles dancing by the fire at tea-time, conkers and tadpoles and warm woolly mittens, and all that stuff so dear to us that foreigners don't understand!" She brushed a hand o'er pearl-dropped lashes. "Anyway, I was coming up north on business."

Well, thought Archie, all that should send King Philip scuttling back to the Escurial. Aloud he asked: "So what happened to the pay-roll?" and Godiva's proud gaze faltered ere she whipped it back into line.

"Why," said she, trying to sound casual, "'twas heisted . . . by some Scotch highwayman or other."

"Highwayman? Scotch?" His face fell like a collapsing scrum. "Oh, stone the corbies! You don't mean—Gilderoy?"

"Something like that," confessed Godiva, tho' her ankles jellied at the mere mention of the loved-hated name, and the Head o' Station B smote impassioned palm to stricken forehead.

"Gilderoy! Scotland's top agent and my deadly rival, who hides his spying self 'neath mask of romantic tobyman, the rat! Oh, madam, what snafu was here! Not only ha' ye lost the goods, the bloody Jocks have got 'em! Hard jewellery, too, better than oil-rigs!" He took anxious chin in troubled hand. "They must ha' known of thy mission—aye, their spies are everywhere, from dole queues to football management." He wheeled on her j'accuse-wise. "I'll bet he smooched it out of you, didn't he, hypnotising thee wi' burning kisses? Aye, thy beetroot beauty betrays thee! Gad, what a technique the blighter's got!" He thumped angry fist on exasperated knee. "And at such a time, when I am in dire need o' the long green to finance a counter-stroke 'gainst Dago deviltry!" Seeing alarmed inquiry o'erspread her perfect visage, he briefed her crisply on the outline of Operation Heretic—which he had gleaned, you remember, by eavesdropping on Frey Bentos talking to himself. (So now you know why he was looking so thoughtful when he trod in that bowl of walnuts; Bond himself would have been equally preoccupied.)

"This much I overheard—that they plan to put an impostor on the Scottish throne, to our eventual undoing in England, and that your man Bentos is up to his tonsure in the plot and meets with La Infamosa and the bogus Stuart in Carlisle this very night," he concluded. "But whither they go thence, who their other confederates are, and where exactly in the border they plan to snatch royal Jim and substitute the lookalike, I know not yet. So 'tis plain I must clobber them wi'out delay before they leave the city." He ground frustrated bicuspids. "Given the cash thou hast lost, I would ha' mustered my Station B operatives to take them out, squeeze them of the details, and then snooker their whole vile Dago apparat—but now, wi' my chaps' pay in arrears and the idle bastards unionised up to here, such hope is vain! Boy, when things go wrong!"

Contrition, we know, was not Godiva's long suit, but the way he punched a nearby oak and doubled up, nursing his fingers, plus the knowledge that the initial goof had been hers, moved her to point to the bright side.

"Nay, all may yet be well!" she cried. "Certes, I'm parrot-sick about the Dacre Diamonds, but there's lots more where they came from, honestly! Shalt have bucks and to spare, once I've written to Coutts—"

Sucking bruised fingers, he voiced indignant scorn. "Tho' it be but Monopoly money to thee, mistress, still 'twould come too late! 'Tis now or never! So . . ." He squared chin and shoulders in resolute unison. ". . . I'll just have to take 'em out single-handed. A nuisance, but thus crumbles the cookie—"

"Can't the Warden help?" cried Godiva, and he gave a derisive snort.

"Ever tried stirring up local government in a crisis? They'd still be filling in forms when this pretender's coronation mugs were in the shops! Nay, here is need o' that lightning decision and ruthless execution which men associate wi' Double-Nought Noble." He shrugged modestly. "And if I have none to aid me i' the clinches and watch my back when the rough stuff starts, what o' that? Won't be the first time."

His careless gallantry rang like a trumpet blast in her shapely ears, for though her final school report ("Spoilt and arrogant pill, deportment unbearable") had been endorsed by many detractors, even Godiva's hairdresser could not have denied her by-jingo spirit (see previous pages). Now her flawless skin gleamed like a body lotion commercial and her bosom quivered with patriotic abandon as she volunteered—nay, demanded—to be taken on the strength, urging her undercover (albeit amateur) status, her award of the Modesty Blaise Rosebowl for unarmed combat at Benenden, and her zeal to make amends by putting the boot in for Queen and Country. To all of which he gave the sexist horse-laugh, she blew her beauteous stack, and a pretty little tiff ensued, thus:

HE: Prithee, madam, leave it out! Here be man's work!

SHE: Yah, right—a man I would ha' cold-cocked a moment since, but that ye pulled that sneaky trick, feigning gammy knee—

HE: It worked, mistress, so there's an end on't.

SHE: Try it again, chauvinist! Nay, by'r lady, an ye
spurn my aid, the Queen shall hear of it, so
there!

HE: Oh, brother! Look, lady, I commend thy spirit,
but here is no soft option where chaps shall open
thee doors and give thee time off to have
babies—

SHE: Vile traducer! Ye impugn mine honour!

HE: Sorry, sorry, mere figure o' speech. Nay, face it,
madam, Rosebowl or no, thou canst not take a
man's part—

SHE: Nor thou a woman's, smartass! [*triumphantly*]
How if La Infamosa should take refuge in some
ladies' loo? What then, ha?

HE: [*doubtful*] True, thy femininity might have uses,
but . . .

SHE: [*suddenly husky-sexy*] And not just for crashing
powder-rooms . . .

Switching gear, you see, the minx. She accompanied the
throbbing words with a forward sway, all pout and smoulder,
and with her lips like tremulous crimson cushions and her patriotism vibrating at close range, Archie found himself wondering
if her assistance might not come in handy at that. After all,
female charm had a place in intelligence work . . . look at Mata
Hari and Pussy Galore . . .

"Nay, if ye put it like that," quo' he hesitantly . . . and then
as she sashayed closer still, giving him both violet barrels,
love's thunderbolt, which had been hovering over his unsuspecting head since their first meeting, zapped him full belt—and

he was clasping her supple softness in passionate embrace, renewed lip-wrestling was taking place, hidden woodwinds were playing "Linden Lea," and the moon-bathed glade was soft wi' the balmy scent of snowdrops and mistletoe (it's February, remember).

The strains of the hidden orchestra gave way to the gentle sclorchhh! of disappearing bath water as their lips drew apart, leaving our hero's emotions in turmoil. What was he doing? He, a double-nought action man, supposedly fireproof, enraptured by pneumatic form and honeyed mouth which only seconds ago had been spitting fire at him—for while his official conscience was carpeting him for canoodling on the firm's time, his heart was telling him that he was hopelessly hammer-locked by Cupid. Duty and common sense were no defence against subtle perfume that worked on him like nerve gas, and he could only nod dumbly as she murmured: "Little need hast thou of aid i' the clinches, but if ye need me to watch your back . . . or front . . . just whistle." Her lashes lowered wi' seductive swish. "Am I welcome aboard, skipper? I'll try not to be a nuisance."

"Oh, all right," he gulped, and deciding that while a burning declaration of love was out of season from Head of Station to part-time assistant, something more was necessary, he added hoarsely:

"Ah . . . um . . . well . . . my lady . . ."

"Godiva," she husked, nestling. "Goddy, to my . . . friends."

"Yes, well . . . Goddy . . . what I want to say is, you see . . . well, I know I'm no Gilderoy (thank God) to dazzle thee wi' Celtic charm and flashy kilt . . ." His manly chin lifted, and true-blue decency osmosissed from every strapping inch of his athletic frame. "Nay, mere honest English am I, four-square and a yard wide, if you know what I mean, and when this beastly business is over . . ."

"Say no more," she whispered. "I know. Oh, and . . . Archie—I may call you Archie, mayn't I, while we're sort of off-duty? Look, I'm sorry about the hanging thingy, really. I get carried away at times, you know, with the feudal tyrant bit, right?"

"Don't mention it. Perfectly understandable." He resisted an urge to tango her round the glade while he devoured her ear-lobes. "Well . . . we'd better be pushing along . . . I mean, the sooner we scupper these Spanish bounders, the better—"

"Yes, let's!"

"It'll take a day or two, I expect . . . you're sure they won't miss you at Thrashbatter?"

"I'll get some passing mendicant to take a note to Kylie. She'll love being left in charge—taking soup and blankets to the Gungemyrites." She gave a tinkling laugh, which was music to his love-smitten ears. "Gosh, some feudal tyrant, I! I'd forgotten all about them, what with . . . this and that . . ."

With an effort Archie dismissed her ear-lobes and became the decisive executive again. "Fear not for thy village, fair Goddy. My dispositions should have all sewn up by now—harken!"

They harked, and sure enough, from the misty bottom came sounds indicating that it was Gungemyre 4, Liddesdale o, and the villagers were doing a lap of honour. Only a quartet of Nixons had made it to their goal, and been overwhelmed by the creeper-swingers, bramble-jumpers, and pit-diggers whom Archie had shrewdly organised; now they were suffering the hideous fate of captured blackmailers, and Godiva shuddered as Trouserless Will's frantic plea for mercy rang through the night: "Hang me, shoot me, but for pity's sake put not breeches on me, or I shall be foresworn! Nay, ye would not have me break my vow!" But they would, forcing him into a pair of tight jeans, while his hapless companions had their bags *taken off* and their bottoms painted in the Dacre colours and decorated each with a carefully adjusted daffodil, whereafter they were bound across their saddles and sent back to Scotland as a terrible warning. Aye, a savage frontier it was, gossips . . .

... and not just on the political front. Have ye noticed, 'midst all the plots and raids and escapes and have-at-you, one fact o' vital import? No, not Lord Anguish's impending hangover . . . no, not the daffodils, either. Give up? 'Tis this: our Heroine, her ice-cool hauteur notwithstanding, has managed to inflame the passions of *both* our Heroes, top hit-men of their rival countries! Explosive stuff, eh? Aye, when they meet . . . but we'll have to find Gilderoy first, where'er he's got to. Quiet, while we scan the misty night . . .

A brooding silence, a quietude so dense as to be almost palpable, hung o'er the mossy hollows and hollow mosses around Thrashbatter Tower, a stillness so heavy that it automatically sank to the bottoms of soundless streams and empty gullies and oozed without so much as a murmur into rabbit warrens and the dens of badgers and similar plantigrade mammals, stifling their earthy tunnels with its sepulchral hush; nothing stirred or was shaken, much, for even the night wind that hardly ruffled the rank grasses and bare branches was mute, and a lonely wayfarer, had there been one about, which there wasn't, might have supposed himself on some dead planet whirling noiselessly in the vast limitless void of space.

Until he got within earshot of Thrashbatter itself, that is, for the great mansion was jumping like a gin-mill with the din of carousal in the servants' quarters, where the hired help were celebrating the absence of their imperious new mistress. A whole tantrum-torn day they'd had of Lady Godiva's domestic tyranny, and the news, brought by an ear-boxed maid, that she had ventured forth alone, booted and spurred, in the direction of Gungemyre, had been received with cries of "Carnival!" "Break out the turnip cordial, Martha, and let's have a ball!" and pious hopes that her ladyship would be done over by raiding Nixons, with luck. So all those lurdens who had managed to avoid being press-ganged to Gungemyre by Archie Noble (the whole male establishment, in fact) and the kitchen wenches were raving it up wi' merry fal-lal and hootennany, with none to let or hinder. For Frey Bentos was also mysteriously absent (aha! where, we wonder?) and the only other member of the Quality on the premises was Mistress Kylie, who simply didn't count as a disciplinary force. Left in charge by Godiva, she had bent a sympathetic ear to the growing uproar of below-stairs revelry, and had even ventured down to see if there were any stalwart stable-hands worth inviting upstairs for cocoa or a game of Scrabble or something, but there weren't. She had returned disconsolate to her chamber, prowled moodily through Godiva's lingerie and cosmetics to see if there was anything pinchable that wouldn't be missed, and was now leafing idly through a luridly illustrated paperback edition of Foxe's *Book of Martyrs*, when she became aware that somewhere beneath her window, just about where the dead silence of the surrounding waste met the din of the staff party, an odd noise was manifesting itself, a sort of rustling punctuated by gasps and heavy breathing.

"It's that damned dwarf who was sneezing in the flower-beds half the night!" was her first thought, but on leaning from her casement crying, "Avoid, shortie! Go snotter elsewhere!" she was startled by a responding exclamation from the ivy-covered wall below of "Demmit, this stuff's playing hevock with mai hose! Is thet yoo, peerless Godaiva? 'Tis Ai, flaying to yur saide!" and reeled back into the room, her maiden heart fluttering like a windsock.

"Gilderoy!" she yipped breathlessly, unable to believe her luck. True, she wasn't the object of his romantic quest, but Kylie knew opportunity when it came thundering on the panels, and in a trice she had flung farthingale and stomacher aside, arrayed her buxom shapeliness in a transparent black negligee, squirted a quick dash of Arpège behind each ear, and was back languishing at the sill, cooing in a deep contralto.

"Who comes?" she husked, like Marlene with a head cold.

"Yur love-smit slave!" was the reply, as with a final heave and crackle he hauled himself up to window level, and her pulses went into overdrive as in the gloom she made out that splendid profile, teeth a-gleam 'twixt pencil moustache and sexy chin-beard. "Ai say, d'you mind if Ai come in? It's deshed chilly out heer, and Ai'm aflame to lay mai heart at yur feet, honestly!"

"Prooove it," drawled designing Kylie, well knowing that with the light behind her he couldn't tell he was at the wrong address. She lowered her face to his, locking on with eager lips, and the ivy rocked and threatened to come away from the wall with the ardour of his response—indeed, for a moment he let go his hold and swung there by passionate suction alone, only grabbing on again as Kylie, her senses ecstatically disordered, came loose with a noise reminiscent of a hippo rising from a swamp, and fell swooning on the carpet.

With one lissom spring he was over the sill and kneeling at her side, chafing her limp wrists and moistening her parted lips with a Drambuie miniature drawn from his sporran.

"Ah, speak to me, Godaiva! Awake, mai love, end tell me whay yur wearing a blonde wig! Ope those violet orbs and—ach, fur Pete's sake! Yur not Godaiva at oll, but thet wee cupcake who played gooseberry i' the coach lest naight! What imposture is this? Where's yur mistress, gurl?"

Kylie's lids blinked open, zombie-like, and she spoke in a breathless quaver. "Honour bright, Miss Hamilton, the gardener's boy was just helping me with my zipper . . . we weren't doing anything wrong, really . . . Where am I? What's o'clock?" Then she focused, blue eyes moist with adoration. "Gosh, I didn't dream it! 'Tis you! Brother, what an entrance! Encore!" And she flung her arms round his neck, smooching hungrily, while the handsome highwayman strove to break the clinch.

"Stop it, woman! Hev ye gone ape indeed? Suppose someone should wock in, end yoo in yur deshabbles! Desist, Ai say, end discourse—whair is Lady Godaiva?"

"Out for the evening," said Kylie dreamily. "Got a heavy date, I ween, and like not to return ere cock-crow. Who cares? We're here, thou and I, and that's a genuine pard-skin rug before the fire . . ."

"Och, peck it in!" quo' Gilderoy, detaching himself with difficulty, and rising to pace the apartment, smiting his brow. "Ai didn't haste me hither through a treckless waste fair hotching with enemies just to engage in wanton delliance wi' an understudy—be she never so sweetly alluring," he added courteously, for he was a fair-minded picaroon. "Nay, mistress, flaunt not thy curves et me, for mai affections are fixed constant otherwhere, so you ken forget it."

"Nought like a spot o' wanton dalliance for keeping in training," purred eager Kylie, fluttering lashes and negligee in saucy invitation, but it was wasted effort, for his eye had fallen on a framed copy of Hilliard's famous miniature of the Benenden lacrosse team, and with a lovelorn whinny he knelt before it and pressed it reverently to his lips.

"Oh, shoot!" exclaimed mortified Kylie, and rose, pouting at her reflection in the pier-glass. "What's wrong with me, anyway? Blonde curls, bee-stung lips, 38-22-36 in see-through material—and you go ga-ga o'er-a team photo!" She sighed. "Faith, thou hast it bad . . . well, make the most o' her likeness, brother, for 'tis the closest thou'lt ever get!"

"There spake naked female jealousy—well, skentily cled jealousy, anyway," said Gilderoy with a reproving look as he slipped the miniature under his shirt. "Divaine Godaiva shell yet be maine, and thet's oll there is to't."

"Mandrake gravy!" scoffed Kylie. "To her y'are as dog meat. What, ye reave her rocks, snog her uninvited, leave her stuck i' the snow—and yet hope to prevail? You've got a mountain to climb, Scotty, and you'll never make it," she added with a smouldering smile, "without an experienced alpine guide."

Gilderoy's amber eyes narrowed, and a speculative glance slithered out 'neath his lowered lids. "Meaning?" he inquired.

"Why, if ye would fair Goddy win, wi' little Kylie first begin," lied the amorous half-pint significantly. "Want to discuss it?" She sashayed towards him wi' artless bump and grind. "Let's sit down, shall we—you on the sofa, me on your knee . . . ?" Before he knew it, she was in his lap, smiling coyly, the hussy. "You'd better hold me, in case I slip . . . yikes, what muscles! Get a grip, Kylie! Now, perpend . . ." She slid soft arms round his neck and nestled against his cheek. "Goddy and I have been buddies since kindergarten," she began, nibbling at his chin, "and none knows better than I the way to her fond heart, or how by my judicious massage it may be softened towards thee . . . if you like," she added, starting to claw the back of his head. "Oh, God, your after-shave! Where was I? Yes, what I'm saying," she resumed, chewing his chin-beard, "is that with me working your corner, boosting your stock to her," she went on, transferring her lips to his Adam's apple, "'twould be passing strange if she inclined not to your suit at the last, know what I mean?" Her control finally snapped, and she buried her pearly teeth in his neck with feline mewings.

"Unfang me, wench!" cried Gilderoy, but he cried it absently, his flawless brow creased in consideration as she began working avidly on his nearby ear. "Ai'm not shoor . . . efter oll, Ai've nivver needed a P.R. on mai previous wooings . . . yet what harm, to hev thee on the inside pitching on mai behaff . . . Aye, but what," he wondered, as Kylie tore open his shirt and began gnawing his chest, "is in it for thee, mistress?"

"For me?" Kylie, panting distractedly, raised dishevelled blonde curls and regarded him with stoned worship. "Oh, well . . . say a candle-lit dinner for two . . . we can have it served up here, nigh to the pard-skin rug, and I can brief thee wi' all need-to-know stuff on thy desired Godiva, her whims, her foibles, her delight in soft centres, her weakness for chaps wi' dimpled chins . . . and afterwards," she lowered coy lashes, "you could practise your approach work, wi' me as a Goddy-model, sort of . . ."

Hand it to Kylie, she's a real mini-Delilah, and could she have read his thoughts at that moment, her yearning heart would have been doing handsprings. For Gilderoy, Godiva-smitten tho' he might be, was not insensible to the pneumatic charms of the pocket-size sex-pot who was e'en now apparently trying to swallow his moustache . . . candle-lit dinner, pard-skin rug, he was thinking—but, no! his pure devotion to the Thrash-batter heiress was proof 'gainst all temptations . . . and anyway she might walk in at any moment and catch them at it. Still, he'd better play this ardent poppet along if he wanted her help in his wooing . . .

"A kendle-lit dinner, four courses wi' chempers end choice o' fruit juice, thou shalt ha', pretty minion," quo' he, flashing dazzling incisors, "but not heer i' the sticks whair maine ene-mies abound. Haste we rather to Merrie Carlisle, the St. Tropez o' the North, whair we may not only daine intimately to the sweet strains o' Billy Bowman and his Ill-Tempered Claviers, but also disco the naight away, or, an't please thee, take in the playhouse, whair Ai'm told the Lord Chamberlain's Men are doing socko with a double bill of *Taitus Endronicus* end *Mai Waife's Femily*—"

"Hot apricocks!" squealed delighted Kylie. "A night on the town!" And she bussed him ardently, swooned briefly in con-sequence, and staggered groggily from his lap. "But a mo-ment, while I slip into something tight, and hey for the bright lights—"

"Yet stay!" She found her wrist caught in fingers of velvet steel, and his smoky eyes glowed like traffic lights on caution. "In return, remember, thy best endeavours on mai beheff wi' thy sweet mistress. Ai expect a furst-cless sales pitch—"

"Shalt ha' the biggest promotion since the Virginia Colony," lied Kylie. "Gosh—I wonder if Carlisle has got a Tramps?"

Thus it was that some little time later the ivy on Thrashbatter Tower was creaking 'neath the double weight of a panting highwayman and a small blonde borne o'er his stalwart shoulder in a fireman's lift—for, as Gilderoy explained, being a wanted man in these parts he'd better not use the stairs. Then, with Kylie snuggled up on his crupper, clinging blissfully as she inhaled his body splash and schemed how she might lure him to a motel for the weekend, they fared forth through the ale-dark night, the flying hooves of mettlesome Garscadden ringing on rock and churning up ooze as they galloped off the miles towards the Cumbrian capital, that sprawling, brawling, lawless, clueless, rip-roaring, hard-snoring frontier settlement known to the Romans as Fort-of-the-Legion, to marauding Scots as the Corbie's Nest, to romantics as the Border City, to fed-up travellers as "Car-*lyle* Station, Car-*lyle*," to optimistic archaeologists as Camelot, but to the reivers, outlaws, and street-smart yokels as Tombstone-on-Eden . . . and who knows what dread menaces await our disco-bound duo in the garish saloons, wide-open auction marts, sin-sodden tea-rooms, and vice-traps like the Thynkynge Man's Strumpet which lie behind its frowning walls?

Well, we'll come to that presently, but first we must pause for station identification on sundry of our other principals, who, like Kylie and Gilderoy, are coincidentally bound for the city, in accordance with our plot. Yes, the surrounding country, which we have hitherto been advertising as lonely, silent, desolate, etc., is now carrying enough traffic to start a good-sized convention. So let's take Olympian licence and soar aloft through the midnight mirk for a satellite view . . .

First, approaching from the south at a breakneck crawl, comes the express hay-wain bearing La Infamosa and the Spanish impostor—but you'd never recognise them as the pair who appeared on the Wizard's cauldron-screen, for now they're in disguise, remember, she as an accountant, he as an exotic dancer, and he at least is acutely embarrassed. For while La Infamosa's baroomphish proportions are modestly concealed in sober tweed trunk hose wi' matching doublet and gabardine accessories, worn 'neath a cloak of sober pin-stripe sharkskin and set off by horn-rimmed cheaters, Gray's Inn trainers, and a copy of the *Financialle Tymes*, the unfortunate impostor is tricked out most inadequately in mini-trunks, studded leather harness, tasselled boots, a platinum Tarzan wig, and Gold-Glo body lotion. To make things worse, he is travelling under the name of Chippendale, and has been subjected to ribald cries from coarse country wenches of "Get 'em off, Goliath!" He for one is relieved when they reach the city under cover of darkness and make their way to the sign of the Thynkynge Man's Strumpet, hard by the leisure complex, and having shown their forged library tickets, win at last to the Priest's Hole Suite artfully concealed between the reference shelves and the Solway Sauna Club. There, with typical Castilian subtlety, they exchange costumes in order to confuse any hostile agents who may be lurking in the shadows of the Dungeon Grill, to which they presently repair for a late snack; the impostor's tweed trunks cause some remark among discriminating diners, but La Infamosa's leather gear gets by because it's a topless joint anyway.

We leave them debating the merits of Cumberland Sausage
à la Reform and Black Pudding au Gratin, and turn our attention to a mean hovel on the city's outskirts, where a disconsolate
Amazon pygmy is sitting with a blanket round his shoulders and
his hairy little feet in a tub of mustard water, while an impatient
Dominican friar prays over him in an Alabama accent. Yes,
Frey Bentos is repenting his harsh usage in slinging Clnzh out
into the freezing night, for the unhappy dwarf has developed
the daddy of all head colds, and can no longer use his blowpipe
for fear of spreading germs. On their way to rendezvous with
La Infamosa, the pair have stopped in at the cottage of a crone
well known for her nostrums (or should it be nostra?), reme-
dies, cures, and antibiotic simples, to try to get Clnzh into some
sort of shape, for Frey Bentos is nervous about going anywhere
without his tiny minder; he also reasons that if you're going to
keep a secret assignation with foreign spies in the middle of the
night, the last thing you need at your heels is a loin-clothed
dwarf who emits a thunderous sneeze every thirty seconds. So
with folded hands and uplifted eyes he seeks the intercession of
St. Catarrh, while the ancient crone concocts a nasal spray of
beetle-bane and worm's wool, and we steal quietly away,
attracted by raucous singing of "Blaydon Races" emerging
from the gloom of the eastern highway.

Things have been average for the Charltons in the last
twenty-four hours. Carved up by Gilderoy when they assailed
Godiva's coach, you recall, they had repaired to a nearby cottage hospital for patches to their green wounds, only to be
refused treatment on the N.H.S. because their stamps were
in arrears; in the ensuing altercation the establishment was
reduced to a charred ruin (fortunately with no scathe to
patients, since the wards were empty on account of Lord

Burghley's "cuttes," but with grievous loss of several tons of filing cabinets, records, forms, correspondence, reports, triplicating ledgers, and state-of-the-art computerised hornbooks), the medical staff were put to the sword, social workers subjected to racial abuse, and great quantities of rubbing alcohol and the better-looking nurses carried off, with cries of "Party, party!" and "A pox on yer socialised medicine!" After a day-long orgy with their plunder, the reivers had regained consciousness in the quiet evenfall to discover that they all had splitting headaches and Wor Jackie had somehow got engaged to the matron; ripe for further mischief, they had ridden away, followed by sighs of "Keep yer feet still, Geordie hinny" and bandages fluttered in fond farewell, and are now on their way to Carlisle for some R and R in the city's night-spots. They travel but slowly, for the horses are as hung-over as their gaunt, unshaven riders, but they'll get there in time for the big confrontation scene which is impending.

Meanwhile, just inside the city gates, a heated discussion is taking place, and if we pass quickly 'neath the frowning portcullis, slipping a couple of groats to the beetle-browed sentries who are frisking tourists for any prohibited substances, such as hay, oats, cheese, rum butter, or grass (get it?), we may be able to do a crafty eavesdrop. We'll have to get close, for this is the gate to the city's Latin Quarter, containing the leisure complex, stews, thieves' kitchen, Scotch ghetto, houses o' ill repute, and laundrettes, and the uproar is deafening. From the garishly lit hells, kens, and young farmers' clubs which line the street issues the heavy metal beat of shawms, recorders, and electronic virginals, quivering the timber and plaster frontages, while the ancient floors vibrate to the thud of acid corantos and lavoltas and the frenzied stomping of churls and hoydens as, crazed by parsnip gin and radish tonic, they gyrate in the psychedelic rays of multi-coloured rushlights, heedless of the protests of gamesters trying to concentrate on fruit machines and Dago Invaders, and the sweet entreaty of a Puritan maid, eyes modestly downcast as she steps daintily o'er the forms of inebriated citizens and shoot-out victims, pleading: "Prithee, who'll buy the *War-Cry*?"

Aye, Merrie Carlisle indeed, swinging on its age-old hinges, with all the riot and colour and free-wheeling excitement our production designer and art director can dream up; its plastic cobbles, worn by the sandals of Hadrian's legions, the hooves of the Knights of the Round Table, the sealskin sneakers of marauding Vikings, and the platform soles and loafers of tourists numerable, echo now to the tread of an astonishing variety of Central Casting (Tudor types) riff-raff: ploughmen and pedlars, gallants and gypsies, ruffians and roisterers, carousers and clergymen, and other equally colourful (tho' less alliterative) figures, such as yokels, wenches, runagates, trulls, mountebanks, broken men, fallen women, Tom-a-Bedlams, and a group of housewives from Cumdivock in on a shopping spree; elegant saunterers ogle slumming debutantes or rub shoulders (and occasionally ankles) with rosy-cheeked milkmaids, sober citizens exchange curses with drunken Sturdy Beggars seeking the price of a posset wi' menaces, swaggering mercenaries elbow mercenary swaggerers (whereof follows bloody debate, clash o' steel, and shrilling o' ambulance sirens), bold-eyed wantons solicit the custom of roaring captains and whispering majors, bearded doxies hang on the arms of painted reivers (sorry, swap the adjectives), and lantern-jawed individuals wearing tin stars marked "Warden" lounge grimly on the sidewalks, scanning the scene, spitting tobacco juice, and ready at the drop of a morion to advance slowly up the street with their hands poised o'er their holstered long-bows . . .

Enough background? Right, back to our eavesdropping on the conversation of two familiar figures lurking in the shadows over there beyond the pillory—one a tall, spectacularly handsome Nordic type whose chiselled features, keen grey eyes, and fair tumbled locks are unfortunately concealed for the moment by a muffling hood, but the active, resourceful hang of his cloak would tell us instantly who he is, even if it didn't have "Noble, S.A.S." stencilled on the back. And who could mistake the statuesque figure of the redhead in the Dick Whittington pantomime outfit, slapping her thighs impatiently as she and her companion remonstrate in passionate undertones.

GODIVA: Thou kidd'st! Ye mean ye have no money *at all*?

ARCHIE: Not a denier! Your knaves saw to that when they slung me i' your cellar. Haply if ye paid them, my Lady Tightwad, they'd be less ready to fleece helpless prisoners!

GODIVA: They get union minimum, and bonus o' Christmas! Ha, some agent thou—I thought Q Branch furnished thee with broad gold pieces in thy purse its secret compartment?

ARCHIE: That went ages ago, in bribes and laundry! Had ye but done your job, and brought me funds, 'stead of letting 'em be smooched from thee by that Scotch gigolo—

GODIVA: He's not a gigolo, so there! He's a
subtle, foining, conniving . . .
gorgeous, knee-trembling . . . ah, be
still, my foolish heart, and let's not go
over all that again! I goofed, all right?
And y'are skint . . . not even a letter o'
accommodation, or credit cards? No
overlooked tanners in thy pocket
lining? Good lack, some organisation!
I mean everyone has *some* money—

ARCHIE: Ha! There spake spoiled darling o' café
society! It's different down here,
duchess, in the real world—

GODIVA: Ah, naff off! See yon ragged
mendicant, he wi' the tin cup and "Old
Soldier, veteran o' Flodden, Flanders,
and Hill 60" on his placard. E'en he
hath coppers in his cup—but not
Double-Nought Noble, oh no, who
lures a girl out on the town when he
can't even afford to go Dutch!

ARCHIE: Lured, quo' she! Nay, here's crust—
who clamoured and smarmed to be
brought along—aye, and tarted up in
Puss-in-Boots finery o' silk and suede
that must ha' cost a jillion, yet never a
stiver in its pocket! Oh, peace, whiles I
consider . . . a way there must be . . .

You see, their perilous mission was like to come unstuck at
the start for want of the entrance fee (they not being members)

to that exclusive niterie, the Thynkynge Man's Strumpet—and if they couldn't get in, how to snooker La Infamosa? Hence their privy bicker, now so heated that they failed to notice the masked gallant cantering up the street with a pert blonde on his saddle-bow, a right comely pair who attracted admiring glances as they alighted at the Strumpet's discreetly lit entrance. There Gilderoy (for 'tis he, masked on account of the reward posters on every litter-bin) flipped Garscadden's keys to the stabling valet, and with a swirl of cloak and sweeping bow ushered enraptured Kylie through the gilded swing doors held open by a blue-chinned gorilla in a steel tuxedo whose snarl of "You a member, buddy?" slid smoothly into a servile "Ta, guv!" as the dashing highwayman pressed a rose noble into his horny hand.

So that's two more of our principals inside, and we'll follow them downstairs to the Dungeon Grill, where they are escorted to a secluded corner by the unctuous maître-d, Gaston (whose real name was Barmy Grisenthwaite from Haltwhistle, but they'd made him change it when he was a trainee at the Hotel du Cap).

'Twas dim and smoky in the Dungeon Grill, where dancing couples smoothly circled the floor while the rushlight spot played on the bandstand where a sultry chanteuse was torching out "I got them pastime-with-good-company blues, baby" to muted harpsichord accompaniment. Too dim to see much, really, but Kylie's eyes widened at the sight of the strapping brunette in studded braces who shared the next booth with an eye-rolling slobberer in tweed trunk hose (aha!) "Topless—i' the provinces!" she exclaimed, and took good care that her escort was seated with his back to the scenery.

While Gilderoy orders up Gretna Wallbangers, let us slide out for another quick eavesdrop on Archie and Godiva . . .

"*Me*—climb in a back window? Art out o' thy ever-loving mind? Fie, sirrah, I'd not so demean myself at Whitehall or Greenwich, let alone this rustic gin-joint! Go, jimmy a slot-machine, or something! Lady Godiva Dacre goes in the front door, wi' bells on, and that's final!"

Right, no progress there, so hie we back to the Strumpet's entrance foyer, where two ill-assorted night-clubbers are demanding admittance in the teeth of the gorilla-commissionaire and maître-d Gaston, who shakes sleek head in firm refusal.

"I regret, m'sieur, I 'ave no reservation in thee name of Bentos, and as wee are foolly booked—"

"You denyin' entry to a minister o' God an' a pore heathen in sore needa sustenance an' salvation?" demanded Frey Bentos. "Now, you hear me, boy, an' hear me good—yo're perillin' yore immortal soul, yassuh, you teeterin' on the brink o' th' infernal Pit, ifn you don't lay out yore welcome mat, pronto! You read me, mah son?"

Pale 'neath his stubble, for he had embraced the True Faith during his apprenticeship in Antibes, Gaston pointed a shaking finger at a sign headed NO SOCKS, NO SHOES, NO SERVICE.

"No one gets een thee dining-room unless 'e ees wearing a ruff!" he protested. "An' your fren' 'e wears no ruff, m'sieur."

"He ain't wearin' a san benito, eether," retorted Frey Bentos, laying a paternal hand on the matted head of Clnzh, who had lost his inhaler up his left nostril and was sniffling pathetically on one cylinder. "But *you* will be, brother, come the Counter-Reformation, unless Ah gits a table—an' away from the musick, at that!" His ascetic features hardened in Torquemada-like fanaticism. "You receivin' me, boy—or you want Ah should start in a-excommunicatin'?"

"That's Popery!" cried the scandalised gorilla, a sturdy

Calvinist. "You can get thirty days for that—or 'ung, I shouldn't wonder!"

"Heretical crapola!" bawled Frey Bentos in stern denunciation. "Ah'm talkin' ole-time religion here, boy, an' if Ah start in a-cussin' an' a-maledictionin', yore hopes o' redemption won't be worth succotash, to say nuthin' of yore jobs! How yore boss gonna like it when his roulette wheel starts payin' out, an' the chef gits possessed by demons, an' yore cocktail waitresses git all wasted an' skinny, like lean kine, huh?"

"Okay, padre, okay!" surrendered the terrified Gaston. "Onlee do me a leetle favour—put thees 'civilisation-challenged' badge on yoor companion, so thee othair customers won't dare complain. Pliz?"

"You just booked yoreself a steamboat ticket over Jordan, friend," crooned Frey Bentos benignly. "Now, if yore goon will jes' check mah chasuble an' this pore homunculus's girdle o' human haids . . . Ah, thank yuh kindly. Pax vobiscum, boys . . ."

Two more for the Dungeon Grill, but down the street our Hero is still stropping his razor-keen wits in vain o'er the problem of admission. How to raise the ready . . .

"Eureka!" he exclaimed. "Suppose I apply for a job as general manager, or scullion, or whatever . . . get an advance on my wages . . . nip out again on pretext that I'm double-parked . . . then we swan in, cash in hand—"

Godiva stifled a weary yawn with derisive fingers. "Oh, why not offer the doorman milk-bottle tops—ye may scavenge them on any dunghill, I ween. Or try hypnotising him . . . eek!" Her withering drawl ended in a girlish squeal as she flung out a hand in agitated point. "Those hairy chaps!" she cried. "I know them!"

Startled, Archie turned to see a line of unshaven huskies in biker gear and steel caps trooping arm-in-arm through the green channel of the gate, spurning the sentries with cries of: "Nowt to declare, buttock-brain!" and "Bring oot yer sniffer dogs an' watch 'em faint!" as they rolled up the street with drunken guffaw and obscene gesture, blowing out lanterns, accosting wenches, and snatching chips from the fish suppers of itinerant diners. At their head staggered Wor Jackie, morion rakishly tilted and top button undone, while beside him Oor Kid flourished a constable's helmet on his rapier point and led the blood-chilling chorus of "Ye'll nivver walk alo-o-one." A sight and sound which otherwhere would have sent honest citizens flying from the streets, but in Merrie Carlisle no one paid a blind bit of notice.

Archie gave Godiva a swift double-take. "You *know* them? You're sure? 'Tis not just a trick of the light? Nay, but, madam, these be the scum o' the Middle March, Charltons, stark thieves of Tynedale, and not your sort of people at all—why, even the Nixons ignore their invitations—"

Godiva interrupted him with noises of escaping steam. "Those are the rotters who dry-gulched my coach yestre'en!" she shrilled. "Aye, 'a plundered my peach brandy, and strewed my frillies i' the snow without ruth or shame, and would ha' offered me randy violence, rot their socks! Well, don't just stand there—summon the law, or take their names, or something!"

"Oh, madam, leave it out!" snapped Archie. "What matter your frillies and potables at such a time, when England's fate hangs by a hair? Anyway, there's a dozen o' them, all expert witnesses, and thou but one to testify they assailed thy wagon . . ." He stopped short with the incoherent yelp of one goosed, wonder and hope shining in his respective eyes, and smote fast-thinking fist into inspired palm. "By George, I've got it! Have I? Yes, yes, 'tis it—the answer, the brilliant wheeze whereby we shall not only win admittance to yon ritzy ken, but recruit needed muscle for our emprise!" Godiva, lips blinking in amaze, found her shoulders seized in joyous grip and his intellect-laden chin thrust into hers in dramatic close-up as he posed the fateful question:

"Was your vehicle in motion at the time?"

"Ah nivver! It's a bloody lie!" were familiar words on the lips of Wor Jackie, but seldom so poignantly uttered as now. One minute he'd been lurching along, singing "John Peel" and breaking windows, and the next steely hands had flung him spreadeagled o'er the hood of a hay-wain and a voice had grated in his ear "Freeze, caitiff! And if ye think this is a packet of Rolo digging into your spine . . . go ahead, punke—make my sennight!" Whereafter grim grey eyes 'neath implacable fair hair had gazed relentlessly into his, and he had been accused of holding up a moving coach in contravention of Section 114B of the Reivers' Code. Hence his sturdy denial, while he wondered where his boys had got to.

"Thou liest, varlet!" snapped Archie, back-handing him across his stubble. "Make it easy on thyself, fellow—this lady hath thy number . . . so gaze on her, look in the mirror, and ask yourself which the judge is going to believe!"

"Holy hell!" gasped Wor Jackie. "'Tis the redhead wi' the great big—"

"Curb thy lewd tongue!" crisped Archie, back-handing again.

"—wi' the great big trunks in her boot, Ah was goin' to say!"

explained Wor Jackie indignantly, and gave Godiva as sheepish a grin as Archie's throttling hands permitted. "Evenin', missus. Got home a'reet, did ye? Champion—"

"So ye admit it! Then list ye, sirrah, and list ye good! Of the plunder, assault, and intended ravishment o' this fair lady, I say nought—"

"Hold the phone!" protested outraged Godiva.

"—but for that ye assailed a mobile conveyance, contrary to all custom and usage, thy freebooting licence—which I doubt not bears heavy endorsements enow—will be justly forfeit when the Union o' Plunderers, Reivers, and Allied Trades get to hear of it . . . as they will," he added, with sinister emphasis, and the large reiver's swarthy features would have paled if Archie hadn't been choking him purple.

"Ye'd nivver snitch to UPRAT, you prat!" he gurgled.

"Hadst better believe it," quo' relentless Archie. "Unless you and your boys do me a small favour . . ."

Thus it was, a few minutes later, that the commissionaire gorilla outside the Thynkynge Man's Strumpet was aware of a group of dishevelled drunks in leather jacks and steel caps in his vicinity, whistling nonchalantly, examining the framed menu with critical murmurs of "Hey, Wattie, there's nae tawtle soop Lady Cawzon" and "Ah'm for the Welsh takeaway, me, an' a bellyful o' devilled leek au chasseur," while their leader approached him with a snaggle-toothed grin to ask the time. From which you deduce that the Charltons, who had been wandering about in an alcoholic daze since Archie plucked Wor Jackie from their midst and strong-armed him into compliance, have now been apprised by their leader that there's work to be done if their licences are to remain intact. Said work being the swift removal of the commissionaire without attracting attention.

To the Charltons, of course, this was money for jam, even in their half-smashed condition. While Oor Kid and a couple of Milburns captured the attention of the passing crowds with an impromptu clog-dance and the others formed a screening wall before the entrance shouting "Taxi!" and "Haud on, Mither's left her handbag in't ladies!," Wor Jackie dealt with the door-man (by the age-old reivers' trick of inviting his opinion on the clashing colour scheme of the overhead canopy, and then belting him on his conveniently upturned chin). Ten seconds later, clad in steel tuxedo and polka-dot bow tie, Wor Jackie was holding the door for Godiva to sweep in, and extending a hand like a shovel in the hope of a tip.

"Hold thyselves in readiness for our more service," whispered Archie, "or UPRAT will get some racy reading in tomorrow's post. Got an umbrella for departing customers? Right, carry on." He shot down the steps towards the Dungeon Grill just in time to see Godiva vanish into the powder-room, and was vainly trying to talk an adamant Gaston into giving him a corner table when she strode forth in all her titivated splendour, red hair lashing like a Wash-and-Go ad, set Archie aside with a languid wave and murmur of "My bird, I think," froze the maître-d in his tracks with one ringing slap of her thigh, and announced imperiously:

"I am the Lady Godiva Dacre of Thrashbatter Tower. A table for myself and my chauffeur"—she flicked a negligent pinkie in Noble's direction—"cocktails o' chilled Charneco in frosted glasses, tidbits and kickshaws on your best china, and summon the chef when I'm ready to order. Incidentally," she added to the awe-struck Antibes graduate, "your powder-room would excite disgust in the patrons of a Bowery doss-house, the tissues are finished, and if you haven't fired the insolent slut-in-charge by the time I leave, I'll have the justices close your squalid establishment as a health hazard." She stirred the crouched and weeping Gaston with a dainty boot. "Well, am I to stand here till next Michaelmas . . . ?"

So, after a chapter which might well have been headed "How to Crash a Tudor Party," we've managed to squeeze four separate pairs of principals into adjoining booths of the steamy Dungeon Grill, none suspecting the presence of the others, for the atmosphere's dense enough to cut up for curtains, and you can't hear yourself think for the thunderous bongo accompaniment to the floor-show—Slave-girl Moolah and her Syncopated Snakes. Disguised as waiters, let's visit each (the booths, not the Snakes) in turn . . .

"Are *you* telling *me*," piped bug-eyed Kylie, amazed asparagus limp in her dainty fingers, "that you're not a highwayman at all, but a Scottish secret agent? An enemy? Nay, Gildy, thou ribbest me!"

"No enemy to thee, Ai vow!" protested Gilderoy, with such fervour that she went dizzy before the blazing sincerity of his eye-slit mask, and the asparagus slipped from her grasp to fall on soggy toast. "End least of oll to thy sweet mistress, the adored Godaiva—for whose sake, ektually, Ai hev pecked in mai career of sordid intrigue this very day. Beng goes the pension, but what the heck—you ken't get splaiced to the fairest flower of English womanhood end spend the honeymoon saigning off her country's spaies, now ken you? Not," he added proudly, "if yur a Glesgow Ekademical. We hiv our code."

"Oh, that's the sweetest thing I ever heard!" Kylie's tender emotions, softened by Gretna Wallbangers, spilled over in crystal tears which fell unheeded into the melted butter. "To set true love above duty to one's country! Still," she added, preserving her mascara with a quick mop o' napkin, "'twas reckless to rush impetuous on to social security—suppose Goddy gives thy suit the frozen V-sign? 'Twill be Skint City for thee, no monthly cheque, no prospects, no paddle . . . unless," she purred, coyly lowering lashes and neckline, "you can hitch your buggy to some lesser star whose doting great-aunt is sure to leave her ten thousand big ones per annum (I'll say it again, ten thousand—wow!) and a place in Sussex . . . oh, shoot!" She bit ruby lip in dismay. "Did I send the old bat a birthday card?" But Gilderoy marked her not, his Tandoori Trotters aux fines herbes neglected as he fixed dreamy eyes on faraway imaginings of Godiva, or the sinuous writhings of Slave-girl Moolah, you couldn't tell which.

"Anyway," persisted Kylie, thirsty for gossip, "ye lost no time in checking in your badge and gun—but did not thy head office take umbrage, or demand two weeks' notice? I thought secret services were wont to terminate defecting employees wi' extreme prejudice . . . do tell!"

"'Twas nae bother," responded Gilderoy lightly, de-Moolahing his gaze. "His Majesty, now vacationing nigh Peebles, wailed end slobbered a bit, as usual, but finally consented to give me a free tresfer. 'Aye, weel,' quo' he, ''tis one less on the pay-roll, onywye. Gang yer ways, ingrate, wi'oot redundancy, fare ye weel, an' leave the jewellery at the desk. Think ever an' anon o' thy auld gossip Jimmy, an' send us a bit o' the weddin'-cake—'"

"Jewellery!" squeaked Kylie. "You didn't give him Goddy's rocks!"

"No option hed Ai," sighed Gilderoy. "Ai pinched them on the firm's taime, to weaken England's balance o' payments and beef up our needy Caledonian exchequer—"

"She'll bust a gut!" cried Kylie, more in glee than consternation, for well she knew that restoration of the snitched valuta would have melted Godiva's resistance to her dashing despoiler. "Oh, well . . . what are we having for a main course?"

"Ah'll have the all-day breakfast—eggs over easy, Canadian bacon, grits, an' cawfee," said Frey Bentos. "An' a raw sheep for mah friend, with nettles, grass, an' weeds on the side. You want it on the fleece or off?" he asked Clnzh, who was devouring the paper flowers with animal gusto. "Aw, what the hell, jes' as it comes, waiter . . . an' would you know, perchance, if two business associates o' mine have checked in—a lady accountant built like Salome an' a male dancer closely resemblin' the King o' Scotland?"

"Ah, we get so many like that, m'sieu'," shrugged dubious Gaston, "but I weel inquire." He coughed discreetly. "Pardon, m'sieu', but could you ask your small fren' not to blow darts at thee snake-dancer? Merci, m'sieu'." He oiled off, and Frey Bentos hit Clnzh with the carafe. "Stop it, yuh little bastard! Ah doan't care if she does remind you of your Aunt Minnie on the Orinoco! Jes' drink your finger-bowl an' shut up! You wanna attract attention . . . ?"

· · ·

While in the next booth . . .

"When's that bleedin' monk goin' to show up?" seethed La Infamosa, snapping her scanty braces in impatience. "I'm abaht perished in this rig—yer'd think the Escurial coulda given us fans or fevvers, the mean birks!" Her marked Cockney accent (so at odds with her appearance, which was statuesque, Andalusian, and virtually starkers, let's face it) had presumably been assumed to disarm suspicion. She glared at the goggle-eyed impostor, burping his way tipsily through his eleventh Alston Sunrise. "An' go easy on that sauce, or you'll be totally ho-an'-hist! by the time 'e gets 'ere, an' we know wot 'appens to yer Scotch accent when yer kettled, don't we?"

"Hoots . . . awa' . . . wi' . . . ye . . . ," belched her companion, articulating with difficulty. "Nozzings too it," he went on, lapsing into fluent Castilian. "I spik da Scotch better'n ennywan . . . yoo wanna heer my Gordon Brown eemeetation, maybe?" He took a deep shlurp of his rum-and-linseed cocktail, muttered "Creesto!," rolled his eyes, and burst into song: "Claaackmaan-an, I'm folling under yoor spell, eef onlee yoo could spik, what a fasceenating tale . . . ah, *caramba*!" as La Infamosa hacked him painfully under the table.

"Belt up, you stupid git!" she hissed, braces swirling and sable tresses creaking in alarm. "You want everyone to know we're Dago agents?"

"I don't care!" hiccupped the gassed impostor, lurching to his feet with dignity. "I gotta go to thee gents," he announced.

"Thou'lt never make it, legless idiot!" cried the Cordovan Firecracker, rising in topless agitation which overturned the table and sent a cascade of crockery on to the dance-floor where it was crushed beneath the feet of samba-happy customers,

Slave-girl Moolah having stormed off in a spitting rage to pick poisoned darts out of her whimpering pythons in the privacy of her dressing-room.

"'Ang on, an' I'll dance yer towards the toilets!" snapped La Infamosa, seizing him as close as her embonpoint would permit. "Ready—I'll lead, you foller . . . wait for it! Now—with a one-two, one-one-two . . ." and she grimly samba'd the giggling inebriate into the close-packed throng . . .

". . . and in case you hadn't noticed, Double-Nought Noble," drawled Godiva, her glass's frosted rim reflecting triumphant violet stars from the effulgence of her bright eyes, "but for my presence ye had still been out i' the street, growing moss. Whose acquaintance wi' those ghastly Charlton persons gained us smooth entry? Who sweet-talked the maître-d? Not the gung-ho professional, oh, no, but the despised Walsingham groupie—"

"Ah, of thy sweet charity, lady, spare me the feminist gloat," pleaded honest Archie, and taking her hand wi' conciliatory smirk he pressed it to his lips, a gesture which would have touched her the more had it not been the hand holding her glass. "Nay, dear Godiva," he went on, sneezing ice crystals and Charneco broadcast, "wi' out thy aid I had been stymied indeed. Let me give you a refill, and drink we to the confusion of these Spanish intruders whom," he added gravely, "we must locate right soon, and on them lower the boom." And his keen grey glance raked the dancing throng, now in the throes of a Dashing White Ancient, with skirl o' pipes and abandoned wa-hey!

"Say the word, skipper," murmured Godiva, mollified by his courtesy. "Yet first, I entreat, don we swift nosebags, for I don't know about you, but I'm starving!" She scanned the gilt-embossed menu, and frowned. "Nay, 'tis in Cumbrian, wi'out translation! Well, of all the snobby affectations! You'll just have to order for me, that's all." She tossed the menu pettishly on to a passing sweet-trolley (whence it was presently seized and devoured with gusto by a ravenous Clnzh) and surveyed the dance-floor wi' Belgravian disdain. "Gosh, the types they let into these joints . . . mark me the bra-less baggage wi' the kinky straps and tasselled boots, holding up the plastered chap in tweed trunk hose . . ."

"American tourists," diagnosed Archie. "Over here to buy up Earl Grey posset and every bloody sweater in Hawick . . . but stay, I've seen that chap i' the tweed bags before . . . aye, those goggle eyes, sandy whiskers, slobbery lips, and the 'Gowrie House for Weekend Breaks' lapel badge . . . but where . . . ?"

"Gossip page o' the *Gull's Hornbook*, perhaps," mused Godiva. "I know what you mean, yah . . . I've seen that drool and shambling gait in whisky ads, was it? Oh, who cares?" she cried, suddenly animated. "That's a lavolta they're playing— come on, Noble, let's shake!" She lissomed smoothly erect, snapping queenly fingers to the rhythm, her alluring lips, hips, and hair-do all a-shimmy in an invitation which Archie, slave of stern duty though he was, could not refuse. Masterfully he swept her into the start position, and now, as their lashes tangle and beams of grey and ultra-violet meet, he feels her vibrant softness and she his steely strength, and both recall that brief passionate canoodle in the enchanted glade o'er Gungemyre— can this be love? Difficult to say . . . oh, he's hooked like hungry tuna, poor sap, but is Godiva just amusing herself with his tousled Redford charms, the wanton, while still carrying a love-hate torch for Gilderoy?—who, by the way, is cheek-to-cheeking with an ecstatic Kylie on the other side of the floor at this very moment . . . but enough. Back to Archie and Godiva as they groove nimbly through the press, he murmuring teasingly in her perfumed ear: "What will café society think, to see the proud chatelaine o' Thrashbatter beating the beeswax wi' her chauffeur, eh?" and she responding gaily (but we fear she means it): "They'll think thou'rt my toy-boy, silly!"

She nestles contentedly 'gainst his stalwart shoulder, and they surrender to the heady beat of Billy Bowman and his Ill-Tempered Claviers as the dance roars to a thunderous climax.

Since it's probably some time since you danced a lavolta, we should remind you that the big moment comes when the chap seizes his partner anywhere between hip and armpit and heaves her high and around in a tremendous arc, turning smartly so as to be on hand when madame touches down. Perilous stuff, with female feet scything the upper atmosphere and occasionally making shattering contact with other ladies' extremities, or with the upper works of vertical males, many of them experiencing their first hernia. Of course, if you're Gilderoy, the Barrowland Bandit, there's nothing to it: he did it one-handed, with joyous Kylie being swept up and round like blonde thistledown, squealing "Whee! More! Bags I again!"; Archie likewise made nought of Godiva's Junoesque poundage, tho' her flying panto boots swept away Billy Bowman and an unwary saxophonist from the front of the bandstand.

La Infamosa, however, was in trouble. Trapped in the dance, she seized her paralytic partner by the slack of his tweed bags and, squawking like a Bulgarian weight-lifter, was just hurling him up and sideways when a courteous finger tapped her shoulder and a mellow Virginian voice inquired: "Pahdun me, ma'am, may Ah cut in?"

You guessed it—Frey Bentos, having recognised her and

the Stuart lookalike, was making contact, and not at the best time, really, for the startled Infamosa released her partner in mid-swing, to the discomfiture of Gilderoy, pirouetting by in a reprise with an ecstatic Kylie hang-gliding on his pinkie. Staggered by the impact of a horizontal body which he instantly, naturally, and mistakenly identified as James VI, Gilderoy exclaimed "Mai God—Yur Mejesty!" and dropped to one knee in courtly salutation, while Kylie, suddenly bereft of support, fell to the floor, skidded several yards to the confusion of various couples, and found herself staring up at an amazed Godiva, who had just landed. Frey Bentos, dance-hardened by countless hops at the College of Cardinals, smoothly piloted La bewildered Infamosa out of the wreckage with a swift one-one-two turn and pas de chat, leaving a disconsolate Clnzh looking for a partner. After which, simultaneous dialogue broke out all over:

FREY BENTOS: Lissen in, honey chile, while Ah gives yuh the li'l ole password: "They got an awful lot o' maracas in Caracas."

INFAMOSA: Blimey, yore Frey Bentos! 'Ang on for the counter-sign: "Inquisition 3, 'Eretics nil . . ."

FREY BENTOS: ". . . after extra time." Okay, that wraps up the recognition signals, so let's cut an improvised rug while we-all start conspirin' . . . Glide, girlie, glide . . .

KYLIE: [*amazed, then roguish*] Gosh, Goddy, 'tis thee—and treading a measure wi' that broken geezer thou wast like to

hang ere thou started fancying him!
Well, thou sly puss, out on the town,
and in male attire, too—

GODIVA: [*ablaȝe*] Never mind my male attire—
who said you could borrow my long
black gloves and pearls, thou podgy sneak,
thou? Aye, and a-reek wi' my Arpège, and
if those are my Polly Pecks—

KYLIE: [*affrighted*] Nay, sweet coz, they fit me
not, being o'er long and large—

GODIVA: [*gnashing*] Flaunt thy size 10 at me,
would ye? Yikes! and my platinum
slave anklet, too—

ARCHIE: Look not now, fair Godiva, but that's
either Gene Kelly in a scapulary or
thine own traitorous chaplain trucking
and pecking wi' the tall tomato lacking
a bra . . .

GODIVA: [*continued*]—and my graduation
earrings, dammit!

GILDEROY: [*kneeling, amaȝed*] Mai liege, what make
ye here, end in those fraightful breeks?
Ai thot ye were still nigh Peebles!

IMPOSTOR: Peebles too yoo, too!

GILDEROY: [*removing mask*] See, Mejesty, 'tis Ai,
thy former employee, et thy command,
tho' denied golden handshake—

IMPOSTOR: [*desperate*] Outta my way, paysan, I
gotta find thee john!

ARCHIE: [*pointing, fortissimo*] And Gilderoy, by
this hand!

GODIVA: [*still going strong, then faint*] So get 'em
off, blonde marplot, or . . . Did you say
Gilderoy? Ah, where?

ARCHIE: Yonder, apparently proposing to the
weirdo in the hellish plus-fours!

At which point, we freeze the shot while everyone takes
stock, thus:

GODIVA, her looted finery for the nonce forgot, stares
stricken at Gilderoy;

GILDEROY, nonplussed as the impostor lurches past him
through the door marked "Gallants," registers Godiva, and
with a cry of "Some enchented evening, across a crowded
room!" prepares to fly to her side;

FREY BENTOS, circling the floor conspiratorially with La
Infamosa and noting with dismay the drunken disappearance of
her companion into the toilets, suddenly realises that the redhead not two yards away is his own imperious employer, and
recognises the necessity of (a) rescuing the impostor from the
men's can before he breaks a leg or passes out, and (b) getting
himself under cover before Godiva sees him and demands to
know why he is capering publicly with half-clad bimbos;

ARCHIE, belatedly aware that the appearance of the tight
chap who's just vanished into the bogs is identical with that of
King James VI, does a lightning deduct and identifies him as the
impostor, from which it's a short step to concluding that the
above-mentioned half-clad bimbo, now being tangoed furtively
around by the known traitor, Bentos, must be La Infamosa—

but what really sets our hero's antennae flapping is that he has just seen the impostor conversing with Scotland's top agent and Archie's hated antagonist, that blighter Gilderoy;

KYLIE, dazed by Hurricane Godiva, becomes aware that she is being accosted by a bashful Amazon pygmy, his gargoyle map suffused wi' blushes as he solicits, by croak and gesture, the pleasure of the next waltz;

and BILLY BOWMAN, half-stunned by Godiva's flying stilettos, crawls gamely back to the podium, surveys the ruins of the lavolta, calls for a crashing chord, and gasps into his speaking-trumpet: "Well, folks, that was just great, but now, in more relaxed mood, we'd like to play for you Master Spyke Jones his arrangement of the Ladies-Excuse-Me Galliard, specially commissioned by our gracious Queen, God bless her, featuring Mad Max Menuhin on cowbells and Bix Bickerdike on solo arquebus, so grab the nearest guy, girls, there are spot prizes for the survivors—a-one, a-two, a-wa-a-a-ay!"

That did it—all imminent assaults, evasions, embraces, challenges and denunciations must be postponed out of respect for Gloriana's favourite disco diversion, and in a trice our principals were perforce high-kicking (as the galliard requires) in ill-assorted couples to the fascinating rhythm. Ignoring the ballroom etiquette of ladies' choice, Archie and Gilderoy both dived for Godiva, but the inevitable florid and paper-hatted tourist from Sacramento scooped her from their grasp crying: "Hi-gorgeous-my-name's-Garfield-call-me-Gar-I'm-in-fertiliser-and-this-is-my-first-trip-to-your-byooriful-country!," and they found themselves dancing with each other; Kylie, recoiling in disgust as Clnzh tried to grapple her knees, made a wild grab for the nearest male and wound up being expertly swept across the parquet by a fanatically glittering Frey Bentos;

La Infamosa, bereft of her partner and beset by a lasciviously pawing mob of yokels and salesmen, snatched up the bewildered Clnzh with a mutter of "Gawd, the fings I do fer Spain!" and danced away, holding him carefully at arm's length . . . but you and I, reader, must tango briskly through the galliard-crazed throng to where the plot development is taking place— here we go, cha-cha-cha . . .

"Yur telling me thet *isn't* James VI who just went i' the shunky?" cried Gilderoy. "Ach, away ye go, Noble, d'ye think Ai don't know mai own liege lord when Ai see him?"

"As if you didn't know he's a Spanish impostor brought hither by that topless number i' the kinky gear!" retorted Archie. "My God, what's that she's dancing with now, a gremlin . . . ? Aye, don't tell me an ace operative like you isn't privy to the whole vile plot—did I not see thee but a moment since, in cahoots wi' the impostor as he nipped can-wards? So ye've gone over to Spain, Scotch renegade! Typical—take that, sa-ha, and that!"

In case that last remark is obscure, we should explain that their dance had lasted about three seconds, for Gilderoy, after momentary surprise at finding himself partnering the English agent 'gainst whom he had been pitted for years, had complained that Archie was treading on his shoon, at which mortal insult steel had flashed forth, and dance had given way to deadly rapier-play, the blades flickering and slithering like the tongues o' tin serpents as the twain lunged and parried and bumped into other dancers, to whom they muttered apology ere resuming their desperate duello. Across the dance-floor they stamped and thrust, wi' imbrocatta, punta rinverso, and those grim hilt-wrestling close-ups that Fred Cavens was so good at arranging, while the galliard surged heedless around them, for this is Saturday night in Merrie Carlisle, and if dance-freaks want to improvise, who cares?

Needless to say it was a dazzling, top-speed, Errol v. Basil thrust-out with the blades grating and whirling too fast for the eye (or the frantically conducting B. Bowman) to follow, and both heroes making full use of the Dungeon Grill's furniture: let Archie, hard-pressed, do a backward standing jump to a table, and Gilderoy seek to up-end him by whipping away the cloth—in a flash Archie had somersaulted to the bandstand, leaving his opponent knee-deep in broken meats and crockery; or, as they fenced their way to and fro through the string section and Gilderoy was trapped 'twixt double bass and 'cello, one swift flick of his point enveloped Archie in the sheet music of "Aida," causing him to lunge headlong through the big drum (in which, of course, he cleverly rolled away, taking half the woodwinds with him). And such was their matchless skill and breath control that they were able to converse as they fought—none of your corny old "Stand and fight, muckrake!" or "You'll not be so lucky as at Panama . . . aaaargh!," but snappy, informative material:

"Ai don't know what yur tocking about! What plot?"

"Don't give me that 'what plot?' routine! Why, the vile Spanish wheeze to hi-jack Jacobus Rex and have that rummy i' the thunder-house substituted—aha! nearly got you there!—so that he can take over when Queen Bess flakes out and undermine our English polity and Plantagenet values!"

"Och, come off it! Who fed ye thet bill o' goods—Smersh?"

"And thou'rt up to thy poncy-ruffed neck in it, I'll wager, so come not the innocent wi' me, Gilderoy!" Clash-clash!

"Yur havering, Ai tell you! Ai nivver heard of yur blested plot—anyway, Ai've retired, ez from yesterday—aha, ye felt the wind o' thet one, smert-ess!"

"Nyah-nyah, never touched me! Retired—thou? A likely tale!"

"Demmit, men, if ye don't believe it, regard me this clipping from the efternoon edition of the *Reivers' Reminder*!" And as they slashed and riposted their way up the stairs past necking couples who were sitting this one out, the dashing Caledonian rapiered a press cutting from the bosom of his doublet, and extended himself in an Italianate lunge which presented the newsprint before his opponent's astonished eyes.

TOP OP COPS CHOP!
QUITS TO SEEK SOLACE
WI' SASSENACH SWEETIE

FRAE OOR COURT
REPORTERS

Espionage circles were fair scunnert the morn when Ebeneezer ("Bonnie") Gilderoy, Auld Scotia's top plaid-and-dirk callant, gi'ed in his cairts tae oor Soavrain Prince, Jacobus Saxtus, wha was fair dumfoonert at sic unwhalesome defection, wis he no', but! "Wae's me!" quo' His Majestie, "Ah shuld hae stood in bed!" Aye, but oor correspondent jalouses that Gilderoy (umquhile weel kent in highway robberie circles, whilk wis his cover, ye ken) has ta'en early retiral tae seek the fair haun' o' that sonsy floor o' th'English nobilitie, Lady Godiva Dakkers (whee-whew!) wha's fortune wid fill Ibrox Park, no kiddin' (see financial pages).

"The money disnae metter a monkey's," the braw Gilderoy tellt oor reporter, "it's luv Ai'm efter . . ."

See Editorial, Page Sax—Here, is a Scotch lassie no' guid enuff, then?

Archie, his rapier limp in disbelief, stood as one gaffed as he conned the clipping—nay, it could not be, 'twas beyond all credence . . . yet there it was, and for a moment he gaped mute ere giving tongue to his amaze.

"EBENEEZER! I don't be-*lieve* it! Ebeneezer!" He rolled down the staircase, whooping with helpless mirth. "Oh, stone me! Not Ebeneezer—nobody gets called that! Oh, thou poor slob—wait till the Middle March reads that! Ebeneezer, I'll die, I'll die—"

"It's no wurss than bloody Erchibald!" cried Gilderoy, his classic profile pink wi' dudgeon. "Anyway, Ai ken change it any taime Ai laike, easy-peasy, bai deed poll—aye, as a wedding gift to mai adored Godaiva when she assumes the hendle of Mistress Gilderoy! Ai think Ai'll be Justin or Damian—no, stay, what about Derren—"

Archie's merriment was stilled in an instant as that aspect of the news story, o'erlooked until now (well, Ebeneezer, I mean to say!), suddenly smote him. His rapier stiffened in twanging fury, and his lips set like defiant concrete.

"Fat chance!" he snapped. "Off the active list ye may be, and unprivy to Dago deviltry as ye say—but know, presumptuous

Jock, that mine own sights are lined up on the Lady Dacre, and ye can stick that in your sporran and toast it—"

"Thou! What, Sexon hireling, not heff-way up the social ledder o' thy class-ridden Southron pecking order—thou'lt give the eye to mai divinity?" scoffed prideful Gilderoy. "Over mai dead body, china! Hev et thee!" And he leaped to the attack, which Archie met half-way wi' jealousy-invested steel and ready gibe.

"That's a laugh! At least I shall woo her wi'out needing an interpreter, thou glottally stopped barbarian!"

"Thet's a demned laie! Mai God, they won't let you pest Potter's Bar withoot a laicence, tocking laike Les Dawson! End she thinks mai eccent's cute, let me tell you!"

"Mere English politesse to the underdeveloped!" mocked Archie. "Why, our ambassador never goes north without beads and hawkbells!"

"Bennockburn, you bestard!" roared Gilderoy, stuck for a punchy retort, but even as he enveloped Archie's blade in a subtle Caledonian parry and prepared to kick him where it hurt, a voice snarled: "Flodden, yah booger!" and a stout cudgel descended on the Peebles Predator's shapely skull. With a cry of "Oh, perfidious Elbion, when a chep's not looking!" he sank unconscious on the top step, and Archie found himself staring into the snaggle teeth of Wor Jackie, who regarded the supine Scot with grim satisfaction.

"Not havin' that," observed the timely Charlton. "'Ey, boss, did Ah do reet, tho'? Ah mean, Ah divvn't like to butt in, but 'e wez gettin' pawsonal, the haggis-bashin'—"

"Forget it," frowned Archie, getting his breath back. "But ask next time, will you? For certes when he comes to, he'll be bawling 'Foul!' from here to Hexham, and demanding a replay."

Then as he regarded the tin-tuxedo'd roughneck, marking the primitive villainy of feature and baboon-like spread of shoulder, inspiration smote him, and he modified his tone. "Why, a seasonable aid was thine, good fellow," he cried, slapping Wor Jackie on the back and wishing he hadn't, for it was like congratulating Helvellyn. "And I can do wi' more of it," he continued, nursing his hand, "for within are sundry enemies o' the State in need of doing over, and well I ween that, reiver or no, thy heart is stout English—why, isn't that an Armada ribbon you're wearing? Good show, spot on! Well, as I was saying, there are rotters downstairs would do our country mischief— the worst type of foreigners, in fact—"

"Mair Scotchies?" Wor Jackie brightened.

"Well, no—but pretty rancid, just the same! Vile Spanishers aye, onion-fanciers and bull-bashers—just the sort," he went on eagerly, "that you and your team will enjoy working over— a thinnish clergyman, a midget, a tosspot in tweeds, and," he waggled suggestive eyebrow, "a rather sporty female . . . oh, 'twill be a gas, honestly . . ."

Come, come, Noble, you say sternly—is this decent, or even necessary? What need o' hired muscle against such eccentric Latin quartet—or of a sales pitch aimed at Wor Jackie's baser instincts? Chuck it, Noble, you add. Ah, but Archie's thinking ahead, you see, reasoning that a heavy mob may be useful in the closing chapters—and if he seems to be emphasising the fun side, well, he knows the Charltons, and Bond was never squeamish in crisis, was he? Get realistic.

Thought creased the reiver's craggy forehead. "Promise not tae squeal on us tae UPRAT?"

"Forget I even mentioned them!"

"Haud on w'ile Ah consoolt the membership," said Wor

Jackie, and was back in a trice, looking doubtful. "'Tis a posh kinda place, isn't it?—an' we're not dressed, like . . . Ah mean, we're just workin' stiffs, an' Ah doot if some o' the Milburns knaws which wine ga's wi' rock salmon an' chips—"

"I'll sign you in as guests!" promised Archie. "Come on!"

"Warraboot Rob Roy heah?" inquired Oor Kid, indicating the comatose Gilderoy.

"Oh . . . bring him along!" Not quite fair, really, to leave the blighter where he might be picked up as a doorway-dosser. Archie took a final glance at the scowling stubble and bulging biceps of the leathery horrors crowding downstairs like so many vengeful Lee Marvins, shuddered, and led the way . . .

And how are things in the Dungeon Grill? Odd, no other word for it. Godiva for once is in a shell-shocked condition, what with her emotional turmoil at discovering that Gilderoy's on the premises, and the fact that she has spent the last ten minutes wedged in a corner booth between Gar (he o' the fertiliser from Sacramento) and his wife, Mo, who has been pouring out unsought information about their three single-parent daughters and her recent shopping spree in Rome at such a rate that our heroine has been unable to get a freezing snub in edgeways. La Infamosa has dropped Clnzh in an ice-bucket and is trying to detach the impostor (who has emerged from the little boy's room like a giant refreshed and thirsty) from the bar, where he is demanding drink and singing "A wee deoch'n'dorus" in Catalan. And Kylie is being galliarded at speed round the floor, for while Frey Bentos knows full well that La Infamosa and the impostor ought to be secluded in the Priest's Hole Suite without delay, he can't resist the temptation to have a go at the spot prize—and there is only one other couple still on their feet: a lock forward from Langholm in size 16 boots and the buxom

Rosebud, treasurer of Foulbogsyke W.I. (remember her, from Chapter One? Gosh, 'tis a small world . . .). The rest of the clientele, weary of worship at the shrine of Terpsichore, are playing touch-rugger and fighting the waiters, Billy Bowman's defiant bandsmen are trying to set a speed record for the galop from *Orpheus in the Underworld,* and although no one seems to be noticing, the joint is being raided. Warden's men, wi' burning turfs on their lance-points, are swarming in from the service doors, blowing whistles, urged on by the night-shirted proprietor of the bawdy house next door, who brandishes an injunction against late-night music which, he claims, amounts to a restraint of trade.

Into this animated scene the Charltons swept like a well-oiled machine, with Archie standing on a chair issuing crisp directions. Their skills honed by years of raid, onfall, ambush, and participation in the Gala seven-a-sides, the reivers homed in on their designated targets like gang-busters—horny hands plucked La Infamosa and the impostor from the bar and Clnzh from the ice-bucket where he was treading water and sneezing right piteous to hear; Wor Jackie himself, having disposed of Gar and Mo with a quick right and left, yanked the bemused Godiva into a smouldering Apache embrace with a leering growl of "Awoy, hinny, tae the Casbah!" and as the alert observant Bowman deftly changed to "Slaughter on Tenth Avenue," flung her sliding across the floor to a waiting Robson in a striped jersey and beret; and Oor Kid Charlton, neatly cutting in on Frey Bentos and detaching Kylie with the age-old ballroom formula ("You dancin'?" "You asking?" "Ah'm askin" "I'm dancing") whirled her expertly away, leaving the dance-drugged Dominican trying to catch the judge's eye with a solo tap routine and wondering what the hell to do next.

For plainly Operation Heretic had developed a stutter, with La Infamosa, the impostor, and Clnzh in the grip of huskies who might well, Frey Bentos reasoned, be plain-clothes rozzers, a theory supported by the presence of whistle-blowing lawmen. What had gone wrong he couldn't guess, but it called for swift evasion on his part—his hopes of the spot prize were up the spout, anyway. With a mutter of "Ah'm outta heah!," the clerkly conspirator rushed through the orchestra, dropping his small change in the pianist's glass, and disappeared behind the curtain shielding the secret stair to the Priest's Hole Suite.

This was what crafty Archie had been waiting for. With friends and foes alike under Charlton wraps, his urgent need was for some quiet spot to sort things out without the Warden's men playing buttinski, and he shrewdly surmised that Frey Bentos's instinct would be to high-tail it for the secret chamber between the sauna and the reference section. His stentorian cry of "Scrum down!" rang through the Dungeon Grill, and the Charltons melded like magic into a solid phalanx, their prisoners among them, and swept irresistibly o'er floor and bandstand, Warden's men and musicians being hurled aside in a confusion of burning turfs and scattered saxophones, none heeding the vain shrilling of their whistles and protests of "Foot up!" and "Not in straight!" as the reivers, with Archie hovering on their flanks, executed a masterly wheel up the secret stairway and vanished from sight.

Nor could there be any question of pursuit, for by the time the Warden's men had recovered their senses, the Dungeon Grill staff had completed that transformation which raided hells and speakeasies have been using since time immemorial—you know, roulette wheels sliding into the wall, baccarat tables becoming buffets, and bedizened strumpets metamorphosing into knitting spinsters. In a moment the garish nighterie had become a Salvation Army hostel, with texts on the wall, Billy Bowman's boys in ill-fitting tails, potted palms on the bandstand, the sultry chanteuse singing "Bless This House," Gar and Mo playing ludo, Gaston proffering mugs of cocoa and asking the leading Warden if he would like to testify, and the secret stairway blocked by a false wall bearing flying ducks and prints of *The Gleaners* and *The Boyhood of Raleigh*. Smart work, eh?

Meanwhile Archie Noble was ascending the hidden spiral like a stoat on adrenaline, rapier at the high port, and at his heels the surging Charltons, their cries of "That was fun!" "Swinging Carlisle!" and "This Gilderoy's a fair bloody weight, gi'es a shot o' the dwarf or one o' the lassies!" ringing in the confined space. He reached the stairhead and found himself in a sumptuously furnished hide-out, walled on one side in Scandinavian light oak from which came wisps of steam and the distant grunts of pummelled sauna clients, and on the other by dusty shelves of reference volumes among which he barely had time to identify the eleventh Britannica (the limp-covered edition) ere he was aware of Frey Bentos flinging open a window in the far wall and leaping nimbly to the sill, like Rupert of Hentzau.

"Yield, false cleric!" baritoned intrepid Archie, while the arriving crowd behind him braked sharply, riveted by the drama, some crying for firemen with ladders, others for a psychiatrist to talk the fugitive off the ledge, and some coarser spirits jeering "Go on, joomp, crackers!" and "Windy!"; Kylie peered through excited fingers, Clnzh stretched out tiny arms and sneezed in pathetic appeal, and Godiva landed a ringing buffet on the ear of her escorting Robson, who had been carrying her in an over-familiar manner.

"Pack it in, Bentos!" commanded stern Archie. "'Tis a fifty-foot drop to the turbulent and polluted Caldew flood, and if its treacherous undertow doesn't get you, hepatitis will!"

Poised on the sill, his ascetic features contorted in a mask of profound dislike, Frey Bentos emitted a snarl of triumph.

"Ah thank yuh fo' th'information, meat-head!" he sneered. "Know, meddlesome English bum, that yore lookin' at the best butterfly swimmer in the Dominican order, as well as the slickest hoofer—an' Ah've had all mah shots, too!" Hate and fury struck malevolent sparks in his fanatical eyes. "An' yuh ain't seen the last o' Bossanova Bentos, not by a heap! Viva Espana!" And with a laugh of pure cackle he hurled himself into the black void.

Tender Kylie, the memory of his nimble ankle-work fresh in her girlish mind, could not repress a shriek of pity. "Ah, will he drown indeed?"

"In the city dump?" Archie Noble laughed complacently. "I knew he'd buy that old fifty-foot-drop-to-the-Caldew line, and end up covered wi' yuggh among the plastic pottles and burst mattresses." He snapped commanding fingers at the Charltons. "Down, fellows, and hale him forth."

But when they had combed the mouldering garbage, no trace of the absconding sky-pilot did they find, save a fractured tassel—and his dance-card . . . and if, fifty years later, a frail and silver-haired Kylie drew it out fondly from the lavender-scented wall safe wherein she stored her "trinkets o' memory," and recounted yet again to her curly-headed grandchildren the story of The Spot Prize That Got Away . . . reader, can you find it in your heart to blame her? You can? Oh, well, suit yourself.

Never mind Kylie's senile droolings—we're still in crisis. Oh, La Infamosa and the impostor may be on ice, but Bentos is out there somewhere, machinating away, and who knows what other devildoms Spain has up its sleeve, eh? Archie has problems, not least wi' Gilderoy around to distract Godiva from her work— or will her passion evaporate when she discovers he's called Ebeneezer? How long can the Charltons, now wallowing in the sauna, be kept in line? Will Clnzh forgive Kylie for refusing him the last dance? Well, we won't find out standing here . . .

"Oh, stop wasting time!" clarioned Lady Godiva. "Shalt ne'er get anything out o' this sullen strumpet by being polite! Start torturing her, can't you—didn't they teach you anything in basic training!"

"I'm asking the questions, madam!" snapped Archie. "And I'll e'en do it by the book—"

"'Tis all I'm asking! Here be weighty tomes enow on these shelves! So pile 'em on her—'tis called the *peine fore et dure,* in case you didn't know—crush her soft silicone-injected flesh 'neath their ponderous mass, and a'll sing like any canary, I warrant!"

"She's never got over being head girl," murmured Kylie to Gilderoy. "Honestly, two minutes late for hockey practice and up they went on the strappado before prep., even the teenies."

"Ai must say, divaine Godaiva," ventured Gilderoy, removing the ice-pack from his head, "thet Ai think yur being just a wee bit unjooly hursh. Ai mean, she is a woman . . . not mai type," he added hastily, "but 'twould be a bit of a waste—"

"Hold thy false Scots tongue, rock-snatcher!" cried Godiva, and smote her forehead in instant remorse, flying to kneel at his side. "Ah, forgive me, gentle Ebby, I don't know what I'm saying, and how's thy poor sconce its hurt . . . , thou treacherous snake, thou! Ah, me," she went on, pressing her temples, "I'm still torn every which way, and know not whether to love or hate thee . . . Get a grip, Godiva! Right!" she resumed, turning on Archie. "Back to basics . . . art thou going to squeeze this defiant broad or no?"

From which you gather that, once they'd got their breath back, our hero and heroine had turned their attention to the interrogation of La captive Infamosa, Clnzh, and the impostor—for while Archie, you remember, had learned the general outline of Operation Heretic during his nocturnal eavesdrop behind Frey Bentos's arras at Thrashbatter, he didn't know the detail of its later stages, exactly, or where La Infamosa and the impostor had been intending to go from here.

"That a Spanish network is already in place in the Borderland is manifest," he had pointed out, "and the only way to uncover it and so secure our green and pleasant land from Continental bondage is to turn this gang inside out, right?"

No one was arguing with that, even Gilderoy, once he'd come to and had the position fully explained to him by Archie, with occasional passionate interpolations from Godiva, which, since they alternated between melting tenderness and blood-curdling abuse (the girl needs help, no question), were of little service to a slightly confused highwayman with an outsize lump on the back of his head. He had got the gist, eventually, and realising that Scotland's security, no less than England's, was teetering on the brink, had agreed to join the home team, "which patriotic survice Ai embrace the more gledly for thet it bringeth me closer to embracing thaiself, mai divinity," he had concluded, turning up his amber gaze to full voltage and giving Godiva's white hand the 'tash treatment. Her limbs had turned to blancmange at his touch, and she had addressed him as "fond heart" and "thieving swine" in the same breath, to the jealous chagrin of Archie, who had sought to tip the scale by whispering: "His first name—wait for it—is Ebeneezer, no fooling, E-B-E-N-eezer, would you credit it?" but to no avail.

Which brings us to the point where La Infamosa—now more modestly clad in a Newcastle United strip donated by one of the Charltons, who had had to be physically restrained from helping her to put it on—was snarling defiance at Archie's questions. She was their only hope, for the impostor was incoherent wi' boozer's gloom, and no one could understand Clnzh's jungle noises. Godiva, her heart hardened by years of disciplining idle juniors, besought Archie to get practical.

"Hang her by the thumbs o'er a lighted candle!" she pleaded. "It always worked on the Third Form—ask Kylie! Or let those ghastly monsters in the sauna work her over . . . nay, though, she'd just enjoy it . . . I have it!—a gym slip, two sizes too small and soaked in brine before a blazing fire, shall so shrink and pinch her corpuscles—"

"Do you mind?" protested Archie, banishing the thought of what this one would be like across the breakfast table, gorgeous poppet though she was. "Anyway, we haven't a gym slip—"

"And precious time flies, while you play Mastermind wi'

her!" blazed Godiva. "Aye, while that stinkard chaplain o' mine blows the whistle on us to his accomplices, and any minute now the maids in this godawful pot-house will be keening at our doors in Filipino, wanting to make up the room—"

"As to Bentos, no man travels fast or far who has fallen head-first into a Carlisle Corporation tip," retorted Archie. "He'll take hours to recover. Nor shall the help intrude—I put out a 'Disturb Not' notice—"

"That just inflames them, fool! Any minute now they'll be beating the panels, whining 'Ello-o-o . . . sorr-ee' . . . Look, let me at her—just five minutes with a nice springy slipper—"

"If you want her to tock," interrupted Gilderoy, "Ai suggest thet you stend beck, and let the dug see the rebbit." He removed the ice-pack, winced, and rose to his splendid height, his matinee idol features aglow with modest confidence. "Ai hesitate to say it, but the fect is that oll wimmen are clay in mai hends, ez these ladies"—he coughed diffidently, indicating Godiva and Kylie—"ken testifay. One touch of mai lips distrects, a second confuses, a thurrd disorientates entairely, end a fourth brings the truth gushing forth laike a burst wotter-main—"

"Stop, stop!" cried frantic Godiva. "Thou'ldst not pollute thy dear, wondrous, lying, deceitful lips by contact wi' that Spanish scrubber!"

"A laight epplication should be sufficient," shrugged Gilderoy. "Of course, if it's her chaildhood memories yur efter, ettitude to parents, deep subconscious stuff, it maight be es well if the ladies left the room—"

With a wild cry Godiva stopped her ears, Kylie gnashed jealous pearls in Infamosa's direction, and Archie, outraged reproof icicling his eye-lids, bellied up to the debonair Scot.

"That's enough of that sort of talk!" he began, and then added uncertainly: "You mean you can snog it out of her?"

"They don't coll me the Scopalomaine Smoocher for nothing," remarked airy Gilderoy, and stepping forward he stooped o'er the chair in which La Infamosa sat bound and helpless, her full red lips and Newcastle jersey palpitating before his electrifying screen presence. He smiled, imps of mischief semaphoring from his smoky eyes, and leaned down into over-the-shoulder close shot.

"We-ell, hull-o thair . . . ," he murmured, and even ten feet away Godiva felt her senses swim, while Kylie began to chew a cushion. "Hev'nt we met before . . . shurrly? St. Petersburrg . . . in the whaite naights? Rothesay . . . at the Fair . . . ?"

La Infamosa gave a goofed whimper, heavy wi' yearn and terror. "Gerraway from me," she quavered faintly. "My muvver warned me . . . ow, Gawd! . . . naow, naow . . . ! Oh, yes . . . yes pleez!"

"Ai've ollways laiked the name Infamosa . . ." His voice was like honeyed curtains slowly drawn. "Ai say . . . Ai think mai horse has kest a shoo . . . end not a smithy in saight . . ." His lips brushed hers gently, and she whinnied; a second touch, and she went rigid, eyes rolling ere they glazed over. Gilderoy stepped back, eyeing her keenly and taking her pulse as she glooped into vacancy, parted red lips upturned and flapping gently. Frowning, he gave them a swift peck, and her earrings began to rattle ere they crashed to the floor. By this time Kylie was face down on the sofa, beating it with her fists; Godiva, forcing herself to watch, muttered 'twixt clenched teeth: "I will be brave . . . it's scientific . . . he doesn't mean it . . . he hates it . . . he hates her . . . I love him . . . no, I don't . . ."

"Raight," said Gilderoy, appraising the besotted tomato,

"thet was the tranquilaiser . . . now for the ten-second whemmy . . . Notebook end quill ready? Turrn yur becks, gurls!" He started to hyperventilate, flexing his moustache, seized La Infamosa's lolling head in both hands, and with a velvet growl of "Yur maine, d'ye heer? Helpless in mai power, har-har! poor fluttering wee herry!" scrunched her lips with torrid ardour what time his foot tapped off the seconds. He desisted abruptly as her sable tresses gave a warning crackle, anxiously lifting her eyelids and sighing with relief.

"Hev to be careful," he explained. "Too much, end they nivver come beck. There's a widow Ai met in the snake-house at Corstorphine zoo . . . poor women still thinks she's Cleopetra . . . Aye, this one's well away. Oll set? Heer we go!" And while Archie stood by wi' quill, Gilderoy began merciless third-degree:

Q: Yur name is La Infamosa?

A: Naow, it's not. I'm Busty Basset.

Q: Thet doesn't sound very Spenish!

A: It ain't. I'm from Catford.

Q: Then whair's La Infamosa, for hivven's sake?

A: 'Ow the 'ell should I know? I'm a temp.

Q: A temp? But, crivvens, how came ye in Dago employ?

A: Yer, well, I used to be in show-biz, see, wiv a troupe o' lady wrestlers, Bess of 'Ardwick's Peeling Belles (gerrit?) an' Master Burbage 'ad us in 'is all-girl production of *As You Like It*, an' I was Orlando, an' my mate Doris was Charles the Wrestler . . . 'ere, we didn't 'alf pack 'em in—

Q: Fescinating . . . but how came the Iberian connection?

A: Ow, well, the boy-players picketed the Globe, the rotten little poofs, an' the show got took off, an' Bess booked us a club tour on the Costa del Sol, wrestlin' in mud, mostly, but sometimes in syllabub an' negus—dead kinky, those Dons are—yer, we 'ad a tag match in cointreau, even, an' that finished us, 'cos we got pinched by the Inquisition for not 'avin a liquor licence—

"She's delirious!" interrupted Archie. "Thou'st o'erdone it, man, and struck her natural!"

"Oh, peace! Tho' it be drawn from thee wi' trem-caurs!" hissed Gilderoy. "Ai'm probing, demmit! Go on, hen, whit then?"

A: Well, they said if we didn't agree to work for Escurial Intelligence we'd go to the stake for indecent exposure. They said I 'ad to impersonate La Infamosa an' go to England wiv this fruitcake wot looks like the King o' Scots, an' meet up wiv Frey Thingummy. "An' if yer don't," sez the Inquisitor, "it'll be fryin' tonight for yore mate Doris, 'oo remains in the clutches o' the 'Oly Office" . . . 'Ere, why you askin' me all these question? Where am I . . . ?

"She's coming out on't!" shouted Archie. "Haste, man, give her a booster shot!"

So fast did Gilderoy react that the sharp splunch! as he locked his lips to Infamosa's drowned out Archie's final words, nor did he de-couple until her expression had resumed its dead-halibut vacancy. Sweat stood in shapely beads on the Caledonian Casanova's splendid brow, and his vocal cords thrummed with relief.

"Bai jove, just in taime—but Ai daren't do it again!"

"Ye mean 'twould damage her permanently?" cried Archie.

"Not hur—me! She must hev been living on gurlick, demmit! 'Tis laike kissing the population o' Marseilles!" He resumed his interrogation with the speed of a pattering comedian.

Q: End whair was Frey Thingummy to take the impostor?

A: Eh? Wot's an impostor?

Q: The fruitcake who looks laike the King o' Scots, thou Ketford dumbo! What was his schedule?

A: Ow, yer . . . me an' Frey Dooda 'as to tike 'im to a command bunker where there's a wizard 'oo's goin' to organise some caper called Operation Jimsnatch . . . but I don't know nuffink abaht that . . .

Q: Keep tocking, gurl! Whair's this commend bunker?

A: Not shore . . . funny name . . . somefink like Ealing . . . underground . . .

Q: Underground? Ealing? Not Hounslow, or Urls Court?

A: Naow, silly! It was Eel-somefink . . .

Q: Ecton? Hemmersmith? Boston Mennor?

A: Naow! Ow, I dunno . . . that's me up to date . . . I'm tired . . . 'ere, where's that lovely big Scotch geezer 'oo kissed me . . . ? More, more . . . ! Signin' orf now . . . over an' aht . . .

And she relaxed comfortably in her bonds, smiling blissfully and singing "Amazing Grace" in a dreamy whisper. Gilderoy shook his handsome head and gave his chin-beard a resigned pluck.

"Thet's our lot, Ai fear . . . she's in a trence, and won't come round for hours, when she'll be medly in love wi' me." He sighed. "Et least we know the impostor hes to be taken to some station on the Piccadilly laine."

"Nay, 'tis not open for another four centuries," quo' dubious Archie. "And yet . . . she said 'underground' . . ."

"Well, it ken't be the Glesgow system—she'd have mentioned the smell . . ."

". . . and 'wizard' . . . and 'Eel-somefink' . . . ," mused Archie, and suddenly (since it's his turn to do something clever) cried: "Of course! *Eildon!* Wi' it's well-known *underground* cavern, home to *wizards* and kindred warlocks! It fits! Bingo, i' faith!" At which Gilderoy lit up, comprehending, and they slapped each other's palms wi' cries of "Right on!" and "Yay!" and "Ma main man!" and other of those sickening expressions of mutual congratulation to which the Elizabethans were so regrettably prone. Then they did a re-think.

For while they knew the rendezvous, other problems loomed, e.g., if the trance-induced Andalusian type was indeed Busty Basset, lady wrestler, where was La real Infamosa? For that matter, *who* was La Infamosa? And such was the Machiavellian subtlety of thought process among Tudor agents that they even started to shoot suspicious glances at Kylie and Godiva, who, their shared jealousy having subsided now that Gilderoy had stopped his osculatory interrogation of B.B., were resuming their debate about Kylie's borrowing Godiva's evening kit, with recriminations going back years to disputed tennis rackets, lipsticks, sweets, copies o' *Buntie*, underwear, and boyfriends, and cries of "Did!" "Didn't!" "Beast!" "Pig!" "Up thine!" and "Sucks to you, too!"

"Neither *sounds* as though she could be La genuine Infamosa," said Archie. "Nay, what am I thinking of! My beloved Godiva, a Spanish agent? 'Tis not on!"

"'Twould be a cunning twist o' plot," mused Gilderoy.

"At this stage o' the story? Nay, too complex by far—no author would dare!"

"True," quo' Gilderoy, "end Ai've just remembered something that proves their innocence beyond doubt. Neether of them," he said impressively, "tasted of gurlick."

"Thank God! That settles it! Mind you, I never seriously suspected Godiva . . . and blondie's a non-starter—bright, but no conspiracy cred . . ."

"Ai concur. Cute, playful, but not intrigue-smert . . ."

"Except in amorous carry-on and Cupid's arts, I daresay . . ."

"Not even in delliance. Leads wi' her teeth . . . Ai've got the marks to prove it . . ."

"So," reasoned logical Archie, getting back to basics, "if neither of them is La Infamosa,* and this Basset is mere stalking horse, 'tis plain that the authentic Sevillian Seductress is still out there somewhere, probably conspiring away like crazy—"

"Cogently reasoned, Noble!"

"—and that louse Bentos isn't going to take for ever to get cleaned up and back on track. Which means," and here Archie's handsome features hardened into a fair facsimile of the Boulder Dam, "that we must penetrate this nest o' Dago mischief 'neath the Eildons wi'out delay, for while by capturing yon recumbent lush we have snootered Operation Jimsnatch, 'tis vital that we squelch this Wizard and his gang before they can take off and do this sceptred isle some new despite—"

"Laike for instance?"

"How do I know? Metrication, political correctness, female clergy, changes in the offside law, Bishops in your own ghastly Scotch Church—who can say what subversion their foreign malice can devise? Nay, in the boot must go, and speedily—"

"But wi' what means? Scottish Commend won't listen to me, now thet Ai'm off the strength—"

"No time ha' we to enlist official muscle—and they'd just foul up, anyway," insisted the sturdy English ace. "We alone must work it—and cop any gongs and credit that may accrue." His reckless fighting smile briefly illuminated the apartment. "Look, this Wizard expects La Infamosa and the impostor to

---

* Author's guarantee: Lady Godiva is *not* La Infamosa. Neither is Kylie. Honestly.

roll up any minute at the Eildons, accompanied by Frey Bentos, doesn't he? And so they shall! Two can play this impersonation game, and there"—he flung out a determined finger at Godiva, who was now perorating on the subject of her favourite rag-doll, allegedly lost overboard when Kylie tried to teach it to swim during a royal water progress on the Thames—"is an Infamosa shall con these Spaniards stupid!"

Heroes seldom goggle, but Gilderoy managed it. "Ye'd hev mai adored goddess penetrate enemy HQ disgaised as the Granada Gorgon? Ye care not, do ye? Heer, but hold on—we ken't pess off a bogus Bentos on them, well known to them as he must be—"

Archie borrowed the goggle briefly, then brightened. "You can say he sprained his ankle, or his tonsure, or something—"

"*Ai* ken say?" Gilderoy snatched the goggle back, distraught. "What d'ye mean—'Ai'?"

"Someone's got to impersonate the impostor, haven't they? Well," Archie pointed out, "certes it must be someone wi' a Scotch accent and all the patter, able to converse at need on haggis prices and Stenhousemuir's promotion prospects—"

"But, demmit, Ai'm six two and splendid of mien, and anyone impurrsonating Jolly Jim—or his double—must needs be a shilpit wee bauchle wi' a face laike a ruptured bunion! Anither thing—the men tocks laike a keelie, end shembles end slavers most scunnersome—"

"Bend your knees and wear false whiskers," Archie dismissed. "Anyway, 'twill be but a brief imposture, just long enough to get into the cavern, case the layout, distract their attention, and as soon as thou'rt spotted, cry 'Geronimo!,' whereon the Charltons and I, lurking without, will sally in and o'erwhelm them, capture their secret files before they can be shredded and so wrap up their whole British network!" Visions of honour and glory flickered in his honest eyes with subliminal speed. "Golly, I could get a K out of this . . . and a few bob, I trow . . . perhaps an estate in Kent from a grateful monarch . . . oh, well, on Wearside, anyway . . . and then . . . ah, then . . . !"

The homely grey of his irises took on a rosy tint which would have made him look like Dracula had his fair face not been shining with nobility. "Then," he glooped reverently, "then I can woo my sweet Godiva on equal terms—well, pretty equal . . . make her Lady Noble . . . open a joint account . . . and who knows, perchance," he went on, blushing slightly, "the patter of tiny Nobling feet . . . Godfrey, after her, and Samantha, because it's such a pretty name, don't you think? And why are you coughing in that sardonic manner?"

"Just a mainor point." Gilderoy's tone was of soufflé lightness. "You'll hev to tock her into this Infamosa imposture furst. Shell we join the ladies . . . ?"

And while they do, let's quit the torrid atmosphere of the Priest's Hole Suite (Sir John Harington hadn't got round to air conditioning yet) and catch up on something we should have checked on ages ago—remember we speculated idly a few pages back on what the opposition might be up to? Yes, it's all very well our hero scheming brilliantly and getting gung-ho, but if he could have seen what was happening 'neath the dreaded Eildons he'd not only have lowered his voice, he'd have resorted to sign language, for the devildoms of Spain are firing on all cylinders . . . or will be as soon as the cauldron technicians have got the thing working again . . .

"'Twas that damned pygmy of Bentos's!" The Wizard's skeletal features were contorted by rage into a knife-grinder's dream.

"Well I wotted the little bugger wasn't house-trained when he tried to drink my cauldron—and then he had to swim in it, yet, polluting its precious magical fluid with his Amazonian smells and microbes! Look at it!"

He gestured bonily at the cauldron, which had been detached, wi' infinite labour and grunts of "Doon your end, Wullie!" from its bed in the basalt conference table, and now lay apart in a tangle of cables and micro-circuits covered with cabalistic wiring directions, while a party of small Scottish warlocks in overalls peered glumly at the liquid's blank surface and agreed that by rights they ought to drain it down to get at the control unit.

"Is't no' under guarantee, whateffer?" hiccoughed Lord Anguish, who, with Don Collapso, had been summoned to a final briefing on Operation Jimsnatch. (Just in time, weren't we?)

"How can it be, Scottish sot?" hissed the Wizard. "'Tis a Spanish model, brought hither by secret ways in crates labelled 'Banana spares—do not bend' and assembled by Escurial experts who, alas, are now sunning themselves on the beach at Malaga while these local cowboys," and his crackling glance shrivelled a couple of warlocks into smoking puddles on the stone floor, "talk of draining and unobtainable parts! I feared the worst when it started to show repeats of old *autos da fe*, and now they tell me it hath a virus in its memory! Aye, a Clnzh virus! Just when our plot is ripe, and I wait helpless for a sight of Bentos and La Infamosa!"

"Shoulda been assembled in Espana," opined Don Collapso, smacking liver lips o'er his ortolan sandwich. "These assemblee keets are nevaire reliable, weeth thair Japanese eenstroctions."

"Got any lizard entrails, jimmy?" inquired the warlock

foreman, and the Wizard, having briefly turned him into a toad
and thought better of it, snatched a flask from his work-bench
and thrust it impatiently into the other's hand. "Ta. Noo, let's
see . . . crivvens, this is weel past it's shelf-life . . . 'bottled in Tai-
wan' . . . jeez, it'll be yin o' they Gobi lizards . . . Aye, weel,
Ah'm no' promisin' nuthin'. Stand by wi' the newt's gall, Wullie . . . jist a wee drap, mind, when Ah intone the magic word
'Dalgliesh' . . ." And he began to chant on a rising note:

> Bogle's blood an' puddock's feather,
> Banshee virus, stint yer blether,
> Belial's granny, Hecate's mither,
> Cauldron, get yer act thegither!

The greenish liquid began to froth and bubble, the cauldron
vibrated as the warlocks clung to keep it upright, the Wizard's
eyes glittered with baleful hope, Lord Anguish gulped a nervous Glayva cocktail, and as the word of power was spoken and
the newt's gall infused, the troubled surface calmed as though
by magic (well, that's what it was, after all), dim shapes writhed
in its depth, and it needed only a supplementary spell from the
foreman ("Go on yersel', McCoist!"), and suddenly the face
and figure of Frey Bentos came into clear view.

"We're the wee boys!" exulted the warlocks, but the Wizard and his companions could only gape appalled at the limpid
screen, until:

"Whit the hell's he daein' in a washeteria?" belched Lord
Anguish.

"Een hees long Johns?" wondered Don Collapso.

The Wizard gave a screech which could only be described

as eldritch. "He's doing his laundry, the Dominican dope! While the fate of Europe lies i' the scale, he labours on his turnout wi' poss-stick and Ariel! Why?" He knew nought of the cleric's immersion in the corporation tip, of course. "Nay, but this shall cost him a few de-merits! Happily," he continued, stabbing buttons and muttering spells, "La Infamosa knows her duty, and is doubtless hasting us-wards even now, with the impostor in tow . . . see, gentlemen, there she is . . . uunnghll!"

His words died in a stricken gulp as into view swam Busty Basset, chairbound in a Newcastle jersey and sunk in beatific stupor; the comatose figure in tweed trunk hose was unmistakably the James VI substitute, and in the background Clnzh could be seen sullenly eating a potted plant. Lord Anguish did a bleary peer.

"That's them, a'right . . . aye, inna Priest's Hole Suite—I mind we had a St. Andrew's bash there a coupla years ago—"

"Silence!" grated the Wizard, adjusting the remote control to take in the whole chamber. Something, he was thinking, has come grievously unglued . . . but he wasn't a double first (Intrigue and Necromancy, Salamanca) for nothing, and even as he lamped the four other figures in the chamber, his talonish fingers were activating the cauldron's identification banks, and his gimlet glare was scanning the parchment print-out:

"Noble, Archibald, English agent and hero (oo classification), b. corporation almshouse, Haltwhistle, 1572 . . . Gilderoy, Ebeneezer (repeat, Ebeneezer, true fact!), Scottish agent, amorist, part-time highwayman, b. Gorbals, 1571 . . . Dacre, Lady Godiva, English aristocrat, Sloane Ranger, and knock-out (wow, check those buns!) . . ." At this point the parchment began to scrunch up and whizz fast-forward until the Wizard

put it on pause with a timely curse. "... b. Mayfair, 1577 ... Delishe, Kylie, English court groupie, Dacre confidante, pushover,
b. Nether Wallop, 1578 ..."

There was lots more, of course, for the Spanish intelligence
service were gluttons for gossip. Thus the watching trio learned
that Archie, working under cover in Cadiz in '88, had actually
travelled home aboard the Armada, spending the whole voyage
hiding in a sack of lentils, as a result of which the crew of the
flagship *Santa Mañana* were disabled by digestive upsets; that
Gilderoy's uncanny power over women was attributed (by a
Jesuit psychiatrist) to porridge and his curious accent, the latter
being a consequence of his removal from Gorbals to Giffnock
in infancy; Godiva's vital statistics, over which Don Collapso
drooled in lecherous disbelief; and the inside story on Kylie, the
gardener's boy, and the jammed zip fastener, of which the head-
mistress had written in her school report, "I wolde nott sullie
this faire page nor thy decent minde, honest parent, with more
fuller disclosure, but do assure ye her pockett monie is stoppt!"

The Wizard's lips tightened, Don Collapso's eyes bugged,
and Lord Anguish's tartan trews paled as they read. Then the
Wizard summed up.

"Woe, woe, and thrice woe!" he exclaimed. "We're rum-
bled. Yet shall this work to our advantage, for see, these heretic
swine who have, by some mischance, put the mockers on our
vital operatives, will suppose themselves i' the driving seat. Little do they know," he cackled, blue sparks flying from his white
locks, "that we are now privy to their conference, and will learn
all that they intend! List, oh list, for now cometh the good
stuff ...!"

They craned over the cauldron, where our four were plain
to be seen, Godiva in full haughty harangue, Kylie agog, Archie

trying to get a word in, and Gilderoy observing his efforts wi' sardonic complacency. The Wizard gave a strangled yelp.

"There's no sound on th'accursed thing!" he cried, and the warlock foreman sighed, put down his mug and his *E'entide Tymes*, rose, peered at the cauldron, gave the Wizard a withering glance, and said: "Ye've got it on mute." Patiently he murmured a potent charm ("Shankly for King"), the mute button clicked off, and the dank cavern walls reverberated to a Benenden contralto raised in passionate protest . . .

". . . and besides, I don't speak Spanish!" stormed Lady Godiva.

"You don't need to! She can't either!" insisted Archie, indicating the unconscious Basset. "Well, not beyond a few elementary phrases, like 'Split, girls, it's a raid' and 'Not guilty, alcalde,' I imagine. She's as English as we are—"

"As you, possibly," observed Godiva tartly. "There are distinctions, don't you agree?"

Archie ground impatient teeth. "Do me a favour! The point is she comes from Catford, so the Eildon conspirators will expect her to converse according, wi' a Cockney accent—"

"Catford? Cockney?" Godiva's slender eyebrows shot north and vanished into her crowning glory. "What, am I to go abroad crying 'What cheer, gossips' and 'Stone the crows' and asking for jellied eels—whatever they are? Doubtless," she sniffed daintily, "thou'dst have me push a barrow into this Eildon place, calling 'Chairs to grind!' or 'Any old whelks?'"

"Or singing 'Knees Up, Goody Browne,'" suggested mischievous Kylie.

"Since you seem to know the words, hoyden," snapped Godiva, "do you play the part—marry, aye, ye have all the brassy vulgarity for't!"

"She's not tall enough!" Archie adopted a winning wheedle. "Nor has she thy queenly presence, thy command, thy style—"

"Thy honest bulk," murmured Kylie.

"—thy wit and resource," said Archie, hurriedly getting between them. "Nay, dear lady, anyone can do the ockney-cay ackchat-bay, honnist, swelp me gorblimey Ginger yore barmy, innit? 'Ah's abaht it, gel?"

"I'm sorry," said Godiva coldly. "I don't speak Danish either."

"Ekshully," interposed Gilderoy, "the eccent's immaterial. Oll you people south of Gretna sound aidentical to outland ears—"

"Dare ye suggest," iced Godiva, "that I sound like that nasally challenged slattern yonder?"

"Nay, sweet nobility!" smoothed the M74 Lothario. "To me thay speech is laike no human vice, but rather as faerie musick that whispereth in Ercady." He stooped to 'tash her limp fingers, and Godiva wilted, murmuring, "Ah, fond blackguard," at his touch. "Ai simply meant thet the Wizard won't know the difference, espeshly if ye swathe thet swan-laike neck in a woolly muffler end say ye cot a chill on the Aisle of Men ferry, so ye may speak i' thet sexy whisper that churrms mai senses quaite. Ai only hope," he added, giving her the wistful amber, "thet Ai can shemble and slobber convincingly maiself . . . ah, but with thee et mai saide, how ken Ai fail?"

Love and hate wrestled in Godiva's senses. "Thou'lt shamble and slobber like any Apollo," she husked, "thou dastard rotter!"

"Gosh, what a team you'll make!" enthused Archie. Jealous as sin, he yet recognised that Gilderoy's line of oil had won her compliance, and quickly got executive before she could change her mind. "Now, then, I'll just run through it all again from the top . . ." And vibrant of voice, reckless of smile, resolute of hair with confidence fairly rippling from ear to ankle, he repeated his plan . . .

. . . while in the shadowy depths of that ghoul-haunted cavern below the Eildons all was sinister activity, Don Collapso and Lord Anguish ordering up mini-brooms and horses, and the Wizard listening in to Archie's every word, chuckling full malevolent as the warlock foreman turned up the cauldron's volume with the dread conjuring words "Firhill for Thrills" . . .

Talk about impending disaster, this is frightful. Those worries that once seemed so important (could Gilderoy get by as James VI if he wore a Hallowe'en mask? will the Charltons leave the sauna as we would wish to find it? what were Kylie and the gardener's boy up to, anyway?) pale into insignificance before the appalling fact that the Wizard has got pole position, and our Fearless Four are heading into deep trouble. At least we know the worst . . . or do we? Probably not. Oh, well, chins up, shoulders back, deep breaths, and any other useless precautions you can think of . . .

Somewhere in the musty files of the Elizabethan secret service—probably tucked away between that forgotten note from old John Forster describing how he found a cypher message among the effects of a vagrant Scottish dentist,* and one of Walsingham's shopping lists ("one browne loafe; one pottle sacke, decaffynated; aspirinne; one new feather for hatte")—there ought to be an à la carte menu from the Dungeon Grill, dated Februarie iii, 159–. Old and tattered now, its gilt edging sadly tarnished, its sauce stains long faded, its entrees almost indecipherable (and probably indigestible unless you fancy

---

* Which, when decoded, gave English intelligence their first hint that Spain was planning something called the "Enterpryse of England" (the Armada, to you)—and if you don't believe us, it's in the State Papers, so it must be true.

singed sheepe's heid wi' nettle gravy), it is naetheless a docu-
ment of mind-boggling historical interest, for if we peer closely
at the back cover, what do we find? Yes, there, between the
blood-stain and the political graffiti "Free Wille o' Kinmont
nowe!," we discern a hastily jotted memorandum:

A. NOBBLE, HYS PROBLEMS
Item, disguize apparel for ye Ladye Dakers and Gilderoye
Item, transport—Charltons?
Item, what to doe wi' B. Basset, impostor, and ye Dwarffe?
Item, will head offis paye for dammidge to Donjon Grille?
Item, ditto, sauna?
Item, floweres and comfits for Ladye D., when occasion
    serves, lest that Scottishe git steal a marche uppon mee!

From which we deduce that our hero was nothing if not
systematic in planning his great counter-strike against Operation Heretic. Starting with Item One, he pointed out that if their
impersonations were to stand an earthly, Gilderoy and Godiva
must wear appropriate costumes—but while Gilderoy reluctantly agreed to don the impostor's tweed trunk hose, etc., and
her ladyship consented to the blonde wig since her fiery tresses
would have been an instant giveaway, she indignantly rejected
the scanty leather braces and tasselled boots of the somnolent
lady wrestler.

"For one thing, fie! 'tis shameless," she demurred primly,
"and for another, while I vaunt not my charms, if I go out in
that lot *and* a platinum hairpiece, I'll start a riot! Think again,
Double-Nought Noble!"

Which he did, to such brilliant effect that two minutes later he was scooting out surreptitiously via the city dump to the nearby playhouse, where the strolling thespians were still partying to celebrate having presented their double bill of *Titus Andronicus* and *My Wyfe's Familie* and got away with it. Cunningly posing as a Warner's talent scout, Archie ingratiated himself with the Welsh leading man and his agent, discoursed largely of contracts, cuts o' gross profits, and swimming pools, listened with feigned rapture to the Taffy's recitation from *Under Milke Wode,* and conned them into lending him feminine attire, a make-up kit, a false beard, and a tinsel crown, which he thought would give Gilderoy that authentic regal touch—and if you think all that is improbable, you've never seen a Burbank operator in action.

Item Two (transport) was a snip. Garscadden was still chomping contentedly in the multi-storey stable, and it was no bother to the Charltons, now sternly summoned by Archie from the sauna where they had been playing steam polo on exercise bikes, to nip out and pinch several steeds (their own being still hungover) from the city's overnight horse parks, and bring them to the kitchen entrance of the Thynkynge Man's Strumpet through streets now deserted save for the usual piles of drunks and corpses. Godiva, in the Priest's Hole Suite's vanitory unit, where Kylie was helping to attire her in the borrowed theatrical finery, overheard our hero's brisk commands to the reivers, and could not but admire his mastery in bending such coarse and fractious ruffians to his will by sheer personal magnetism and the threat of snitching to UPRAT if they played not ball.

"Truly, while Gilderoy is something else, yet is this Noble no common man," she sighed, and frowned distraught at the mirror. "Ah, sweet Kylie, how am I to choose? Nay, my judgment is all shot; I dither, I swither, I can't decide—"

"No contest." Designing Kylie, buttoning briskly, was prompt. "Go for Noble every time. Just your type, and after all, what's Gilderoy but a male model who talks through his nose, and Scotch to boot, yugghh—"

"Not them, lackbrain!" railed Godiva. "This gown o' green Flemish velvet—doth it not clash most foully wi' accessories of scarlet fur? Should I wear the sequined farthingale? And what o' the plumed bonnet wi' bells on—or the yellow ermine toque and spangled veil? Oh, 'tis all too much! That I, thrice on the cover of *Gloriana's Glasse,* should be lumbered with playhouse castoffs—"

"You're going to a conspiracy, not Ascot," Kylie reminded her. "Here, what about this psychedelic ruff all prettily set wi' glass marbles and turquoise ribbons? Go on, why not? 'Tis just thy size, and the Wizard's cave is sure to be pretty dark, anyway . . ."

Meanwhile, organised Noble, zipping through his schedule at speed, was disposing of Basset, Clnzh, and the impostor by ordering Oor Kid and a spare Robson to convey them to Thrashbatter, there to be mewed up in the cellar for the duration. "And guard ye them right jealously," he enjoined Oor Kid, "for should th'impostor win free, our hopes might yet be marred. And keep thy paws off the Catford bimbo, understand, or UPRAT will get an earful on Monday morning. Another thing—you take orders from Mistress Delishe, who accompanies thee, she being unfitted for the rough stuff at Eildon, in that she is young, blonde, daffy, and plumply soft o' limb . . . why are you licking your lips, Charlton?—if you've got crumbs in your beard, use a handkerchief, for heaven's sake . . ."

Items Four and Five would have to await a court of inquiry, and Item Six he couldn't do much about beyond dropping a stern hint to Gilderoy (who was in evil mood on account of the false beard and tinsel crown) not to take advantage of his proximity to Godiva in the forthcoming operation.

"Edventage? Don't make me leff!" scoffed the gorgeous Gael. "Ai don't need to take it, brother—Ai've got it. End if you don't laike it, when this caper's over we ken take up the debate where it was interrupted by yur friend wi' the cosh and faive-o'clock shadow—of oll the ceddish tricks, bashing a chep from behaind—"

"With you, rattlemouth!" Archie's teeth gritted in furious gnash. "Any time, any place, wi' unbated tuck! But for the nonce, our mission . . . ye know the way to Eildon, I presume? There's only one cave, clearly signposted, so even a Glasgow Academical can't miss it . . . the Charltons and I will be right behind you, awaiting thy Mayday call—"

"Armed wi' coshes, ez usual, Ai suppose . . . stinkard!"

"Scotch tyke!"

"English twitte!"

That wrapped up the planning stage . . . aye, and now 'tis time for heave and ho in earnest, for this is H-hour dawning as the first light creeps timidly o'er the red battlements of the scarred old city, blinks with distaste at the human debris snoring in the gutters, and starts to shine with obvious reluctance. The last vital decisions are taken: in the vanitory unit Godiva reaches a compromise (the yellow toque *and* the scarlet fur accessories, for what the hell, if you've got to go over the top, get airborne); Gilderoy wonders if he can get away with kerrying the tinsel crown, because he's demned if he'll wear it; at the kitchen entrance the Charltons are rubbing their stubble and slapping their calves as they warm up; Kylie listens eagerly to Archie, glancing sidelong at Oor Kid's rugged profile and brawny thews as she asks wide-eyed: "And you say he'll do *everything* I tell him? Gosh, happy birthday—I mean, right, okay, gotcha, Noble, yah . . ."; the three prisoners are brought swiftly down the back stairs and loaded into the hotel's laundry-wain, two of them still stupefied (with love and drink, respectively), and Clnzh discreetly concealed in a pillow-case with a dead python in case he gets peckish on the way to Thrashbatter.

Well . . . here we go. Once again, as so often in its long and perilous story, the old country's fate is on a knife-edge, and not for the first time (or the last) its only hope rests with a small band of determined head-cases. Not the kind to win graves in the Abbey or an entry in the D.N.B., but if you look carefully enough in the footnotes of history, you'll find thousands like them, just as unlikely and every bit as eccentric: the crazy English optimist ready to bash on with dauntless enthusiasm and inspired lunacy; the proudly heedless heroine capable of prodigies with her nose in the air and her mind on something else; the Scotch adventurer whose careless bravado masks a skill and craft which make him a priceless (but unpredictable) ally; the blonde scatterbrain, overlooked, who may yet have the vital part to play; and, not least by any means, the uncouth frontier bandits who are only there for fear of losing their licences—and for the hell of it and anything they can pick up. (With luck, they'll always be there.)

But now, as we tighten our girths, look to our weapons, adjust our toques, surreptitiously drop tinsel crowns in the dustbin, tell Oor Kid that Robson can drive and it's ever so cosy in the back . . . and Archie casts a final steel-eyed glance over his ill-assorted command, it's time for those brief but heartfelt farewells so dear to the island race in time of peril . . .

"'Bye, Goddy, take care, and I'm awfully sorry about the rag-doll . . . no, really, the blonde wig and yellow chapeau go smashingly together, no kid . . ." "You're sure? You little bitch, you're smirking. No, come on, do I look okay, straight up? Oh God, this scarlet fur's a disaster . . ." "Well, happy hunting, Gilderoy—we have our differences, but I can't think of anyone I'd rather go into the jungle with . . ." "'With,' quotha? Ai'm going to be a helluva long way in front o' thee, Sessenach— but it's ollways the way, if there's dirty wurk, send for the Jocks . . ." "I'll pretend I didn't hear that . . . ah, sweet lady, how well red-green-and-yellow become thee—may I cadge one of those turquoise ribbons as a guerdon . . . ? Ah . . . I didn't mean all of them, actually . . . oh, well, thanks awfully—see, there they go into my bosom, next to my fond heart . . ."

Touching, reader, is it not? But as Gilderoy on fleet Garscadden and Godiva on nimble palfrey wheel away through one of those convenient posterns which are always unguarded in the best romances, with Kylie fluttering anxious kerchief and Archie swearing softly as he tries to stuff several yards of haberdashery inside his shirt, it's time to zoom aloft and see what's happening elsewhere. Merrie Carlisle may be feeling anything but, and won't get over its hangover for hours, but the rest of the Borderland is buzzing like a bee-hive, and nowhere busier than in that gloomy rockbound chamber under the Eildons, where the Wizard hugs bony elbows and turns the warlock foreman into Paul Newman (that's how good he's feeling, the vile necromancer) ere returning to gloat over the images which he conjures up in his cauldron, for now he is hep to every detail of our heroic principals' schedule, and wants to be sure that all his rotten snares are in place . . .

First, he looks in on Frey Bentos who, his habit newly laundered tho' unironed, has been gamely trying to thumb a ride as he heads north to Scotland through the Debatable Land, and getting nowhere in that unchristened country. Hay-wains and ox-carts rocket past, ignoring his cries of "Pax vobiscum, buddy!" and his board marked "Eildon"; pack-horses leave him choking in their exhaust fumes, their riders deaf to his ex-communications; and finally the Wizard, from policy rather than pity, dispatches a witch-ridden mini-broom to pick him up, making a note to charge it to the unhappy Dominican's account . . .

Next, the cauldron shows Lord Anguish, trews and ginger whiskers flying in the wind as he rides furiously down Liddesdale, his foam-flecked charger in overdrive as it skids past peel towers and bastels, horse and rider leaving a stench of molten rubber and whisky fumes in their wake. Astonished Armstrongs and bewildered Beattys, to say nothing of startled Storeys and exclaiming Elliots, returning from night forays, hastily swerve their stolen herds on to the hard shoulder as the tartan tornado sweeps by, ignoring their cries of "Joy-rider!" "Get the polis!" and "Is it a bird? Is it a banshee? No, it's Supertrews!" For Lord Anguish, his flanks heaving and his sporran smoking, is bent on a desperate mission—well, it must be desperate to bring him to Liddesdale, the foulest robbers' roost in Europe, where even the toddlers have records and the very sheep go in fours.

But wait, you say—wasn't Anguish's job to enlist Bangtail's Boys to do the actual Jim-snatching part of the conspiracy? So shouldn't he be in Teviotdale, or wherever, recruiting the heavies? Dead right, but as you recall, Archie signed off Bangtail in Chapter One, leaving the Boys at a loss as they wended slowly homeward with their miserable plunder of felines and poultry. So Lord Anguish, poor slob, arrived just in time for Bangtail's funeral, his happy cry of "Awright, youse yins, get fell in!" dying on his lips at the sight of the open grave, with Slackarse, Fire-the-Sheep, Blacklugs, Grunt, and Wandered Tom singing "You'll Never Walk Alone" while the cats and chickens stood with bowed heads, some of them weeping openly.

Half-stewed though he was, Scotland's premier sot and traitor realised that there would be no action from the Boys until they had received counselling and given valedictory interviews to the tabloids. Desperate, he remembered the Nixons as rascals ripe for any mischief, so, pausing only to vodka his horse and pick up a couple of cashmere cardigans in Hawick (never miss the chance), he rode pell-mell for Liddesdale and that peeling beetle (sorry, beetling peel) where old Sir Prising Nixon was at that very moment being advised that Trouserless Will's blackmail raid had finally returned from Gungemyre, and was exclaiming in pop-eyed amaze: "Daffodils? *Where?* I don't believe it . . . !"

We draw a veil over him and the fast-approaching Lord Anguish, and join the Wizard for another peek at the cauldron . . . and again we suck in startled breath, for if Lord Anguish careering down Liddesdale was a shock, what are we to make of Don Collapso, armed cap-a-pie and marching along the Solway sands with a band of swarthy chaps in morions at his heels, singing "It's a long way to Barcelona"? Let's recap . . . surely this Collapso ought by now to be in the hunting retinue of James VI (nigh Peebles), getting ready to lure His Majesty astray so that he can be heisted and the impostor substituted in accordance with the Wizard's diabolic plan (see pages 60–61)? You bet he ought, but with the impostor in the bag, the Wizard has had to rethink his strategy, and the first step in his revised plan has been to despatch Don Collapso by supersonic warlock-broom to that mini-Armada which, you remember (and if you don't remember, try page 59), has been tooling around the Solway Firth manned by Mediterranean football hooligans posing as peaceful shrimp-shooters, the swine. And that is why a round two score of them, with the disgusting Don C. calling the step, flourishing his rapier and shouting *"Adalante, bravos!"* and *"Empujar sobre!"* (which is "Push on!" in Spanish*) are heading into the story, tho' what fell villainy they purpose we can only guess . . .

One thing's for sure—the odds against Archie Force are getting perilously long. Gosh, if only they knew what they were walking into . . .

"But they don't, heh-heh!" cackled the Wizard, chewing his bony gloves in excitement as he continued his cauldron scan, homing in on our intrepid principals in turn—Godiva and Gilderoy followed at a distance of a few miles by Archie and the Charltons, all heading north by devious, untravelled ways; and Kylie's laundry-wain making due east for Thrashbatter Tower. "See how they blunder into my web!" gloated the malevolent sorcerer. "Poor, feeble, simple English cretins—"

"British cretins, if ye don't mind!" objected the warlock foreman, who sported an SNP badge, and was promptly turned from Paul Newman into Quasimodo for his insolence. "Oh,

* Well, near enough.

here, mac, that's a bluidy liberty!" he muttered in medieval French, but the Wizard was intent on the screen, gloating repulsively as he noted that, for various reasons, the morale of his intended victims was already showing signs of wear . . . as thus:

LADY GODIVA, her haughty spirit bruised by the knowledge that she was appearing in public in an outfit that would have caused hoots of mirth even on the *Clothes Show,* had suffered a further shock when Gilderoy, making light conversation as they cantered along, let slip that the Dacre Diamonds had passed into the Scottish exchequer, from whose bourne no bijouterie returns; consequently love-hate feelings for him at the moment were roughly five per cent infatuation, eighty per cent sheer loathing, and fifteen per cent don't know; even her palfrey was giving him dirty looks;

GILDEROY, not unnaturally, was cheesed and frustrated, wondering if he should try to kiss her into adoration again, and calculating doubtfully whether Olivia would have succumbed to Errol if he'd been wearing tweed trunk hose and moth-eaten sideburns;

ARCHIE, far behind them, was having to play his UPRAT threat to the hilt, for the Charltons were growling mutinously at the prospect of entering Scotland without reiving visas or collision insurance; there were even ugly mutters about danger money and nonemeat vouchers, and our hero's brow was dark and his knees grimly flexed as he parried their moody lance thrusts and reminded them sharply that they were meant to be riding to attention;

KYLIE, who had hoped to discover en route to Thrashbatter just how far she could arouse the animal passion of Oor Kid without having to pull the communication cord, had found her style cramped (literally) by the presence in the laundry-wain of a drying-out impostor, a lady wrestler in a noisy trance, and an agitated pillow-case whence came yowls suggestive of a pygmy who didn't care for dead python, or vice versa.

"Everything on schedule and alle systems goe!" chuckled the Wizard as he scanned the cauldron and cocked a satisfied ear to the distant whine and splutter of a mini-broom engine being switched off at the cave entrance overhead, signifying the arrival of Frey Bentos. The Wizard brought up one final picture on his liquid screen and rather wished he hadn't, for this was real PG stuff—James VI frowsting in bed (nigh Peebles) and looking like a hibernating orang-utan in a night-cap as he dreamed contentedly of his forthcoming hunt, Latin, gluttony, syrupy wines, witch barbecues, and the Noe Smoaking signs which he intended to put up all over Scotland. The Wizard switched off, irritably restored to warlock shape the shambling hunchback who was pestering him for a set of church bells to swing on, and began sticking pins in a campaign map of the border . . . and if we sneak a quick peek over his shoulder we can get a final fix on everyone.

That's Carlisle at the bottom, with Eildon about fifty miles north through country which is wild and nasty even by Tudor standards, as Godiva is discovering as she and Gilderoy press on into it, with Archie and the Charltons in their wake. Just over the hill Lord Anguish is spurring down Liddesdale, farther south Kylie is nearing Thrashbatter, and from the west comes a whiff of garlic where Don Collapso and his gang are marching inland from the Solway. The exact location of the slugabed King James is irrelevant, since his hunt doesn't take place until tomorrow, when he will have drooled his way to within striking distance of our plot, assuming his attendants have got him out of bed by then, and sober.

So that's everyone on course, but it's going to take them all day to get where they're going, and we have no intention of following them step by step, beguiling your impatience with reassurances that it won't be long now, the story's bottoming out, the plot mechanism's in place and running smoothly, and our nail-biting, cliff-hanging, all-action finale will soon be busting out all over—nay, we can't wait *that* long, it must be fast-forward wi' a vengeance, bridging the tedious hours, turning the accomplishment of lunch, tea, and supper into a stopwatch, leaping smartly o'er Time's chasm and coming to earth with a whoosh and a thud twelve hours hence . . .

. . . to find ourselves suddenly plunged into clammy darkness that enfolds us like a black shroud, and all around is eerie, deathly silence, broken only by the faint whimper of benighted stoats, the grumbling of badgers that can't find their burrows, and the fitful moaning of the fell wind. Somewhere, over the hills and far away, 4 a.m. is chiming from the clocks of gate-locked towns, snug and secure, but we can't hear them, for this is the desolate heart of the grim Borderland, with nothing but fog and filthy air for miles, and we long for the sound of a human voice, even if it's only the distant bickering of an impatient highwayman and a raging noblewoman who has just put her dainty foot in something wet and awful, and wants to know where they are and why the hell they're having to lead their goddam horses . . . but never mind them—what is that frightsome vision that blights our sight—yonder, over there, through the goblin-haunted mirk . . . aye, 'tis the outline of three sinister hills, lit by the baleful glow of hellish subterranean fires issuing from the craggy jaws of a most discouraging cave above whose sepulchral arch is graven in letters of sulphurous smoke the dread legend: "Eildon. Get in layne . . ."

Yes, this is it . . . we're there.

"Ai'm sorry, but Ai'm not in the hebit of kerrying tissues on naight forays! A ghastly oversaight, no doubt, but Ai didn't expect to hev to shoeshine an urrl's dotter who hedn't the sense to look whair she's wocking! If yur shoon are menky, scrub them with gress or somewhat—"

"Grass, marry come up! I'd not touch 'em wi' industrial gloves! And if thou wert a gentleman, I'd not have to! Ah, me, this is what comes of associating with minor public school-boys—"

(Infatuation nought per cent, loathing one hundred per cent. It's dark, you see, and without visual or body contact Gilderoy's charm depends on his voice, which isn't exactly loaded with sex-appeal at the moment.)

"Oll raight, oll raight! Sit still end Ai'll see what Ai ken do . . . och, goodness, 'tis not menky at oll! It's just wotter!"

A tremulous sigh from the gloom rewarded him. "Ah, that touch . . . those strong, thieving fingers on my foot . . . so gentle, so vile . . . nay, unhand me! Nay, don't . . . go on handing . . ."

"Godaiva!" Impatience fled, and his voice throbbed like a motor mower. "Ah, furgive me, mai own—whay are we quor-rulling? The touch of thy silken enkle inflames me! Give me yur lips, enchentress . . . where are they? Ach, demn, Ai kent see a blested thing—"

"Here, here—thou arrant wretch! Ah-h, oh-h . . ." For a moment the night was filled by snoggish sighs ere they plunked apart. "Nay, again, again . . . dear bounder! Ah, how I detest thee . . . wow! My head swims . . ."

"Maine, too. Nay, though it be torchur to desist, we must, lest we become love-puggled, for clear wits we must hev for what laies ahead . . . see, the yonning mouth of thet ghestly kevern beckons us to duty—"

"Gosh, yes, and I'm wearing this godawful get-up! Oh, well, let's get on with it . . . but stay—should we not await Noble's arrival, to liaise about admin and distress signals?"

"Distress mai ess, if you'll purdon th'expression. Hev Ai not mai trusty blade, Keeliecleaver, to unseam our foes, end thou et mai saide to inspaire end, et need, to clock them from behind wi' ornaments? We can do wi'out Noble's tardy aid . . . ah, but one more embrace, dear Godaiva, ere we split . . ."

"Just one, then, sweet cad! Encircle me wi' thy defiling arms, but touch not my lips or I'll flip . . ."

They cuddled, with yearning whimpers. Then, with Gilderoy bending at the knees and trying to slobber in Latin, and Godiva masking her beauty 'neath the yellow toque's spangled veil, and practising Cockney vowels, they stole forward over the swampy moor to the mouth of the sulphur-smoking cave, waiting until its lurid glare changed from red through amber to green. Slowly they entered hand in hand, the infernal light glinting on the marbles of her psychedelic ruff and casting weird shadows of tweed trunk hose on the dry-ice fog that closed behind them . . .

"Here they come, like mice to Danish Blue!" gloated the Wizard, as the two bizarre figures, one waddling and muttering: "Weeny, weedy, weeky, ye ken!" and the other like Zandra Rhodes in fancy dress, appeared on the cauldron-screen. Down the cavern's sloping floor they came, trying not to notice the strange shapes and bright ghoulish eyes that haunted the shadows under the nitre-dripping roof, down and down, round darkling corners, past acid puddles green as colour-supplement desserts, and the Wizard heh-heh'd and snapped spidery fingers at the warlocks in overalls.

"Down cauldron! Chair-locks to condition puce! Transformers on tarry awhile! Now void my sight and await the highsign—move!" The warlocks disappeared behind the sofa (the sofa?) and the Wizard assumed a pair of dark glasses and a benign expression as he turned to greet the approaching footsteps of wary Gray's Inn trainers and cautious slingbacks.

The sight which met the eyes of Godiva and Gilderoy as they rounded the last bend was as big a shock to them as it probably is to you, gentle reader. No green smoke or gruesome lighting, no flickering sparks or seething cauldrons, but a warm and cosy snuggery such as any comfort-loving sorcerer might repair to in his quiet hours—Habitatte wallpaper with pentacle motif, china bats flying up the wall, mandrake root reclining chairs, toadskin sofa stuffed with lizard wool, henbane cigars in a mantichore-skull humidor, drinks cabinet with flasks and alembics in smoked glass, and low posset tables bearing back numbers of *Thaumaturge* and *Spello* magazines as well as (a shocking affectation on the Wizard's part, but testifying to his literary taste, and a terrific talking-point) the first chapter of *Don Quixote, in manuscript,* with a scribbled note "Any good? Value yr opinion. As ever, Miguel." And hurrying towards them, falling over the furniture in his haste and beaming like a benevolent Dr. Who, came the Wizard, conical smoking-hat on head, flourishing his evening wand in greeting.

"Thrice, thrice welcome, senor and senorita!" he babbled, overacting feverishly. "Here at last! Well, well, am I glad to see *you*!" He peered myopically at Gilderoy. "Fantastic, by Belial!

James VI doesn't look more like James VI! You're sure you're not he? Heh-heh—just a little comedy there . . . But those knock-knees, that slobber, the whiskers—and you can do the accent, I wager!"

"Aye . . . umquhile," croaked Gilderoy, essaying a light drool. "Aiblins . . . and whilk, the noo. Up the Hibs . . ."

"Astounding! And this is La fabulous, La legendary Infamosa! How I have longed for this moment! Ah, but permit me!" Glittering wildly, the Wizard lifted Godiva's veil, and our heroine's heart did a quick triple toe-loop as his dark glasses seemed to scorch her make-up. "Hellzooks, senorita, if thy guile and malice match thy beauty, I'm glad you're on our side—but I can't wait to see you without the peroxide head-doily," he added craftily, and noted with wicked glee how her violet eyes paled in sudden fear. "But where is Frey Bentos and that cute little poison pixie of his?"

Here we go, thought Godiva, and assumed a Liza Doolittle whisper whose hoarseness was a rasping plea for glycerine and lemon.

"Flaming hell, guv'nor," she husked, enunciating with care. "He cometh shortly, with—wiv, I should say—our bleeding luggage. God strike a light," she added bravely, "what with the laryngitis, I am about jap-lacquered. Straight up." And if that doesn't blow our cover, she told herself miserably, nothing will.

But the Wizard was all apologetic concern. "But what am I thinking of? Certes, thou'rt cream-crackered after thy journey—sit, sit, I pray, gracious Infamosa—and do you, honest impostor, take the weight off those trunk hose." Smarming, he ushered them to the recliners. "There, park thyselves, unlax, shed the shoon an ye will, and tell me, was't brass monkeys on the Isle of Man ferry? Tut-tut! Now, try some of those pilot's-thumb canapes—they're delicious with hemlock dip—while I rustle up some soothing gargle, or a cockatricetail . . ."

Amber hope and violet doubt met in the glance which Gilderoy and Godiva exchanged—was't possible their disguises were Wizard-proof? But even as they sank into the enveloping recliners, hope nosedived and alarm went rocketing, for the Wizard, swizzle-stick and shaker in hand, was watching them in a marked manner, and his tone was roopy wi' sudden menace as he continued:

"Are you sitting comfortably? Then I'll begin . . . But stay!" he cried, and triumph was in his cackle, "Here comes the belated Bentos—and without any luggage, unless these shades deceive me! What happened, Frey—trouble with the Customs?"

Terror froze Godiva's toque and chilled Gilderoy's false beard—for there, sidling out from behind the drinks cabinet, his habit sadly creased but his currant eyes fruity with malevolence, came the tall Dominican, inclining his tonsure in ironic greeting.

"Evenin', folks," crooned he, in honeyed Southern menace.

"My dancing chaplain!" gasped Godiva, and instinctively added: "You're fired, libertine!"

"Och, demn, it's a trep!" exclaimed Gilderoy.

"Push the button, mac!" bawled the Wizard.

And ere our twain could stir, hoops of griping steel shot out from all over the recliners, clamping their wrists, ankles, waists, farthingale, and trunk hose in 'prisoning clutch, overalled warlocks sprang from behind the sofa crying: "Nyah-nyah-nyah!," green smoke flecked wi' crimson fire gushed from the skirting-boards to shrivel the Habitatte wallpaper, the china bats came to life and swooped squeaking o'er the victims' heads, the posset tables clanged back to reveal the bubbling cauldron, and what with one thing and another, the value of the place on the housing market dropped at least fifty per cent in the twinkling of an eye.

But 'twas not the sudden transformation from snug bachelor digs to ooze-walled fiend's den that caused Godiva's lovely lips to part in roseate tremble, or Gilderoy to emit involuntary two-tone whistle—in fact, if the joint had changed into the Albert Hall they wouldn't have noticed. Blind to all else, deaf even to the glottal gloating of the warlocks and Frey Bentos's viciously blown raspberry, they stared stricken at the figure emerging from the dazzling orange explosion which had taken place between the cocktail shaker and the swizzle-stick.

For the Wizard had vanished, and in his place stood a female embodiment of evil who looked like a cross between Snake Woman and the Wicked Queen in *Snow White*. Clad in a low-cut evening sheath of black silk which appeared to have been applied to her voluptuous form with an aerosol spray, her sable tresses tumbling to shoulders whose whiteness, like that of her flawless features, had a curious greenish tinge, she stood undulating sensuously what time she smoothed her elbow-length gloves, posed with elegant hand on sinister hip, and regarded her captives from coal-black eyes whose pupils glinted fiery red. Her purple lips writhed in a smile of unutterable malevolence, and if she had invited the assembly to put the blame on Mame they would have assented without hesitation. She didn't walk, she slank to a muted "Big Spender" drum accompaniment, slowly swirling her glossy coiffure, and came to a pulsating rest before the helpless chatelaine of Thrashbatter.

"So-o-o . . ." Her voice was a sort of contralto hiss, heavy with sneer, and Godiva knew instinctively that if ever she needed a baby-sitter, this one would barely make the short-list.

"So . . . thou'rt the presumptuous puss who would impersonate La Infamosa, ha? Well, take a good look at the real thing, sister, and eat your heart out. Or"—and she thrust her flawless bone-structure close to Godiva's own, and bared gleaming gnashers in a threatening grimace—"perhaps I'll do it for you!"

To quote Gilderoy, dem end blest! Just when we'd decided that La Infamosa must be one of those Rebecca types, much discussed but never seen, on she sashays, evil incarnate—and what an entrance, what timing, what guile to pose as the Wizard all this time, red-herringing us stupid . . . but forget that, she's got two of our team in her toils, and tabs on the others . . . What? You say Archie's still out there, full of zip and resource? Please, stop whistling in the dark. It's going to take the daddy of all turnarounds to contrive a happy ending now. Right, here we go, but don't expect miracles . . . well, not many. (Here, suppose she is a cannibal? Don't think about it.)

Say what you will of Benenden, it trains its daughters well—or perhaps it was just Godiva's noblesse which obleeged her, once she had exclaimed "Cripes!" and regained her composure, to turn to Gilderoy and say, wi' grace right courtly:

"I'm sorry. My goof. 'Twas my imperfect Catford patois which betrayed us, and landed us in deep doo-doo. Well," she added on a rising scream, "don't just sit there—do something!"

Gilderoy was quick to respond in kind. "Nay, blame not thyself, fair Godaiva—hed Ai but worn thet tinsel crown, oll maight ha' been well. As 'tis," he shrugged at the top of his voice, "what the hell ken Ai do, pinioned es Ai em?"

"Nothing!" gloated La Infamosa, flinging up elbow-length arms in passionate triumph. "Y'are in my power, poor deluded fools! Two down, and only that English oaf and his pack of bums to go—aye, and the blonde butterball to boot . . . which is not a bad idea," she added, giving one of the warlocks a swift kick wi' her dainty stiletto. "But first, a few well-chosen taunts and jeers at your expense, to satisfy the conventions and give me my kicks, eh?" She burlesqued her way across to Gilderoy. "So this is the Heathery Heart-throb, is it?" Cruelly she tore the false beard from his chin with *scrrch!* of spirit gum, and considered the clean-cut face architecture beneath. "Mm-m, not bad, if you like insipid juvenile beefcake . . . Big boy, aren't you . . . ? Well, I may toy with thee awhile, if I've got the time and energy, ere I doom thee to fiery torment below. Let's try you on for size." She did a languorous stoop, pressing her purple lips to his (which weren't purple, actually, but pinkish) and munching amain, and Godiva, repressing a cry of "Lay off, he's mine!" watched with jealously bated breath, looking to see her stagger, bemused and cross-eyed, under the uncanny power of Gilderovian osculation. But to her amaze, when La Infamosa surfaced after one final passionate gnaw, her evil beauty remained unboggled, and her red pupils betrayed no hint of squint. Was she immune, this sorceress, wondered Godiva, and then she noted that Gilderoy was gaping like a landed hake, and stunned reverence was in his pleading glance.

"More, more!" he panted. "Gi' me the gurlick, tho' Ai die of it! Oh, come on, Infamosa, be a sport, one more time . . ."

Godiva's senses swam, but with feeble strokes, and she could no longer restrain a wail of "Lost, lost! He is ensorcelled quite!" as, to compound her anguish, came La Infamosa's contemptuous sneer.

"Pah! 'Twas like kissing cold liver. Thou'rt welcome, duchess. But take heart—ye shall share his fiery grave, when the time comes. That'll teach you to impersonate me! And in those

Carnaby Street dishclouts, too! Where did you get 'em—Oxfam?"

Distraught though she was, Godiva's haughty spirit rallied at the taunt. "At least I don't have to go around disguised as a carnival magician!" she retorted. "Not that I blame you—nothing like a wizard's robe for concealing the fact that you have to wear a girdle and uplift bra, is there, thou false—or should I say falsies?—seductress!"

"Girdle? Falsies?" Sparks flew from La Infamosa's crimson eyes and gnashing teeth. "'Tis a lie! I can give you two inches round the top any day, thou puny punk, thou! Aye, and scant twenty inches is my waist that hath never known confining clasp o' corset yet . . . Hot Hecate, I'll show you . . ."

And in her rage she made as though to rend away her clinging finery, while the warlocks jumped up and down crying: "Take it off!" "Down in front!" and "Jelly on a plate!" and even Frey Bentos glanced about him to see if there was an anachronistic Polaroid in the place. But Godiva, figuring that she might as well die game, trilled with scorn.

"Save it for thy Dago public, droopy! Why, thy whole act is phoney as a two-groat sundial! Cheap villainy at its worst, wi' thy chintzy conjuring tricks and imitation toadskin upholstery and photo-copies of *Don Quixote* in vain attempt to impress the Joneses—and talk about Oxfam, that plastic sack you're *trying* to wear would look bad on a scarecrow, even if it did have a better figure, which wouldn't be difficult . . ."

Vulgar abuse and railery, born of jealousy at seeing her adored swain beglamoured by this necromancing sex-pot, and rage at being bound helpless in clothes which she wouldn't have put out for Guy Fawkes—is that what you're thinking? Or perhaps just true-blue defiance in the face of defeat by beastly foreigners? No, neither. Don't under-rate Godiva—she's needling with intent, to throw the enemy off-balance, although what good that can do when she's 'prisoned by hooping steel and Gilderoy is muttering: "What happened? Whay do Ai taste of gurlick?" remains to be seen. But she's game, our heroine . . .

"And another thing!" she cried. "Do with us what ye will, the bitter cup of failure is thine, and I hope you slop it down that ghastly dress and can't get the stain out! Aye, tear thy hair, Infamosa (assuming it isn't a wig), for Operations Jimsnatch and Heretic are down the tube! Thy impostor is where you'll never find him—and if you have some loony idea that you can drug that gorgeous beast over there with thy poisoned kisses, and get him to do the job, forget it! He's too tall by half a head, and his slobbers wouldn't fool a two-year-old, so there!"

Spirited stuff, which moved La Infamosa no whit. If anything, it bucked her up, judging by the way she laughed in fiendish triumph, stripped off one of her gloves with a flourish, swung it round her head à la Gypsy Rose, and flung it to the clamouring warlocks.

"Thy wit matches thy dress sense, poor Godiva!" she mocked. "So I know not where th'impostor lies, eh? And I couldn't squeeze it out of you, could I?" Her dress creaked, but split not (to Godiva's annoyance) as she sank down beside the recliner and hissed in our heroine's shapely ear. "We Spaniards are experts wi' rack and thumbscrew, remember—how if I have the boys work thee over downstairs? They'd love it, and so would I—thy screams would be music such as I love to hear—"

"What perfume do you use—creosote?" inquired Godiva, tho' her flawless flesh crawled at the villainess's threat.

"Creosote—there's a thought!" mused La Infamosa, cruel

yellow flecks appearing in her crimson pupils. "Hot and bubbling, and so refreshing to madam's tender skin! But that's for later—we ha' no need of it at present . . . as you shall see." She lissomed to her feet and swayed across to the cauldron, licking purple lips in anticipation as she gazed on its blank surface. "What is the word of power?" she asked the warlock foreman.

"'Dig a hole for 'im!" cried the eager mechanic, and at once the liquid began to bubble and give off static ere it settled to a smooth sheen. Godiva watched, a nameless fear revving up her heart, and though Gilderoy's expression was still that of one who has got in the way of the Pontypool front row, a close observer might have noticed that his cinnamon eyes were clear and watchful.

"This is a recording," hissed La Infamosa. "The events you are about to see took place some hours ago, and we apologise for the sound quality, due to conditions beyond our control. One of these scum," she added venomously, her basilisk eyes playing over the warlocks, who fidgeted uneasily, "dropped a spanner in it—and his shrieks as burning marl consumed him were both tuneful and gratifying. Watch, heretic dogs, and learn the power of La Infamosa!"

The screen cleared on an image of Kylie preparing for bed in her chamber at Thrashbatter, and the sight caused the warlocks to elbow each other in lewd glee, and Godiva to emit a stricken cry of distress.

"My black see-through negligee! And my open-toed mules! Nay, this passeth all—disrobe at once, thou purloining slut—in the bathroom!" she added, as the warlocks crowded forward.

"She can't hear you," chuckled La Infamosa, as Kylie was seen preening before the mirror. "My, what a plump little pigeon it is . . . you could have danced all night, eh, Bentos? Now, hist, and see . . ."

They watched as Kylie dabbed Arpège, and there were cries of "Ssh!" as Godiva ground furious teeth. Then, humming merrily, the little blonde tripped to the chamber door, opened it a crack, and called right melodiously: "Coo-ee, Charlton . . . there's a tap dripping next door—can you come up and fix it?" Silence followed, Kylie frowned, called again, and pouted angrily when no activity ensued.

'Twill be the spider in the basin next, the randy little trot, thought Godiva grimly, and sure enough, Kylie was seen to brighten, take a deep breath, and squeal in most realistic terror: "Charlton, Charlton, haste to me—there's a dirty big moth i' the warming pan—nay, 'tis a frog, wi' eyes like golf balls! Speed to my aid, good Charlton! Charlton . . . ? Oh, come on, do as you're dam' well told!"

This time it worked. Clumphing footsteps were heard on the stairs, and Kylie shot giggling across to the four-poster and disposed herself Dietrich-wise, dimpling decoratively—and screamed in real horror as the door crashed open to reveal Don Collapso Baluna at his most repulsive, paunch quivering, rapier a-flourish, and licentious leer at full voltage.

"A moth, senorita?" he chortled playfully. "Nay, a booter-fly, all a-flooter een black gauze, wheech I shall add too my collection! Ay-ay, luscious lepidoptery!" And he waddled at speed towards the bed, while Thrashbatter echoed to off-screen discharge o' musketry, crashing o' crockery, and Spanish war-cries.

"Switch it off!" begged Godiva. "I can't watch! 'Tis too horrid! My best negligee, to be ripped and torn by swarthy ravisher—"

But it wasn't, for even as Don Collapso loomed lustfully o'er his cringing victim, morioned men burst in at the window crying: "Ah-ah, naughtee excellencee!" "Fair shares among mates!" and "We'll tell Senora Baluna!" Foiled, Collapso had no choice but to place the swooning Kylie under guard, after which the cauldron cut to a montage of action shots, in which the brutal invaders were seen firing shots, trampling floors, pursuing kitchen wenches, carousing on elderflower wine, overpowering Oor Kid and the spare Robson, and releasing the impostor and a disgruntled Clnzh from the cellar, along with Busty Basset, who appeared to have emerged from her Gilderoy-induced trance, for when the licentious soldiery would have mishandled her, she kicked them in the slats right Catfordly, announced her retirement from Spanish service, and vanished at speed into the night.

Finally, having commandeered wagons and loaded them with looted doormats (highly prized by Spanish infantry for siestas in the trenches) the brutal invaders set off north at the double, leaving all the lights on—a typically wanton act of Castilian vandalism. To Godiva's dismay, her negligee (containing Kylie) was also carried away in a cart guarded by the watchful Clnzh; he'll probably eat it, thought Godiva dismally.

(So now we know why Don Collapso was sent to recruit heavies from the shrimp-shooting Armada: to o'erwhelm Thrashbatter and release the impostor—and that wasn't the only o'erwhelming he did in the course of that night, as we shall see presently, alas.)

"Seen enough?" jeered La Infamosa, as the cauldron-screen went blank. "So Operation Jimsnatch is down the tube, is it? The impostor was where I'd never find him, was he? I'd offer you copies o' the tape, but you won't need them where you're going—the heat would spoil them, anyway." And she laughed spitefully on a shrill rising note, which eventually only the warlocks could hear, and Godiva's brain quivered and her bosom reeled at the import of what she had seen. But either the laugh or the movie had evidently restored Gilderoy's Infamosa-disturbed senses, for now he gave vent to a defiant "Tchah!" and derisive chuckle rich in carefree Giffnock bravado.

"Ai don't believe it!" he jeered. "Thet was no genuine image, but a studio simulation bai professional mummers—mere Dago propagenda to create alurrm end despondency end sep our moral faibre! Courage, fair Godaiva," he clarioned, and her heart did chin-ups at his ringing confidence, "she's getting desperate! But her phoney visions shall nought avail her an we keep our cool—"

His words were cut off as La Infamosa, with a scream of rage, peeled off her second glove and lashed him cruelly back and forth with it, her skin quite emerald with fury, and as the flimsy material played havoc with his moustache and swept the brave utterance from his lips, Godiva came on as substitute.

"Hit someone your own size, coward!" she shrilled. "Lay off, I say! Ah, sweet Gildy, provoke her not . . . you skunk, it serves thee right! Oh, what am I saying! No, no, I didn't mean it . . . ah, beloved, it wrings my heart to see thee clobbered by any but me, vile, adored robber that thou art! Alack, I am confused!"

She can say that again; even in the perilous pass to which they are come, her emotions are still rent Gilderoy-wise. But at last La Infamosa, having vented her spite, tossed aside the glove which was now tattered and full of bristles and, having got her breath back, regarded them with heaving eyes and bosom, the former glowing evilly red.

"Studio simulation, eh?" she panted. "Mistrustful swine, I was going to show you the sequel, Infamosa's Vengeance II, featuring the nocturnal surprise and capture of that poor balloon Noble and his ragged gang—aye, while you were blundering lost i' the dark, they were already sitting in a peat-cutting nigh the cave mouth, supposing thee within and awaiting thy Mayday call, and Don Collapso's party, forced-marching from Thrashbatter, caught them flat-footed and facing the wrong way! Well, I shan't show it you now, so there!"

"Ai'm not surprised," quo' cynical Gilderoy. "Hed difficulty faking it, did you? Couldn't get stunt doubles for the Churltons, Ai suppose? Hed to abendon the production, did you? Too bed."

For a moment it looked as though La Infamosa's wrath would burst her brassiere, and the warlocks held on to each other in gleeful anticipation, but though it creaked and something went *ping!* round the back, her heaving fit passed, and it was in a smouldering hiss, charged wi' hate, that she addressed her captives.

"Aye, y'are all the same, you recliner-chair critics—doubt my cauldron's images, will you? Then shalt see for thyselves whether it showed true or no!" She hip-swivelled imperiously to the warlocks. "Have them out, my faithful hell-spawn! Bind them wi' convenient thongs, and make 'em good and tight—especially hers! No, his too—he's just as bad! Then hale them below, that they may see the truth, and take it wi' them to the fiery crackling doom that awaits them!"

She added an exultant "Hah-ha!," tossed her raven mane, and swayed pneumatically from the room, followed by Frey Bentos, while the warlocks sprang on our peerless pair, unlocked the recliners, and pinioned their wrists behind their backs with cries of "See's a convenient thong, Wullie!" and "Pit yer finger on the knot, ye midden!" For a moment Godiva and Gilderoy were face-to-face as the warlocks argued about reefs and grannies, and as their eyes met, passionate violet and manly amber, silent messages passed between them:

"Why aren't you making a break for it, for God's sake?"

"The odds urr too great, dear Godaiva. We must baide our taime."

"Until she sticks us in the fiery crackling doom thingy! Great!"

"Trust me, mai love—"

"Trust thee, thou pearl-pinching caitiff? That's a laugh!"

"Nay, adored object, oll is not yet lost. La Infamosa—"

"Aha! So that's it! She hath thee in thrall, the ensorcelling bat! Ditch me for her, will you, betrayer? Oh, how I do loathe thee! Ah, crafty worm . . . kiss me, tho' it be for the last time . . ."

Their lips met, briefly, as the warlocks stood with their shaggy heads on one side, going "Aw-w-w . . . ," and then they were dragged from the chamber, Godiva swaying slightly and murmuring something about atomic lips, down slimy steps lit by guttering torches, and so out on to a great stone gallery whence they could look down into a huge echoing vault cut from the living rock, its smooth floor broken by narrow fissures from which smoke wreathed up, bespeaking volcanic fires beneath. The only light came from the greenish phosphorescence of the damp-trickling walls, and one bright rosy glow which Godiva, with a gasp of despair, identified as the blush of shame mantling the intrepid cheeks of Archie Noble, Double-

Nought and now hapless prisoner, chained to the wall in his underfugs and deep mortification.

Still, he was better off than the captured Charltons, hung by their heels from a massy chain that spanned the chamber like a gigantic washing-line, Wor Jackie at one end and Oor Kid at the other. Yet even in that dreadful strait, their arms bound and their mouths gagged, the indomitable reivers were defying their enemies by swinging to and fro, clashing their steel bonnets together in a metallic tune which Godiva, her heart swelling with national pride, recognised as "Colonel Bogey."

La Infamosa, lounging on the stone balustrade, swinging an elegant leg and sipping a cockatricetail of smoking amber liquor, flicked languid manicure at the sorry scene below. "Satisfied now?" she purred, and her two captives, sick as mud though they were, yet responded with unruffled dignity, Godiva raising queenly profile in silent disdain, and Gilderoy muttering, "Ach, knickers!"

"'Twas featly done, Don Collapso," commended La Infamosa, and the obese hidalgo, who was standing by chomping a victory tortilla, smirked greasily. "King Philip shall hear on't, and will right well requite thy valour. Thy table manners are something else," she added, ducking gracefully to avoid the tortilla fragments which flew from his oily lips. "But enough! Have your men bring that creature i' the Y-fronts to the death chamber, along with these two, and do you, Frey Bentos, attend us also. Warlocks, to your cauldron maintenance—I expect perfect reception for Operation Jimsnatch tomorrow, or else! Away, about it!"

"Worrabout thee clanging Charltons?" inquired Don Collapso.

"Let 'em clang till they rot!" snarled La Infamosa. "Have dishes o' tripe and black pudding, such as they relish most keenly, aye, and rhubarb plate-cakes and rum butter, wi' flagons of Newcastle brown and State Management bitter, laid on the floor beneath them, inches from their salivating chops, so shall their slow starvation be exquisitely anguished!" Hellish glee flared in her crimson eyes, and she shimmied with feral delight. "And have one stand by crying 'Who hung the monkey?,' so that they may die remembering their greatest and most lasting shame!"*

So now was frenzied bustle in the echoing vault 'neath lonely Eildon, with Don Collapso's two-score morioned pikemen springing to disciplined command, numbering off and marching in all directions. Four of them herded Gilderoy and Godiva down a steep stone tunnel festooned with chained skeletons and Madrid Expo pennants, La Infamosa cha-cha-ing ahead of them, silken hips swaying and stilettos tapping a vaunting tattoo, accompanied by Frey Bentos on maracas and Don Collapso on tortillas. Two other morions descended to the chamber where the Charltons were having their swing session, and with brutal jest and rough usage unchained the self-conscious Noble and frog-marched him thence, ignoring his pleas for breeches and a size 16 shirt. Downwards they hurried him, by winding ways where bats squeaked and peculiar things squished and wriggled underfoot, into a gloom that grew ever

---

* Trust La Infamosa to know the embarrassing story of those sturdy North Countrymen who, during a war with France, found a Barbary ape washed ashore from a shipwrecked vessel, and, being unfamiliar with the species and naturally assuming it to be a Frenchman, hanged it.

hotter and more stifling, till he was aware of a female voice ahead of him, and his heart smote wi' love and angst as he recognised its clarion quality:

"Any idiot can see 'tis for bedroom wear alone, being o' gossamer fineness, but you have to go traipsing over half Scotland in it, rolling in carts and caves, thou butter-curled half-wit! 'Sblood, if it's rent or besmirched—"

"Nay, Goddy, leave it out, I beg! How was I to know I'd be kidnapped in't? I'm sorry, honest, I was just trying it on—"

And then Archie found himself blinking in the pale and eerie light of a most loathsome dungeon containing racks, strapaddos, iron chairs, smouldering braziers, whipping posts, iron maidens, and like equipment of the Spanish Ministry of Culture; portraits of Philip II, Torquemada, Sixtus the Fifth, Fiftus the Sixth, and the Inquisition pelota squad hung on the mouldering stone walls, and to one side yawned the mouth of a ghastly pit from which thin orange fumes wreathed up from unseen burning depths, but what Archie found particularly disquieting was the row of steel see-saws on the pit's lip, their outer ends projecting over the fiery void, and the notice: *Attention! Victims must be launched separately, to avoid pit congestion which can cause serious fiery-depth cloggage! Penalty for improper use—three guesses?*

Trouserless though he was, our hero's keen wits registered at once that this was not the staff canteen. The horrid significance of the see-saws was plain from the fact that their inner ends were tethered to the dungeon floor by slender cords which, when severed, would permit the weight of a victim seated on the outer end to take over, precipitation into the pit resulting. Typical, thought disgusted Archie, but now the human occupants of the chamber took his attention, starting (naturally) with his adored Godiva, pinioned but proud between her guards as she tore verbal strips off Kylie, cowering in a filmy black negligee and plainly wishing she'd chosen flannel, for Don Collapso's eyes were coming out on stalks as he ogled her and tore a libidinous enchilada 'twixt pudgy fingers, and even Frey Bentos's austere features bore an odd expression which suggested that cold cells and hair shirts were not uppermost in his mind (of course, he may have been thinking of the spot prize they hadn't won). Clnzh regarded them both with baleful jealousy and took threatening practice puffs at his blowpipe, but ever and anon his gargoyle eyes would soften as they strayed to hapless Kylie, and his tiny feet would shuffle in an imaginary samba.

Reclining sinuously in an umpire's chair above the instruments of torture, her slim red-taloned hands toying with a branding iron, was La Infamosa, and the sheer villainy of her strapless gown and the purple-lip and crimson-eye accessories told shrewd Archie that this must be the queen hornet in person. And since Godiva, Kylie, and Gilderoy were bound and under guard, and the place was stiff with extras in Spanish uniform, he quickly deduced that something, quite apart from his own discomfiture, had gone amiss. Well, play it by the book, thought our hero, so he waited courteously until Godiva had run out of names to call Kylie, coughed diffidently, and turned to Gilderoy, as the senior British officer in the mess. At the sound of his crisp throat-clearance, Godiva gave a glad cry, and her eyes shone with loving pride at his nonchalant bearing, so befitting a captured English agent in his underwear.

"Ah, there you are, Gilderoy, old man," he baritoned.

"Good evening . . . My lady . . . Mistress Delishe. Well, Gilderoy, snafu about sums it up, eh? Bad show, I think. Still, better luck next time—"

"Next time!" La Infamosa's voice cracked like an electrified knout, and her flawless coiffure writhed and hissed Medusa-like. "English fool—here is thy 'next time,' and thy last! Aye, gaze on't—down yonder, and die as many imaginary deaths as ye have time for before the real thing! Behold, I say!"

Not having been introduced, Archie confined himself to a curt bow before glancing into the pit, and wished he hadn't. Far below white-hot lava churned in red and yellow streaks, and flames leaped up the shaft as though trying to get at him; don't let the enemy see you're rattled, he thought, and addressed Gilderoy again.

"Ye're wondering, I doubt not," he continued wi' aplomb, "how we came to be nabbed. Blame myself, really—letting the men play five-card brag to beguile our weary vigil, while I myself kept ceaseless watch, heavy-lidded tho' I was, and then this chap—Milburn, I think his name is, ugly big sod with bad teeth—well, he had three threes, and, would ye believe, two o' t'others held three kings and three tens, most extraordinary thing . . . anyway, 'twas the biggest pot ye ever saw, eyeball to eyeball, bragging their backsides off, and I must needs turn from scanning the deep o' night to adjudicate when Milburn wanted to cover the kitty—and before I well knew't, some hairy swine had a blade to my throat yelling 'Yield, perro Ingles'—you know the way they do—and, well, they were all over us, you see." He shrugged string-vested shoulders and ran deprecatory fingers through rueful hair. "We fought like bull-dogs, natch, but with three of our chaps clutching cards and shouting. 'Up twenty!' we were sorrily outnumbered . . ."

"And who won?" demanded Gilderoy.

"What? Why, the Dagoes, of course, or we wouldn't be here in rotten durance—"

"Nay, man—the threes, the kings, or the tens?" cried the other, and even Don Collapso waited agog for the result while the morioned guards laid lightning bets.

"Oh, I see . . . nay, 'twas ne'er played out. Have to split the kitty, I expect. Tough on Milburn, of course—"

"Oh, heer, that's hurdly fair—he hed the three threes!"

"And wanted to cover the kitty, remember! Which means he's entitled to the pot up to that point only—"

"End the other twain ken split any further stakes? Well . . ."

"Eet calls for a re-deal!" stated Don Collapso emphatically. "Soopose een the toormoil of thee fight, someone saw hees opponents' curds?"

"I hadn't thought of that! D'you think someone did . . . ? I'm sorry, I didn't catch your name . . . ?"

"Collapso, grandee of Espana—"

"How d'ye do, I'm Noble. 'Tis a moot point, of course—"

"Awn the rivuh-boats," put in Frey Bentos, "gennelmen would ha settled it with a single cut, or pistols awn the texas deck—"

"Ai don't think trensetlentic rules ken applay in this case—"

A blood-freezing contralto hiss cut through their discussion, and Don Collapso and Frey Bentos started guiltily under the red glare of La Infamosa's malevolent eyes as she slithered from the umpire's chair and glided towards them, twirling the branding-iron like a baton. "Imbeciles! Nay, traitors, even, to parley wi' the enemy in this vital hour when Operation Heretic is in count-down, and your every thought and deed should be bent on our great enterprise!" Viciously the iron smote a taco-burger from the trembling hand of Don Collapso, and was then dropped on Frey Bentos's sandaled toes. "Anyway, the hands are void, since their holders e'en now hang by their heels en route to that great brag school in the sky—where you shall await them," she continued, her fell smile traversing our quartet, "after a rather more painful voyage. To the see-saws wi' them!"

Our gang were seized in violent hands, and dragged towards the dread machines, with cries of horror from Godiva and Kylie and sturdy protests from our heroes—and Don Collapso.

"Not the ladies!" cried Archie. "'Tis against all usage!"

"Stay thy hend, cruel Infamosa!" contributed Gilderoy. "How would you laike it, demmit?"

"Spare thee leetle one, lady boss!" pleaded the hidalgo. "Pliz, I beg of yoo!"

"Who—the blonde fatso?" Infamosa's purple mouth was moist with evil anticipation. "Nay, Don Collapso—think how she will crackle and splutter when the flames lick her plump flesh, toasting her to a small crisp! And what's she to thee?"

"I need a new secreetary!" cried the perspiring don. "And she ees so yong, and fair, and queevers so appeeling in her negligee—"

"And you would have her for thy amorous sport, thou lustful lard-bucket!" sneered La Infamosa. "Why, 'tis a worse fate than the fire—still, she can fry when you've finished with her . . . all right, help yourself."

"Unhand her!" raged Godiva, as Don Collapso laid sweaty paws on the trembling groupie. "She would rather die!"

"Speak for yourself!" cried Kylie. "Nay, give us a break, Goddy, I don't want to crackle and splutter—"

"Selfish strumpet! Have ye no shame?"

"Lots—and I want to keep it as long as possible—"

"Take her hence!" commanded La Infamosa. "Nay, Don Collapso, not so fast! Work now, play later, and while y'are about our business, the pygmy shall guard her! Clnzh, thou worm, see her borne to the vault o' prisoners, and watch her well—and I mean watch, or the rack shall stretch thee up to size. Away!"

Weeping piteously for appearance's sake, but quite relieved, Kylie was borne out by guards, with Clnzh hopping eagerly in their wake, and La Infamosa hugged her smooth shoulders and shivered with schadenfreude as grinning morions ensured that the three prisoners' bonds were secure before seating them on the outer ends of see-saws, their backs to the burning void beneath them. Godiva, in the centre, was like to swoon with the acrid airs that drifted from the pit, but her two lovers, with heroic consideration, took turns in blowing vigorously in her direction. One result of this was that when Infamosa started taunting them, they were too goofed to respond, and the task of hurling defiance devolved on Godiva alone. Fortunately, she was up to it.

"Hadn't you better keep your distance, dear?" she inquired sweetly. "They say silicone melts, you know . . . and if you start sweating in that grisly dress 'twill look even more like a used bin-liner than it does now—"

"Sucks to thee, vain English rose," jeered La Infamosa. "We'll see presently how that clown's outfit o' thine stands up to high temperatures. It isn't minimum iron down there, you know." She took a sword from one of the soldiers and played the gleaming point around the cord of Godiva's see-saw. "Shall I . . . ? Nay, sit a little longer, all three, and learn how, in the day that dawns in the world above which you shall never see again, my plans go forward to fruition." She turned to Frey Bentos. "Is the impostor ready?"

"Sober, slobberin', an' talkin' Scotcher than Harry Lauder," replied the Dominican. "Why, if Mary Queen o' Scots could see him now, she'd holler 'That's ma boy!' "

"Then be off wi' him, and lurk at the appointed spot. Don Collapso—to Peebles straight, to attend on Jacobus Rex his hunt, and when the time is ripe, wander him sideways wi' some fair excuse. Lord Anguish hath already gone to drum up his snatch-party, so all's in train, and by this evening Scotland will have a new king—but they'll never know it!" Her eldritch laugh echoed from the walls and rippled o'er the dungeon floor. "So, begone! And you, good morions," she added to the soldiers, "to the kitchen for well-earned chilli con carne and garlic-burgers, whereafter ye may siesta early, in case we have need of you in the afternoon. *Vamos,* and success attend you all!"

In an instant the dungeon was devoid of soldiers, Collapsos, and Bentoses, speeding eagerly to their various destinations, and La Infamosa, glowing greenly with excitement, turned to her victims three.

"So much for business," she hissed, and bent the rapier in her hands like a whip. "Now for pleasure. Which one first, eh?" She swayed slowly along the line of see-saws, tapping the blade lightly on each cord in turn, and we'd be tampering with the truth if we said that our intrepid three weren't watching with interest. They could feel the distant fire below them, and the icy breath of doom in the dungeon's clammy air, but as they watched the voluptuous black shape pause in malicious consideration, and met the gloating red eyes with their own (fierce grey, disdainful violet, and calculating amber), each was busy with his (and her) thoughts—well, wouldn't you be?

Godiva was thinking, what a beastly way to go, but at least it won't last long; Archie was wondering if he could break his bonds with a mighty wrench, launch himself forward with a sudden spring, and blip this frightful female on the jaw; Gilderoy was speculating whether he could make a deal . . . and then the glittering blade flashed up, hung for a mind-freezing instant, and swept down . . . to bury its point in the wooden framework of the rack.

"No hurry," chuckled La Infamosa. "It's such maddening fun, deciding who's to go first . . . I'll have to think about it. Don't worry, the fiery depths won't go away . . . and neither will you." She stretched luxuriously, gnashed shining teeth in an ecstasy of satisfaction, and Mae Wested her way to the door, where she fluttered a white hand in mock farewell. "Catch you later, amigos," she whispered, and they were alone in the dungeon . . .

One flight up, in the green-glowing gloom of the rocky vault where the swinging Charltons, exhausted by the snappy rhythm of "Colonel Bogey," were now clashing their helmets to the less taxing tempo of Tchaikovsky's "Chanson Triste," so appropriate to their condition, Kylie was discovering that see-through gauze was but poor insulation 'gainst clammy stone. Bound and shivering in a corner, our blonde scatterbrain was prey to such conflicting miseries as imminent hypothermia, the prospect of a long weekend at the mercy of the revolting Don Collapso, and the plight of her bosom chum and associates in the dungeon below, for the significance of the see-saws had not escaped her, and she shuddered at the thought of her friends being given the Margery Daw heave-ho.

"Alack, poor Goddy!" she moaned. "And yummy Gilderoy, and that Noble's a bit of all right, too, wi' his dimpled chin and tousled locks—nay, forget it, unhappy Kylie, whose fate is the dimpled blubber and greasy embrace of El Ponderoso! Ah, how to aid them, and my poor self! There must be a way, surely . . ."

She gazed distraught round her rocky prison, seeking inspiration, but finding none in the melancholy clank of the penduluming Charltons overhead, or in the regular tramp of Clnzh on sentry-go, marching and about-turning with his little blowpipe at the slope. He alone stood guard, for the morioned troops were all in the distant kitchen, whence came their faint chanting of "Hand me down that can o' beans" as they waited impatiently for their breakfast, while the cook-sergeant, labouring to prepare tripe and black-pudding for the prisoners' torture, went spare. Never if not now, thought Kylie . . . if only she could get a hand free, and Clnzh would look the other way, she could surely release the chain from which the Charltons hung, undo the thongs of Oor Kid who at the moment was passing just overhead, his helmet doinging a melancholy B-flat against his neighbour's . . . nay, 'twas hopeless! Her bonds were tight, and Clnzh wasn't looking the other way.

In fact, Kylie realised, he was watching her sidelong, shooting her wistful, pouting glances as he strode up and down. Now he was ordering blowpipes and standing at ease, sniffing in a hurt, sulky way, what time his teensy feet stirred impatiently, and his girdle of human heads jiggled to a Latin beat . . . and Kylie's heartstrings went *zing!* wi' a sudden hope. Visions swam before her . . . of Clnzh's yearning arms seeking to encircle her knees on the heaving parquet of the Dungeon Grill, his pleading Piltdown face upturned, his grieving dole when dance-

happiness was denied him . . . could it be that, where pleas for
release would have been vain, music and her negligee'd curves
might charm the savage breast?

Breathing a silent prayer, she murmured softly "Ay-ay,
conga!" and saw the pygmy shoulders stiffen; his eyes rolled at
her, gleaming with a beady wild surmise, and as she whispered
"One and two and three—boomf!," wi' provocative shimmy of
torso and her sauciest wink (and they came no saucier than
Kylie's), he quivered like a galvanised frog, and his blowpipe
began to rattle a heady bongo solo on the echoing stone.

"Oh, Charltons . . . yoo-hoo!" called Kylie softly. "Look,
the classical stuff is great, but d'you think you could rustle up a
rumba . . . ?"

But suppose Clnzh doesn't rumba? For all we know, he can't dance a step—and even if he can, what wild series of curious chances is it going to take to free the Charltons, overpower the morions, stop La Infamosa deep-sixing our see-saw-bound trio, prevent Operation Jimsnatch being a roaring success, and keep Godiva's negligee in bandbox condition? At this stage, frankly, we can't say, but don't panic: wild series of curious chances are our forte—it's the imponderables that are worrying. Like, where on earth is Lord Anguish, for we've a feeling it all depends on him . . .

Dawn was breaking o'er the broad Borderland in strict accordance with the immemorial laws of romantic poesy and legend, which meant that everywhere sleepy vales and drowsy meadows, faerie castles and dew-pearled woods, were awakening to smiling day under the caress of Phoebus's rosy fingers—except in Liddesdale, where it was bucketing stair-rods, as usual. Wherefore the natives of that sodden defile, stretching mildewed limbs and combing the rust from sleep-tousled heads as they paddled around their leaking towers and scowled at breakfasts consisting of last-night's dishes of spurs warmed up, called down savage curses on Master Fishe who, they reminded each other, had sworn a mighty oath that overnight showers would die out before dawn, giving a generally fine day with above average temperatures, and would now be sitting smug and content among his astrolabes and owls' entrails by distant sunny Thames, caring for nought beyond Potter's Bar ("which place he calleth the North, aye, gossips, truly!").

But one at least in the wild glen did not share the general griping discontent, although you wouldn't have guessed it to look at him. Lord Anguish, his trews drooping and his sporran wilting from very weariness, his ginger whiskers bedraggled from twelve hours of enforced abstinence (for he must keep a clear head who negotiates in the small hours with wily old Sir Prising Nixon), might look like a collapsed tartan tent, but his heart was light as he scrawled "Angooishe" on the sheepskin contract which bound the Nixons "tae seize, reave, and mak awa' wi' the person o' oor liege and lawful prince, James, sic as he is, for considerations stated hereunder . . ." It had cost an arm and a leg to hire the Nixons, but he consoled himself that apart from the down payment, the rest of the deal could be reneged on.

". . . American rights, sixty–forty . . . participation in gross profits o' any theatrical presentation based on the Work . . . aye, aye," mused Sir Prising, combing his white beard with a pensive dirk. "That minds me, we've never seen a penny for the Kinmont Raid from that thievin' bastard Buccleuch—talk aboot creative reivin', yon man should be in jyle . . . aye, weel, twenty per cent o' residuals on said majestie's memoirs, whilk sall be computed on the gross, and not on producers' net profits . . . even split on marketin' o' Jimsnatch shirts, mugs, and cart-stickers . . . aye, weel, mebbe . . ."

"Stop greetin' and sign the bluidy thing!" cried Lord Anguish, his temperance-frayed nerves on edge. "And mind Clause 2B: 'Time bein' o' the essence'—which means noo, an' your bums no oot their beds yet!"

"Watch this and wonder," replied the border war-lord. He

made his X in blood drawn from a convenient servitor, threw
the contract to his clerk for triplication, strode to the window,
flung aside the Percy-skin curtain, and in a voice which lifted
slates from the tower next door, bellowed the blood-curdling
words of Liddesdale's ancient rallying-cry: "Wakey-Wakey!
Shake loose the border! Ivverybody oot! Get yer cold feet on
the warm flair! Swords and lances! Let's be havin' ye! It's a contract job, wi' money up front!" The response from the towers
and bastels to those last three stirring words was immediate.
Sturdy reivers sprang to arms, gulped their coffee, checked
their policies, rummaged in drawers for clean Scotland jerseys,
and in some instances even cut themselves shaving, such was
their haste. Their women hurried to prepare packed lunches,
sent the children early to play-school, stood ready at the doors
with their husbands' best jacks and mufflers, and entreated them
to ride carefully and light a bale-fire if they were going to be late
for supper. Loons and grieves led prancing hobblers from the
stables and warmed up the saddles, the Riccarton Junction Silver Prize Band searched frantically for the sheet music of "A
Hundred Pipers," at his window Sir Prising gazed in eagle-eyed
pride and tried to think of an appropriate quotation from
"Marmion," and at his elbow Lord Anguish gasped "First the
day!" as he swallowed a quart of Glenlivet neat and called for a
refill, for the spectacle of Liddesdale taking the war-path was
enough to fright the bravest, let alone Scotland's premier drunk
and traitor.

All along the valley the horses stood in the old traditional
three-two-three formation, and Riccarton Junction's answer to
Sousa got their act together with a bass rendering of "Blue Bonnets" as the Nixon riders, each in a Scotland jersey with thistle
crest, filed out of their towers, pacing slowly to the steady

drum-beat. At the head of each file marched its leader, bearing beneath his arm a steel bonnet which he passed neatly to his mates as they broke into a trot, while from the commentary tower came the enraptured cry of the local minstrel:

"My wurrd! We couldn't have a better day for it! There they come, ready for the fray, and my goodness! there are some big fellows there, I can tell you! There's Dicky's Tricky, with hands like frying-pans, riding his sixty-fifth foray for Liddesdale—only two more and he'll have equalled the record set by his father, old Legless Jock Nixon, who was a great loose rider in his day, always in the mauls—I wonder if he's in the crowd this morning? My wurrd, he'll be the proud man . . . and there are Mad Molly Nixon's boys, Dand the Man and Dand the Beast, a great second row, known as the Twa Corbies . . . oh, and there's Trouserless Will, still struggling to get out of those tight jeans . . . I don't think I'd care to say 'Daffodils' to him today, ha-hah! My wurrd! And here comes old Sir Prising himself, to lead the foray . . . my goodness, that's unexpected, after the beard injury he sustained at Reidswire! But he's a tough old bird . . . I was talking to Vidal Nixon, the trainer, earlier on, and he wasn't sure the beard would be fit, but evidently it is . . . And now comes the ceremonial of lining out Sir Prising's steel bonnet, and it's thrown in from his tower door, and up they go for it . . . oh dear me, a bit of lifting there, I fancy, they're still not quite used to the new rule . . . yes, there's the whistle, and down they go, and out it comes—against the head! My wurrd! I can't see whose head it is . . . Hungry Jock's, I think . . . aye, there it goes, rolling into touch . . . Aye, well, his widow'll have something to say about that, I imagine . . . but there goes the steel bonnet along the line, and there's a man over! It's Sir Prising, and he scoops it in, and they're away . . . !"

With a thunder of stirrups the great cavalcade swept down the valley, Sir Prising at its head, the steel cap flourished aloft, and hot on his heels came Lord Anguish, breast and stomach swelling with triumph and raw spirit. At least, he thought, he'd got the show on the road, and all that remained was to guide them to the spot marked X to which, by noon, Don Collapso would have lured the Scottish monarch. Elated by his success, his besotted senses stirred by the headlong rush of the foray and the cries of "Up and under!" "Drive, Liddesdale, drive!" and "Change at Carstairs!," his lordship surrendered himself to the exhilarating charge, and took another swig at his saddle-jerrycan. It's the only way to raid, he thought . . .

". . . at this rate he'll be three parts gassed afore he's half-way there," observed the warlock foreman gloomily, as he viewed the Nixons' galloping advance on the cauldron-screen, and then cringed as La Infamosa turned her red-eyed glare in his direction. "Sorry, missus," he cringed, "Ah wis just makin' a comment, like. Keep the heid . . ."

"Silence, blot!" she hissed, and made a spiteful pass over his shaggy head, intending to turn him into a marmoset. It didn't work, because in stripping off her Wizard's guise of robe, hat, beard, and rubber mask, she had also discarded the wand, and as any necromancer will tell you, without a wand you may as well climb back on your truck. (She doesn't know that the warlock foreman, sick of being metamorphosed, has hidden the wand in his tool-box. Well, it's a relief to know that she is shorn, as they say, of her magical powers and skill in grammarie; let's hope it's permanent.)

Foiled, La Infamosa bent her gaze on the cauldron, and noted that the Nixon cavalcade, sweeping northward out of

Liddesdale in full cry, was suffering its usual thinning out as reckless riders rode slap into trees, tripped over tussocks, and remembered previous engagements. But there were plenty left, she reflected, and they were heading in the right direction at full throttle, with Lord Anguish, admittedly well kettled but still in the saddle, consulting his map and shouting hoarse directions.

In obedience to the remote control, the cauldron image cut to a green and sun-kissed valley where the royal hunting party (no longer anywhere nigh Peebles, and getting perilously close to the spot marked X) was winding its way through boskage and verdure at a leisurely pace. Despite the presence of King James VI, it could not be described as a gay party; His Majesty's brow was o'ercast wi' care, his lip drooped petulantly to his saddle-bow, his rachitic shanks clung but irritably to the flanks of his palfrey, and all told his appearance was that of a monarch who wished he had stayed in bed. The hunt had been a frost so far, with not a beast sighted, let alone slain, and only four thieves and vagrants hanged and one hamlet put to the torch (for thrifty James believed in combining the business of hunting with the pleasure of law enforcement on his border expeditions). Had he but known it, the absence of game was due to the crafty planning of Don Collapso, who had secretly despatched his retinue of small Spanish attendants ahead to chivvy away harts and fawns and even rabbits with cries of "Shoo!" and "*Vamos*, beasties!"

Now, riding some way behind with the Russian ambassador, who looked and sounded like Akim Tamiroff with a head cold, the subtle Spaniard took satisfied note of His Majesty's sagging garments and occasional mutters of "Eheu! Me miserabile! Ach, the bleezes wi' this, Ah'd sooner hae a nicht on the toon wi' John Knox!" and judged the time almost ripe for his intervention. Even the one-liners of the king's jester, Archie Armstrong, running alongside with his foot in a bucket, were failing to lift the royal gloom.

"Here, gossip James, Ah've got a good yin!" cried the buffoon. "Listen tae this!" And he struck an attitude. "'It'll get worse afore it gets better!'" He collapsed in mirth, wiping his eyes. "One in a row, boo-boom, eh?"

The monarch sighed heavily, and the jester tried again. "'A patch is nae disgrace!'" he chortled, watching anxiously for the royal smile. He didn't get it. "'Never up, never in!'" Still nothing. "Aw, c'mon, gossip," he pleaded. "Gi'es a break!" King James drew rein wearily, and turned morose whiskers on the motleyed fool.

"Where the hell dae you get your material, Armstrong?" he wondered. "*The Sunday Post?*"

"Ah'm daein' ma best!" cried the sweating clown. "Jeez, yer worse'n the Gleska Empire, so y'are!" He thought desperately, and brightened. "Here's one ye hivnae heard! Wait fur it: 'Aye, weel, ye ken noo!'" He went widdershins in delight, while the king groaned deeply and sagged even lower in his saddle.

Seeing his chance, Don Collapso urged his mount alongside the king's and greased ingratiatingly. "Yoor jestair's drolleries are leetle to Yoor Majesty's liking? Eef yoor grace would permeet me—"

"If it's mair flamenco dancers," grunted moping majesty, "Ah'm no' interested. Goadless hussies stamp-stampin' aboot—an' castanets isnae mentioned i' the Scriptures, Ah may tell ye—"

"Nay, nay, sire," soothed the portly Iberian. "Trost mee to know yoor royal taste. I heer," he added confidentially, "that they're boorneeng a coupla weetches een thee next pareesh . . ."

"Ach, when ye've seen one, ye've seen them a'," gloomed His Majesty. "Forbye, it just pits me in mind o' hell-fire. Can ye no' suggest somethin' a wee bit cheerier?"

"Thee boorneeng weel be followed by a sermon in Latin," urged Don Collapso. "Two hours, easy, weeth allusions to thee Socinian heresy, an' questions afterwards."

King James considered. "Two hoors? No kiddin'?" Then his face resumed its unhappy simian expression. "Ach, but his pronunciation'll be just one damned vee efter anither—"

"Wice wersa," insinuated the cunning Castilian. "Wincit weritas, yoo better beleeve eet! An' then there's to be an open deescussion on passeeve smokeeng . . ."

"Zatafact?" The royal visage did a slight beam, its nose aglow with anticipation. "Here, that's mair like it!" He turned to his esquire. "Right whee-ol! Forward, ho!" he commanded, but Don Collapso plucked at his sleeve.

"Yoor pardon, sire, but I could onlee get teeckets for two. So how about thee boys attend us heer, huh, an' yoo an' me take een the show? Eef you don' like, we leave at thee eenterval— but thees preecher, he's a reel pulpit-buster! I know yoor gonna like heem, yes sir—eet's heem an' thee Devil, feefteen rounds to a deceesion, no fooleeng . . ."

In the cauldron La Infamosa watched gloatingly as the two figures ambled off into the greenwood, Don Collapso talking with animation, while the royal retinue, waiting till they were out of sight, produced pipes and pouches and turned the air blue with illicit fumes.

"Ah, that Collapso!" She licked purple lips. "A diplomatic genius! Now, if Bentos is on parade and waiting . . ."

The cauldron image changed again, this time disclosing a hidden glade with an enormous X whitewashed on the turf. The

impostor was seen sitting on a log, regally attired, critically titi-
vating his beard in a hand-mirror and humming "Campbell-
town Loch" to get in the mood, while Frey Bentos paced up and
down anxiously, kicking toadstools, peering over bracken
fronds, taking an hour-glass from his pocket and holding it
doubtfully to his ear, and chewing his tassels in impatience.

"Excellent!" purred La Infamosa, and took another look at
the Nixons, now seen in long shot as they careered across a
meadow, Sir Prising out front with his white locks streaming,
then the sozzled Anguish supported by two riders as he tried to
orient his map at the gallop, and in their wake the grim black
squadron of the remaining Nixons, lances couched, eyes glaring, girths bursting and the more reckless spirits shouting
"Look, no hands!" as they swept by, the woods echoing to that
terrible refrain for which Romberg would write music several
centuries later:

> *It is the thunder of Sir Prising and his band*
> *And royal watchers better understand*
> *Oor . . . cry . . . of . . .*
> *JIM!*
> *It's a time he'd best be hiding*
> *JIM!*
> *He's oor pigeon an' we're efter*
> *HIM . . .*

The overalled warlocks chewed their claws in terror, and
even La Infamosa shuddered delicately before consulting the
cauldron's next image—a map with X at the centre, the two tiny
blips of King James and Collapso nearby, and at a greater distance but closing fast, an irregular mass of erratic blips, some of

which fell away and lay flickering feebly (the Nixons). La Infamosa heaved an ecstatic sigh, her eyes sparkling scarlet pleasure, and if she'd had the wand handy the warlock foreman might easily have become George Clooney, or even Tom Cruise.

"Ten minutes and counting!" she hissed, greenish ripples of excitement mantling her flawless shoulders. "Ten minutes to the coup o' the century! What rewards, what dignities, what honours will His Catholic Majesty not heap on his loyal servants— and, in especial, me? Speaking of rewards," she continued, and the warlocks could have sworn that her gleaming teeth were momentarily transformed into fangs, "there is the present delight of tipping those three patsies below into the fiery soup! Yes, time for a little relaxation, I think . . ."

Chuckling evilly, she brought up the dungeon image in the cauldron, and looked her wicked fill on the three helpless figures precariously seated on the lip of the pit of doom. It crossed her mind to check on the vault where the Charltons hung, and for a moment her polished talon rested on the button, hesitating . . . (no, please, don't let her look!) . . . before she decided that she couldn't wait any longer for her dungeon fun, cut back to the map, and tossed the remote control to the warlock foreman.

"Summon me when the balloon goes up," she commanded, "and if I discover that in my absence ye have been watching the Globe Theatre Follies, right exquisitely slow and lingering shall be thy doom, so watch it!" She swayed sensuously from the chamber, followed by silent raspberries from her stunted acolytes.

"Slow . . . slow . . . quick-quick, slow . . . ," exclaimed Kylie desperately. "Look, why don't you just stand on my feet and I'll *walk* you round the floor? You ham-footed little jerk!" she added to herself, smiling winningly as she and Clnzh moved in an erratic circle, the small Amazonian scowling in concentration as he strove to follow her gliding steps. "Slow . . . slow . . . nay, thou'rt terrific!" she lied aloud. "Wow! Move over Astaire, the Brazilians are here! Now the turn . . . easy, boy—yes, I know Master Nureyev is wont to lift his partner o'er his head . . . all in good time . . ."

From which you deduce that Kylie's brilliant idea of conning Clnzh into releasing her so that they could tread a measure, has worked like a charm. Mind you, dancing with a partner two feet tall and short in the arm poses its problems, but her chief worry was how to disable the prancing pygmy long enough to enable her to free the Charltons. Clnzh might be tiny, but he was tough, and Kylie was no Boadicea. No, guile must be her weapon, and as they cut a passionate rug the length of the chamber and back, Kylie trilling gaily and Clnzh emitting ecstatic grunts, it came to her . . . the Charltons, head-clanging at speed to "Minnie from Trinidad," were swinging wildly only a few feet away . . . if she could just work Clnzh into position . . . his shaggy skull was exactly level with the steel caps as they swung, bonged, and rebounded . . . go for it, Kylie, she thought . . .

"Ay-ay-ay!" she hummed, hip-grinding like crazy while Clnzh, eyes bugging eagerly, tried to climb up her legs. "Ah-ah, naughty!" she reproved, wagging a playful finger, easing him gently back until he was within a yard of the clashing caps. Wait for it, she thought . . . and as Oor Kid and his neighbour swung towards each other with the ponderous power of two Compostella censers, she took Clnzh by his little shoulders . . . and shoved.

The result was gratifying in the extreme. Two pendulous Charlton steel helmets smote simultaneously on either side of the pygmy's matted cranium with the sound of a tall ship hitting a reef, a beatific smile o'erspread his primitive features, and it was plain to see that he was gathering primroses by the Orinoco's brim as he sagged at the knees and collapsed serenely on the floor.

He hit it approximately three-fifths of a second before the Charltons did, such was the speed with which Kylie withdrew the bolt retaining their chain. As it slackened, the twelve pendant reivers descended, steel-clad heads first, striking the cold stone in a positive carillon of sound which totally out-tocsined all their previous efforts, reverberating through the vault in a mighty chord which, had he been privileged to hear it, would have persuaded Wagner to re-title his opera *Die Meisterclangers*. (They tried to repeat it, later, in peacetime, diving head-first off cliffs and charging about in quarries, but the blend of helmets must have been wrong, for the distinctive purity of the chord eluded them; it became a family obsession for a century or two, and even today modern Charltons often wear a grim, thoughtful look as though they were listening for something.)

Anyway, at the time it made one hell of a din, and as Kylie strove to unknot Oor Kid's hands, she became aware that the sound of Spaniards eating in the distant kitchen had died away to a soft munching and slurping, punctuated by cries of *"Que pasa?"* and *"Que clango?"* and "That's no way to finish a rumba!" Any minute, she knew, they would come to investigate, and she couldn't hope to undo twelve sets of bonds in time . . . her eye fell on the dagger in Clnzh's girdle, and with a hysterical squeal of joy she seized it and hurled herself on Oor recumbent Kid with the demented energy of an Australian sheep-shearer. Two lightning zips, one gag-muffled scream of pain, and the Charlton was free, blaspheming horribly as he nursed his congested head and Kylie strove to get his circulation going.

"Hurry, hurry!" she moaned, chafing his hairy hands. "Get restored, I pray thee, and aid me in releasing thy brethren! We must limber up ere the Dagoes are upon us! Jump up and down, run in circles, come on, you idle blighter—gosh, I bet if I promised my negligee to the first man on his feet, you'd be doing the hundred in evens!"

The mere idea was enough to get Oor Kid staggering afoot, but even as Kylie turned knife in hand to the next Charlton, came the sound she had dreaded—the unmistakable tread of forty reluctant Spanish soldiers munching tortillas as they came to see what was up. She could see their morioned shadows on the wall beyond the arch leading to the kitchen; two seconds would bring them into view—and while Oor Kid was shambling about like an arthritic baboon, eleven of the Dirty Dozen remained trussed as Christmas turkeys. She had failed to beat the clock.

Deep in the dank and slimy dungeon tunnel, no sound penetrated from the levels above, and La Infamosa stepped daintily along all unaware that overhead the Charltons had just hit the floor with enough noise to drown out the launching of the *QE2*. She paused by the open dungeon door, her malicious ears eagerly pricked for sobs of despair, pleas for mercy, or yowls of "They can't do this to me!," but all she heard was good stiff-upper-lip chit-chat, on this wise:

"Nay, sweet Godiva, if die we must—and frankly that's the way the smart money's going—at least we die together, two souls in bonds o' mutual love—"

"Hold it raight there, Noble! Let's just get it straight—if there's going to be any of thet unaited-in-death stuff, 'twill be in mutual love wi' *me* thet her ladyship goes down the pipe—"

"Thou, weasel Scot? Nay, what crust is thine, to speak o' love to an Englishwoman, thou outward forroner!"

"Listen, mec, Ai saw her furst!"

"Aye, and robbed her in thirty seconds flat! Some love, i' faith!"

"Heed him not, divaine creecher! Ah, Godaiva, if only Ai could daie for thee, Ai would do so gledly—"

"Not half as gladly as I would! Ah, love, for thy sweet sake I would endure a thousand half-gainers into yon molten stew—"

"Thank you, gentlemen!" Godiva's queenly contralto would have done credit to a Guards drill sergeant, both in passion and volume. "I am beholden to you both, and 'tis one hell of a consolation! But prithee . . . *DO* something, can't you?"

"Ah, sweetheart, if I but could!"

"Nay, dearest, if *Ai* but could . . ."

At this point La Infamosa decided to make her entrance, and their debate ended abruptly as first a slender arm appeared, then a shapely leg, and finally the rest of her, sliding sinuously round the door and tossing her head ere she posed theatrically, considering them and wishing she had a spotlight. A vicious thrill possessed her as she read the instinctive fear in their eyes, and thought to herself, *caramba,* this is living! Slowly she sauntered towards them, plucking the rapier from the rack, and paused before Godiva. Her glowing eyes rested on each in turn, and merciless was her smile as she laid the glittering point against Godiva's cord.

"Well, milady," she husked. "Any last request?"

My God, thought Godiva, this is the end of all things . . . life's last lesson, for while we all know that death's inevitable, it's a some-day thing, and even when sentence is passed, it's still in the future . . . and it comes as a blinding shock when the moment finally arrives in all its horror, and you realise it's a matter of seconds to . . . nothing. An icy vise seized her heart, her flesh crawled, and she felt her limbs trembling and wanted to scream . . . and then Benenden came through in the pinch, as it does with real heroines, and it was with outward composure that she raised her peerless red head for the last time, and drawled in a voice which she hoped wasn't shaking too much:

"I'd ask for a hair-do . . . but one look at you tells me you haven't got the facilities. Pass, thank you."

La Infamosa drew in a hissing breath, and half-raised the rapier, only to let it fall.

"Just for that . . . wait a little longer," she mocked, and to Archie she said: "And our English hero . . . any last words, heretic? Like . . . 'goodbye,' maybe?"

Interesting she should ask that, thought Archie, for he had been giving the matter some thought—as every right-thinking hero should, of course—and was undecided whether to take the straight patriotic line, by singing "Heart of Oak," or wax wittily defiant with "Happy Days Are Here Again," or a memorable gag of the I-think-I-could-eat-one-of-Bellamy's-pies or On-the-whole-I'd-rather-be-in-Philadelphia order. Had he been to a certain school he could have cried "Floreat Etona!," but "Floreat Haltwhistle Almshouse!" didn't have the same ring, somehow. In the event, being plain English, he decided there was only one thing for it.

"God save the Queen," said Archie Noble.

"Typical!" sneered La Infamosa. "Well, He won't—nor the King o' Scots, neither." She turned to Gilderoy. "And thou, haggis?"

"Es a metter of fect," said Gilderoy, "there is something Ai'd laike to say . . . Godaiva, Ai'm just sorry thet the lest kiss Ai received in this life was not from thay incomparable lips . . . but from others which left a decaidedly nesty taste in mai mouth." He gave the merest flicker of repugnance in La Infamosa's direction. "Thenk God," he added, "et least Ai won't hev to endure *thet* ghestly ordeal again."

Something in his tone caused Godiva to stare at him, and beyond her Archie stiffened suddenly and looked also. Gilderoy was smiling serenely, his gaze averted from La Infamosa, and the Spanish fiendess's lovely face was blank for an instant before contorting in malevolent fury. Three swift steps she took towards Gilderoy's see-saw, and for a moment it seemed she would slash the cord through—and then she stopped, percolating with rage and wounded pride.

"Is that so?" she spat. "Well, that's where you're wrong! Aye, here's that shall wipe all memory o' her insipid smooches from thy memory ere I beam thee down, Scotty! Take this wi' thee to hell—from La Infamosa!"

And casting aside her rapier she gnashed spiteful incisors, wiggled her hips, tossed her head, and stepped almost to the edge of the pit, flexing her purple lips. Gilderoy's eyes were closed, and his expression was one of shrinking cringe, but Archie saw, wi' sudden surge of hope, that he was hyperventilating like an air-starved grampus—and then La Infamosa had seized his head and her mouth clamped on his with the sound of a paddle striking home on wet blancmange. His splendid frame rocked 'neath the impact, and he swayed perilously on his seat; Godiva saw his biceps swell and the veins stand out on his magnificent neck; weird creaking noises seemed to issue from his ears—and then Godiva cried aloud to see that La Infamosa's glossy locks were flapping like curtains in the breeze, her nerveless hands were falling from Gilderoy's head, her body was sagging as though filleted, and she would have staggered and fallen had she not been locked by some amazing lip-magnetism to the Peebles Predator's features. The green highlights of her skin were paling to alabaster, her ankles were jellying visibly, and steam rose from her décolletage.

"My God!" cried Archie. "'Tis his force-five whammy— she'll never come out of it, like the woman at the zoo who thinks she's Cleopatra! Nay, Godiva, look not on't! 'Tis too horrible!"

"Betrayer!" cried Godiva. "Vile seducing gorgeous monster—nay, desist! Put that woman down, I say! Oh, shut up, Noble! Don't try to tell me he isn't enjoying it, the wondrous swine! Oh, I could spit! Unhand her—nay, unlip her, rather, thou adored recreant libertine!"

La Infamosa's limbs thrashed weakly as Gilderoy, in danger of falling from his seat, put every last ounce of voltage into one final osculatory surge—and then their lips parted with the rasp of plaster peeled from buffalo hide, and she reeled away like Jersey Joe when Marciano nailed him, out on her feet, eyes crossed and no longer glowing crimson but glazed and sightless, her five-inch heels buckling and her black silk sheath drained to the hem. For a moment she tottered, clinging to the Iron Maiden, and then subsided on the rack, inanimate save for the faint whisper of the Spanish version of "Roll me over in the clover" issuing from her trembling purple lips.

Archie heard it not, for his ears seemed to be filled by the rousing strains of the *Superman* theme, and had his hands been free he would have punched the air and swapped jerseys with his colleague, who was slumped exhausted like the last survivor of Fort Zinderneuf, his lips peeled and his pencil-slim moustache reduced to a charred fragment. As it was, Archie decided to sing "Rule Britannia," while Godiva stared in mingled fury and amaze.

"Why . . . why, thou wertn't ensorcelled by her vile kisses upstairs at all!" she cried. "You were kidding all the time! Of all the sneaky tricks to play on a girl, thou vile, god-like chauvinist! Nay, thou dreamy detestable, thou! How I love and despise thee!"

"Arose, arose, arose from out the azure main!" carolled Archie, and stopped abruptly. "Hold on, though—how long will she be under? See, she stirs, tho' feebly. Is she zonked indeed?"

Gilderoy, wheezing for breath, raised eyes whose amber was sadly bleared. "Mai . . . God!" he croaked. "How . . . she . . . stenk! Ai've tasted gurlick . . . but thet's ridiculous! Ai'll hev to . . . drink . . . nought but . . . engostura bitters . . . for months! Oh, help ma boab!"

"Will she recover?" cried Archie. "And if so, when?"

Gilderoy shook doubtful head. "Ken't say . . . Ai'm afraid. Ged, but she's tough! Heving mai hends taied . . . didn't help, of course. Ten minutes, maybe . . . perheps less . . ."

"What ruddy good's that?" clarioned Godiva. "Are we to sit bound and helpless, then, until she surfaces and gives us the message? Why," she demanded, "couldn't you have got her to untie you while she was 'neath the influence? You great oaf! For Pete his sake, ye had that scrubber Basset jumping through hoops!"

"Besset's British," explained Gilderoy. "These Letin types . . . different metebolism . . . end Ai've hurd thet Spenish scaientists hev been wurking on snog-resistance . . . she may hev hed a course . . . never known such lip-force . . ."

"She's moving!" yelled Archie. "'Od's boots, she's coming out of it! We are undone!"

"We're nothing of the damned sort!" snapped Godiva. "That's what I've just been saying—don't you men ever listen?"

"Quaiet!" cried Gilderoy. "Dammit, she must be faire-proof!"

For La Infamosa was doing a Sleeping Beauty, lids flickering, limbs twitching, and a long dreamy sigh animating her bazoom. Again she sighed, and slowly struggled into a reclining position, shaking her bemused coiffure and turning a vacant stare on the captives, who sat rooted (not that they'd any choice) as understanding returned to her eyes, which began to glow faintly pink. She tried to speak, but no sound came, and when she attempted to rise, her motor coughed and died. A moment she lay, heaving gently, and then suddenly the crimson beams blazed forth 'tween her vengeful lids, her stiletto heels stiffened with two sharp clicks, and to their horror she slithered from the rack and began to snake along the floor towards the fallen rapier, her face a mask of evil determination.

"Mai God!" cried Gilderoy. "'Tis the Laurel Benk Recovery!"

"What's that?" shrieked Godiva.

"A rare but terrible re-ection to mai embrace!" gasped Gilderoy, his chin-beard dilating wi' apprehension. "The senses clear entairely, but use o' the limbs returns only gredually . . . 'tis named efter a sixth-form gurl Ai met et a school dence . . . took me unawares end dem' near brained me wi' a hockey-stick—"

Godiva screamed as La Infamosa's talons closed on the rapier-hilt and she continued to inch in serpentine fashion towards the see-saws. Nearer and nearer she crept, her eyes lasering ill-will, until her colubrine writhings brought her within range of Godiva's cord. Gasping and hissing she extended the blade, and with teeth-gritting effort began to saw weakly at the slender hemp.

"Ai luv you, delectable Infamosa!" roared Gilderoy, in desperation. "Ged, but yur beautiful! Ai yurn for yur embrace—kiss me, you fool! Away in the long gress, you'll no' get your feet wet!"

For a moment it looked like working. La Infamosa shivered, stopped sawing, and the crimson glare was replaced by roopy devotion—and then the fit passed, her eyes re-blazed, and she gnashed feebly and began to attack the cord again with painful slowness, back and forth, back and forth . . .

Suddenly a strand parted. Godiva felt the slight jar of it, and closed her eyes. She could hear the faint rasping of the blade, and Archie's audible straining against his bonds, even above the frantic endearments which Gilderoy was bellowing in a vain attempt to reassert his influence . . . another faint snap and tremor. Goodbye, world, she thought, and as the fiery horror beneath closed over her imagination, she forced herself to open her eyes—and there in the dungeon doorway was her negligee, with Kylie inside it.

Too late, thought Godiva, even as her blonde associate's piercing cry of "Stop that at once, you rotten cow!" pierced the fume-laden air. La Infamosa, half on her knees, was sawing at the last strand with the strength of a convalescent maniac, but at Kylie's shrill command she paused involuntarily, turning her head, eyes widening in amaze as a golden-haired fury in black gauze came hurtling towards her with a ringing squeal of "Banzai, Benenden!" With a superhuman effort the Castilian nemesis swung round her glittering point, and as Kylie came in to land it sliced rippishly through the negligee, missing the soft skin beneath by a whisker. Godiva gave a quavering cry of "Ruined beyond repair!," Kylie sank her small teeth in La Infamosa's hand, the rapier clanged on the stone and rolled into the pit, taking most of the negligee with it, Archie and Gilderoy gallantly averted their eyes, Kylie hung a plump left on her opponent's ear, and Godiva's last memory before she swooned away was of the Bond Street milliner murmuring: "Certes, moddom, 'tis the latest boudoir-gear o' Paris, woven to gossamer lightness, so fine ye may read small print through it, and who's the lucky man . . . ?"

Then a massive arm was about her, the aroma of rescuing reiver was in her queenly nostrils, and she oped fluttering lids to find herself gazing up into the unshaven, snaggle-toothed leer of Oor Kid. Instinctively she kneed him in the groin, and as he staggered, clutching himself and groaning "Haud up, missus!" she became aware that she was free, and elsewhere in the chamber Kylie was hastily wrapping herself in a bathrobe emblazoned "Eildon Dungeon," Gilderoy was enfolding La Infamosa in a passionate embrace, and now Archie was hastening to her all glad-eyed and romantic, seizing her in masterful arms, raining kisses on her bewildered cheeks, and crying: "Saved, dearest Godiva! Rescued, i' the nick o' time! All's well, my life, God's in his heaven, and the saints are marching in—"

"All's well my aunt's embroidered rug!" cried Kylie. "The only marching that's being done in this beastly burrow is by forty Spanish stinkers in tin vests who e'en now are probably carving thy hapless gang o' head-clanging misfits into bite-sized chunks! Or hanging them up again," she added.

"O, woe and fiddlesticks!" cried Archie aghast. "Ye mean we're not in control—we haven't won? Speak, mistress, fill me in!"

Which she did, with graphic description of how pike-wielding moustachios in morions had arrived before she could free the Charltons, but she had scooted out unseen, bethinking of her dungeoned friends, followed only by Oor Kid, whose intentions she suspected (this with a coy blush) were dishonourable rather than merely fugitive.

"But he's been quite useful," she concluded modestly, "for while I could ha' handled (no problem) that slinky she-devil in the black dress with the thigh-length slit and fitted hips and how she gets into the dam' thing without two strong men to help, never mind how doth it stay up wi'out glue or guy-ropes, I'll never know—anyway, he was pretty timely, lending me a hand, and then turning you lot loose. Gosh," she added, prettily agog, "it must ha' been passing hairy, was't not, sitting poised o'er yon fiery void! Were you scared? I'd have been up to high doh, honestly—"

"And the Charltons lie upstairs, captive o' forty Spanish heavies?" interrupted Archie. "Nay, we must to their aid—where's Gilderoy?"

"Where else?" grated grim Godiva, her momentary weakness quite dispelled by the sight of La Infamosa locked in the Rutherglen Romeo's heaving clinch. But even as they looked, he desisted, breathing hard, and as he laid the unconscious hidalga gently on the rack they saw that her beauteous face was blank, her dress sagged in exhausted folds, her stilettos drooped limp, and her entire being was tranquilised to yonder.

"Phew! That's settled her," said Gilderoy, wiping his brow.

"Aye, ye may chalk off La Infamosa. Ai hated to do it, in a way, for they're not building them like thet any more—not in Spain, I mean," he added hastily, seeing Godiva's violet gimlets upon him. "She's in dreamlend for keeps, anyway, and fit for nought but taking the veil or singing in naight-clubs, enamoured end hurmless. End now, sweet Godaiva, let me—"

"Sweet me no sweets, false lover! What, wi' her kisses hot—"

"Squad, 'shun!" roared Archie. "Nay, dear heart, forgive, but 'tis action time, and ye can brush him off later. For Operation Jimsnatch may e'en now be under way, and we powerless to prevent until those overhead Dagoes have been dealt with. So pay attention, everyone!" He stood erect, flawless brows aligned, tossing back eager curls from resolute forehead and dominating them wi' his reckless fighting smile. "Right! I've got it all worked out. This is what we do . . ."

Well, he's said that before, and look what happened. Mind you, the boy's a trier, and our team's luck hasn't run out yet—at least they've 'scaped the fiery doom, thanks to little Kylie (who'd have thought she had it in her, eh?)—and if only they can put the skids under the enemy aloft . . . But we can't wait around for Archie to develop his plan, for political crisis is boiling up in the outside world, with the impostor on hand, the Nixons arriving, and King James walking blissfully unsuspecting to his doom . . . well, not blissfully, exactly, by the sound of him . . .

Seated on a decayed tree-stump, nursing his aching dogs and moodily watching the centipedes gambolling, His Majesty of Scotland heaved a profound sigh as he prepared to deliver one of those weighty pronouncements which had won him pre-eminence among royal philosophers of the day. Henri of France might be better-looking, Philip of Spain had a bigger palace, Elizabeth of England could curse more fluently, Mohammed of Turkey had more wives, and Sigismond of Poland was rumoured to be a better adagio dancer, but when it came to scholarly sound-bites, James was at the tape before the rest had started, as his present utterance proved.

"I'm fair forfochen!" he exclaimed, and meeting Don Collapso's uncomprehending stare, translated wearily. "See me— I'm aboot jiggered! 'Tis weel for thee, Collapso, big creeshy thing that y'are, and can go stravagin' a' ower the woods, but I'm gey weak i' the legs and shamble in my gait!" He replaced his shoon, glowering. "Tae froochy wi' this, I've had it! I'm gaun hame—"

"But, sire, eet's onlee a leetle foorther!" cried the perspiring hidalgo, his eyes fixed on the blasted oak a mere Number 5 wood distant, which he knew stood in the X-marked glade. "Joost' roun' thee bend—"

"Roond the bend ye maun surely be," quo' James emphatically, "if ye think I'll stir anither fit. Oot upon thee and thy twahoor preacher—I doubt he exists at a'!" His goggle eyes narrowed, with a suspicious creaking of lids. "I was a fule tae harken tae ye," he grumbled. "A foreigner—aye, and a Pape! Oh, I see thy design, sir ambassador—to weary me oot and put me aff my supper, so that ye may pull some diplomatic nifty on me when I'm pooped—ah, but I'm fly tae thy Castilian subtlety . . ." He broke off, sniffing. "But what's this? Smoke? Have ye dared tae have a crafty drag ahint my majestic back, Don Collapso?"

"Nay, sire, nevaire!" protested the don. "'Tis a habit loathsome too thee eye, harmfool too thee longs—"

"I said that!" peeved the king, nostrils flapping. "Nay, but someone's at it—"

"They moost have started boorning thee weetches!" crowed Don Collapso. "Let us hasten, Majesty, beefore they're all gone!"

"Witches, smitches!" scoffed James. "'Tis vile tobacco! Oh, I thank thee, Lord, who vouchsafedest tae us kings senses abune those o' common folk, bestowing on thy servant a hooter divinely infallible!" He inhaled vigorously. "Aye . . . 'tis an ecumenical blend o' Three Nuns and Presbyterian mixture, beyond question . . . and cometh frae whaur we left the hunt! Wae's me, the impiddence! My ain courtier loons, puffin' and blawin' their beastly butts the meenit I'm oot o' sicht! Right," he cried, "I'll sort them!"

And before Don Collapso could stay him, the royal patron of ASH was scuttling back the way they had come, his aching feet forgotten in the excitement of the chase. By the time the Spaniard had heaved his massive guts in vain pursuit, the outraged monarch was out of sight, bawling, "Flaunt your vile Woodbines afore the face o' kings, would ye, ye whiffers? Summon the Royal Archers! Get the polis!" Cursing, and with only a backward glance at the distant oak, Don Collapso waddled in his wake, his mind already busy with the excuses he would cook up for the Escurial.

"Where in tarnation is that Anguish?" fretted Frey Bentos, for the umpteenth time. "Him an' his posse shoulda bin here yonks ago! Ah wouldn't mind bettin'," he fumed, "that tartan bum has got hisself a jug o' forty-rod and is layin' under a hedge this minute, stewed to hellangone! An' you," he added savagely to the impostor, who was sprawled at ease on the grass dividing his attention between the Premier League Tables and the Shorter Catechism (necessary lore for aspiring Scottish monarchs), "better start takin' an interest, if you want to rest yore ass on the throne of Albion, never mind succeed the heretic Elizabeth! Sumpn's amiss, goddammit!"

"Keep your tonsure on," yawned the impostor. "They'll get here."

"You wanna bet?" snapped the austere Dominican. "Ah knew we shoulda never trusted that lush to awganise th' snatch! Clnzh coulda zapped this guy James with a tranquiliser dart,

easy! Boy," he brooded, "Ah shore miss that Clnzh, with his little blowpipe an' human haids an' all . . . An' another thing—
where's Collapso an' the Stooart monarch, huh? How we goin'
pull a kidnap ifn we don't got a victim, jus' tell me that!"

"'Tis thy problem," said the impostor. "Mine is the chief
end of man and the likely relegation of Raith Rovers, whoever
they are."

Frey Bentos chewed an anxious tassel, and then his habit
stiffened in sudden resolve. "Ah cain't stand it!" he muttered.
"Ah'm gonna look fo' them. So don' you-all go 'way, now, you
heah? Ah won't be gawn more'n a few minutes, so jus' you keep
a-studyin' them books, an' if Collapso shows wi' Jacobus, keep
outta sight till Anguish gits heah? Got it? 'Bye, now . . ."

And he slid into the bushes *and was never seen again.*

[Historians are divided as to why Frey Bentos, a mature and
experienced agent, should have deserted his post at this critical
point. Some think he did not, and that mere impatience sent him
in quest of his associates, but the generally accepted belief is
that his fall into the Carlisle Corporation tip had damaged his
nervous system, rendering him, in medical phraseology, slug-
nutty. This seems more probable than the strongly held minority view that he was abandoning his duty to go in search of
Busty Basset, of whom (according to its proponents) he had
become enamoured; if this were so, he must have fallen for her
at one hell of a clip, since their acquaintance had been limited to
a brief whirl round the dance-floor of the Dungeon Grill. Supporters of this theory point out that she was a professional
dancer, and that Frey Bentos was unusually susceptible to the
terpsichorean muse, so the Basset Solution, as it is called, cannot
be discounted entirely, unlike the fanciful speculation of an
American academic, that the Dominican simply went into the

bushes to take a leak. Obviously this was not the case, or he would have been back in two minutes tops, and would not have been shanghaied by crimps in West Hartlepool a week later, an incident for which there is irrefutable evidence in the State Papers and the sports edition of the *Sunderland Echo*. What is less clear is how the unhappy cleric came eventually to be sold as a galley-slave to the Barbary Corsairs, among whom he eventually won his freedom and, renouncing both faith and nationality, rose to prominence as a corsair chieftain, Bentos Bey, the Drawn Cork (or, according to some authorities, Hawk) of Islam. This is beyond the scope of the present work, but we thought you'd like to know. Suffice to say that Frey Bentos vanished at a climactic stage of Operation Jimsnatch, and that his absence was of crucial importance.]

Right, is that it? Finished with the historical interpolation are we? We can get on with the story? Oh, good . . .

Well, while Frey Bentos was tooling off, possibly to look for Anguish and/or Collapso, possibly on a frolic of his own, leaving the impostor alone in the X-marked glade, and King James was waddling back to the hunt as fast as his little bandy legs would carry him, with blood in his eye and reek o' Capstan Full Strength in his nostrils, what of Lord Anguish and the Nixons? We left them, you remember, homing in on their quarry, with only a few miles to go, and Lord Anguish map-reading and refreshing himself from time to time with the good proof spirit. With the result that the closer they got to the X-glade, the more sincerely puggled became his lordship . . . but we can do no better than quote the famous old border ballad, "How They Sought King James from Ghent to Aix, or Thereabouts Anyway," whose poignant stanzas are, unfortunately, incomplete, but give a pretty fair indication of the trend things were taking:

> *Now Liddesdale has ridden a raid*
> *Tae lift King James by Eildon lee,*
> *But by noon o' the day*
> *They had lost their way,*
> *For Anguish their guide, fu' stoned was he.*
>
> *Sir Prising sate on his muckle steed,*
> *And a waesome tear was in his e'e,*
> *"O, Anguish is drunk*
> *And our hopes are sunk,*
> *Unless his map ye can read tae me."*
>
> *Then up and spake bold Trouserless Will:*
> *"Sir Prising, gi'e the map tae me,*
> *Wi' my reading specs*
> *I'll find the X,*
> *So guid King James shall oor prisoner be."*
>
> *"O, tak' the map, bold Trouserless Will,*
> *And your skeely*specs fu' well tae see,*
> *My dochter's hand*
> *And a gowd hat-band*
> *Ye shall hae for this service done tae me."*
>
> *He has ta'en the map, and his reading specs,*
> *But of the X no trace found he,*

* skilful

"O, the lens is broke
And I rue the joke
The false optician has played on me."

"De'il tak' the map and your lousy specs,
We must trust tae luck King James tae see,
Just look for a loon
Wi' a kingly croon,
Who shambles and slobbers, for that is he!"

Sae now they ride to the Eildon wood,
They seek a king wi' a goggling e'e,
And whiskers lank
And a spindly shank,
Wha drools in Latin—for sure 'tis he!

And now it's back to the dungeon tunnel, where nitre still drips from the festering walls, slimy things continue to wriggle underfoot, and Gilderoy, Godiva, Kylie, and Oor Kid await in breathless silence the return of Archie Noble, who has nipped upstairs to see how things are segashuating. We last saw him, remember, outlining a three-point plan for a) escape, b) rescuing the Charltons, and c) scuppering Operation Jimsnatch, the essence of which was that he, Gilderoy, and Oor Kid should sally aloft and batter the Spaniards into submission with their bare hands—perfectly feasible, he contended, since they would be three hardy Britons against a mere forty foreigners. On being reminded that the enemy were equipped with firearms, to say nothing of swords, pikes, and armour, whereas his side possessed only Clnzh's knife (Oor Kid's offer to use the Iron Maiden as a club proved impracticable when it was found to be too big to go through the door), he had been forced to rethink; hence his scout ahead to assess the situation.

Now he was returning, and his waiting friends caught the sound of his soft foot-fall, the barely audible rustle of his alert hair against the roof, the faint tap of his finger-tips as he guided himself by touch, and the sharp yowl as he walked into the wall. As he emerged into the guttering torch-light, nursing his knee, they saw that his stalwart cheek was pale, and cold fury was age-ing his boyish good looks by the second.

"Speak!" they whispered. "What gives?"

"Nay, 'tis too much!" quo' he, in trembling voice. "Those Castilian beasts are torturing the Charltons! Myself I saw it, creeping to the gallery whence I took a quick butchers into the vault where they lie bound . . . ah, the horror on't!" He paused, shuddering. "They brought from the kitchen great platters of tripe, which they thrust, all flopshus and steamy, down their collars; greasy black-puddings were bound i' their armpits, rum butter smeared on the inside of their socks—"

"Forbid it, heaven!" gasped Godiva, while Kylie stopped her ears. "Can even Dagoes be so cruel?"

"Worse was to come," tight-lipped Archie. "Flagons of ale were poured up their trouser-legs—"

"Not the Newcastle broon?" cried Oor Kid, aghast. "Nay, 'tis a' sticky an' claggy an' hellish! The dawty boogers!"

"—and new plate-cakes, gushing wi' juice, crammed piece-meal up their sleeves—"

"Bay heaven!" Gilderoy shook passionate fist, banging it painfully on the roof. "Never again will Ai show murcy to a Speniard!"

"You mean you have in the past?" asked Kylie. "When . . . just for interest?"

"A figure o' speech, demmit, to express mai caring end consurn!"

"Dids't find a way out?" demanded Godiva, sticking to essentials, and Archie shook reluctant head.

"Ai hev it!" exclaimed Gilderoy. "We must bai-pess the vault end win to the upper level where the Wizard hed his ops room—"

"Wizard? Who he?" asked bewildered Archie.

"The one Besset told us about—the Spenish mester-maind! You never met him—ekshully, he proved to be La Infamosa in dreg—"

"—wi' magic wand and hat right pointy," put in Godiva. "Aye, and wi' a cauldron wherein which he . . . she, I mean, might see all that passed i' the world!"

"Prithee, hang on! Why," demanded Archie, "should La Infamosa assume wizard guise?"

"Why but to hide her corset and falsies from the public view 'neath cloak o' Lurex, the ill-made tramp—"

"Ai think, sweet Godaiva," said Gilderoy, wi' diffident cough, "'twas rather to confuse counter-espionage, diverting ettention to Busty Besset es a precaution, rather than to conceal her physique—"

"Her physique, eh? Well, you should know all about that, thou wanton fondler, thou—"

"Nay, bate thy rage, dear lady," pleaded Archie. "For we must haste to this ops room right speedily, to see what it may offer. Right? So, follow all, silent as creeping mice for our lives!"

He led the way up the tunnel, ignoring the arch leading to the vault whence came the piteous cries of Charltons in torment, and the brutal laughter of their captors as they mercilessly applied tripe and plate-cake to their writhing victims. On and up they stole, Archie and Gilderoy to the fore, Godiva behind, then Kylie followed by Oor Kid, he breathing heavily and she squeaking and slapping as he pinched her through the bathrobe. By many a twist and turn they went . . . and then before them was light shining from a door ajar, and an unseen Glaswegian voice that glottaled right merrily:

". . . look, gaffer, it's true, Ah'm tellin' ye! This Wizard—the one that pit in th'emergency call tae heid office tae hiv his cauldron fixed—a right crabbit auld midden he wis . . . aye, weel, whenivver he loast his temper he kept turnin' me intae a' sorts o' things an' bodies. Is that no' right, fellas?"

"Right, enough, Hughie!" came a chorus of warlock voices. "He turned ye intae a puddock, an' Paul Newman, an' a wee hunchity-back so he did!"

"But when he pit aff his lang goon an' pointy hat, here he wisnae a wizard at a', but a right wee smasher in a black dress that she was fair burstin' oot o'—an' when she wisnae lookin' Ah pinched the wand—here it's, but! It's magic, gaffer!"

"Magic yer granny!" growled a deeper voice, and Archie, eye pressed to the crack of the door, saw that the warlock foreman, watched by his admiring mates, was displaying the wand to a warlock inspector in a bowler hat, evidently a new arrival.

"Here an' Ah'll show ye!" cried the foreman. "Haud still, Wullie!" He pointed the wand, and where a small warlock had been there suddenly stood a red-haired human in a yellow jersey.

"Inna name o' Asmodeus!" cried the warlock inspector. "Whit's yon?"

"A Partick Thistle goalkeeper," said the foreman. "Ah'll prove it . . . catch this, Wullie! See, he drapped it!"

"That's a helluva thing tae turn anybody intae!" The fore-man rummaged for a parchment. "Ah'll hivtae report this. We cannae hiv customers, wizards or wee smashers tho' they be, takin' liberties wi' oor employees! Here, how does it work?"

"Ah dae ken. Ah jist thought whit Ah wanted him tae be, an' p'inted the thing. See . . . noo he's Wullie again . . . Here, this is fun!"

So intent were the warlocks that they never heard the faint metallic *ping!* from beyond the doorway—it was Archie Noble being struck by the inspiration of the century. Such was its dazzling impact that he rocked on his perfect heels, quivering hand to genius-smitten brow . . . and then he was whispering urgently to Gilderoy and Oor Kid, while Godiva and Kylie stared in decorative attention, catching the excited words: "Right, I've got it! Here's what we do!," and wondering what new idiocy was taking shape behind that boyishly handsome countenance, its ruffled curls alight with can-do, chiselled lips and keen grey eyes illumined by a fighting smile of unparalleled brilliance.

The warlock foreman never knew what hit him. One moment he was falling about with mirth as he surveyed a row of Seven Dwarves, with the inspector as Snow White—and the next tanned heroic fingers had snatched his wand, one arm had been seized by what appeared to be a mountain gorilla in a steel cap, and the other by a handsome superman with a charred moustache who snarled: "Just tray something, shortie, end you've surviced yur lest cauldron!"

And now everything moved with lightning speed as Archie, wand in hand, faced the stricken Disneyfolk. "As you were!" he snapped, giving it a curt wave, and in an instant Snow White and Co. had resumed the shapes of seven confused warlocks in

overalls and one in a consternated bowler, all checking themselves to make sure there was nothing missing.

"Right, against the wall, legs apart, arms spread! Frisk 'em,
Charlton—and mark me, warlocks, this wand doth itch for
more employ, and I'm thinking slugs and crawlies, savvy?
Ladies, this is a big scene, so try to look apprehensive and
admiring—got kerchieves to twist, have you? Yes, yes, the hem
o' your bathrobe will do . . . Oh, splendid, dear Godiva, thy
ivory hand plucking bits from thy ruff . . . Right, Gilderoy,
bring that squirming mechanic over here, would you . . . by the
cauldron . . . come along, come along . . . time's burning up the
track . . ."

So bursting with zip and executive action was Archie that
Gilderoy's chin-beard stiffened resentfully, and little bits of
burned bristle sprang from his singed upper lip, but he contented himself with plonking down the warlock foreman in a
marked manner. Not so Godiva, her momentary pique at being
ordered about melting to admiration as she marked our hero's
brisk command and stylish port; patronising chauvinist he may
be, she thought, but he's a right little knee-trembler when he
gets masterful . . .

"Now, overalled fink," Archie addressed the scowling foreman, "they tell me this machine doth show what passeth i' the
great outdoors. So, unless ye would go into it head-first, show
me the King o' Scots his situation—now!"

Trembling, the warlock touched the remote control, and
before their startled eyes appeared a sunny forest clearing
where unhappy courtiers stood mumchance while burly retain-
ers tended a fire wherein burned meerschaums, briars, church-
wardens, packets o' twenty Players, Hoyo de Montereys, and
great store of cut plug. Shambling up and down, reading the

riot act and looking like a triumphant mandrill in a plumed bonnet, was a richly clad personage whose awkward gait, Latin pronunciation, and occasional slobbers could belong only to Jacobus Rex, and lurking in the background, fat and foiled, they espied the gaudy rotundity of Don Collapso.

"His Majesty's purson is preserved!" cried patriotic Gilderoy, all animus forgotten. "Jim for King, th'imposter ken't sing!"

"Aye . . . but what o' th'impostor?" quo' keen Archie, and at his behest the warlock switched channels while they watched in such suspense that Kylie began to chew her bathrobe and Godiva so far forget her wonted hauteur as to wrench the hated psychedelic ruff clean off her swan-like neck.

For there was the X-marked glade, and sweeping through it at full tilt, snatching the protesting impostor up to their saddlebows, were the Nixons, led by an exultant Sir Prising waving his snowy locks while his steel bonnet streamed in the wind, and roaring:

> *Noo Liddesdale has cotched the king,*
> *They hae lifted him up on the Eildon lee,*
> *The work is done*
> *The prize is won*
> *Noo bonnie residuals shall we see!*

They did it again, and then a third time, replacing the vainly protesting impostor in the glade and charging through to scoop him up for the benefit of ballad-mongers and woodcut engravers (who had appeared mysteriously, trust the Tudor paparazzi to have got wind of things) and who kept crying: "One more time! Look this way, Your Majesty! Great, just great . . ." Then they clustered round, asking how he felt, and had it come as a total surprise, and how did he think it would affect the succession to the English throne, always assuming the guid Scots lords (in their cork-heeled shoon) rustled up his ransom? To no avail did the impostor protest that he wasn't King James at all, but an itinerant Spaniard—in fact, he quickly gave up, with Sir Prising's wrathful eye fixed on him and Trouserless Will holding a poniard to his ear and muttering: "Look, mac, you're the bluidy king, get it! Think we've come a' this way tae snatch a phoney?" By the time he had been trussed and flung across Sir Prising's saddle, with the woodcut experts running alongside for one last quick carve and the balladeers demanding a final quote, he was proclaiming his royalty and assuring his auditors that he bore no grudge against his kidnappers, and forgave them freely. Finally, after the Nixons had posed, grinning, with their quarry, they thundered away towards Liddesdale, but not before Trouserless Will had been signed up to endorse a new line of bespoke reiving wear.

As the full import of what they had seen came home to the watchers, a silence fell on the Wizard's chamber . . . as so often happens when, suddenly, after a long and bitter struggle against impossible odds, the game is seen to be won, and the thing's done, quite unexpectedly and for reasons not fully understood . . . and it's all over. Archie was first to take it in, and while within him a football hooligan was yelling "Yahoo!" and punching the air, he schooled his speech to complacent nobility and modest candour.

"Ne'er was Dago deviltry more fittingly snootered!" said he. "They send an impostor to replace the king, and what befalls? The impostor gets nicked by mistake, while the true king is laughing sandbags! We may ne'er know what providence prevented Don Collapso from luring Sunny Jim to the spot marked X, or contrived that Bentos and Anguish should not be there to explain the snafu and, perchance, guide the snatch-gang to their true target. Providence, did I say?" He lifted prideful chin. "We did our bit! And proud am I to have captained such a team. Gilderoy, your hand. Mistress Delishe, ye ha' played a blinder. But what," he added, turning glowing gaze on Godiva, "can I say to thee, peerless pearl o' womanhood, wi'out whose steadfast support, timely assistance, girlish enthusiasm, and, dare I say it, inspirational love, I could never have—"

His stirring words drew emotional cries from his hearers. "Who says you keptained the demned team?" "Well, at least I can get out o' these beastly clothes at last—not that there'll be a rag fit to wear in this grisly hole!" "Oh, Goddy—little Kylie wants to go home! She's bushed, and like to weep!" and "Warraboot ma brithers doon yonder, then, sufferin' the tripe torture, ye selfish git!"

Concealing his chagrin at being interrupted just when he'd been hoping to embrace Godiva and murmur to her about broad sunlit uplands, Archie laid a hand on Oor Kid's grimy shoulder.

"All under control, honest fellow," he promised. "If you'll all just step this way . . ."

But Godiva and Kylie were already rummaging in a futile hunt for La Infamosa's wardrobe, and finding only cupboards full of skeletons, mandrake root, and necromantic equipment. Archie sighed, turned the warlocks into potted plants with a flick of his wand, and led the way nonchalantly down to the gallery overlooking the vault, where the captive Charltons lay moaning in congealed pools of tripe and rum butter, while their captors, sadism unsated, debated what further torments they might devise with tortillas and other Mediterranean dishes. Gilderoy and Oor Kid waited expectant as he rapped the balustrade with peremptory wand.

"Attention, Dagoes! Look this way, and watch the birdie!"

Automatically the forty Spanish soldiers turned, baring teeth and crying "Cheese!"—and suddenly there were forty stone statues grinning up at the gallery, some posed in matey groups, others showing their best sides. Archie flourished the wand airily.

"I thought of turning them into garden gnomes, but it occurred to me that as statues they'd make splendid ornaments on either side of the drive at one of Godiva's country places," he explained to an astonished Gilderoy. "A fitting wedding gift, from groom to bride, don't you agree?"

Gilderoy didn't, naturally, and he was not alone. For when the Charltons had been released and more or less de-triped, and Archie had spoken a few crisp words of commendation and told them they had twenty minutes to prepare for kit inspection, Wor Jackie expressed interest in the Spaniards' translation into sculpture. His brothers were already knocking experimental bits off the statues and daubing them in an extremely vulgar way, but they gathered round, goggling hairily, as Archie explained indulgently. Wor Jackie picked a thoughtful lump of black pudding from inside his shirt, and regarded the wand with a predatory leer.

"Girraway!" he pondered. "An' it can turn fowk intae owt ye like, ye say? Wat'll they think o' next, eh?" He shook shaggy head in admiration. "Can onybody work it, gaffer?"

"So it would seem . . . Here—give that back!"

For the wand had been deftly snatched from his hand, and

before our hero could stay him, Wor Jackie had sprung away, snaggle teeth bared in an unholy grin, designer stubble bristling wickedly, and his bellow of unbelievably dirty laughter echoed booming through the vault as he waved the wand at the Spanish statues.

Archie turned—and gulped in disbelief, for where petrified soldiery had stood, there were now forty voluptuous dancing girls in gauzy trousers and flimsy veils, undulating in beauteous bewilderment. He had a fleeting impression of tresses blonde, red, and sable, of kohl-darkened eyes and crimson lips, of complexions from creamy white to dusky gold—and then he was striding forward in subalternly outrage.

"Put those women back at once!" he cried, and grabbed for the wand, but succeeded only in dashing it from the reiver's grasp. It spun in the air, a whirl of silver light, struck the stone floor, rolled slowly across it to one of the narrow fissures—and was gone in an instant, down to unknown volcanic depths. But the forty damosels were still there, and as the Charltons roared in delight, Archie's first irrelevant thought was: someone's going to have to write to those Spaniards' next of kin; well, it's not going to be me. And his second thought was: who'd have thought that an uncouth primitive like Wor Jackie had ever heard of the *Arabian Nights?*

He became aware of the Charlton's massive paw on his shoulder.

"Ye can blaw the gaff on me an' the lads tae UPRAT if ye feel like it," grinned Wor Jackie. "We'll not be gan reivin' for a while anyways." He crushed Archie's hand in a mighty grip. "A' the very best, lad. It's been nice knawin' ye." He swung round to address his brethren. "Noo, then, tek time! There's forty o' them—that's fower for me, an' three each for the rest o' ye. So joost haud back, noo, while we git them fell in an' sorted oot . . . A'reet, lassies, fattest on't reet, slimmest on't left, an' git thasels numbered aff . . ."

Baffled and flat-footed, our hero did the only thing possible for a junior commander when stroppy other ranks are beyond the scope of disciplinary action: he left abruptly. After all, he reasoned, his priority must now be to hasten to King James to urge instant action against the scattered conspirators, apprise His Majesty of his narrow escape, and point out (in all modesty, hem-hem) to whom he owed his preservation. As he observed to Gilderoy, if they didn't tell him, he'd never know, and what was the good of enduring one dam' thing after another if you didn't get some credit at the end of the day?

So they shot upstairs again, closing their ears to the excited giggles and enthusiastic guffaws as the Charltons introduced themselves to the new arrivals, collected Godiva and Kylie, heaved a resigned sigh over the row of potted plants, on one of which hung a bowler hat, and descended once more to the dungeon to scoop up La Infamosa for delivery to the authorities.

But when they reached that grim chamber, she was gone, leaving not a wrack nor stiletto heel behind, and to this day her disappearance remains unexplained, tho' old borderers still re-tell the legend of a mysterious mini-broom, piloted by an Amazonian pygmy and having as its sole passenger a veiled beauty in a slinky black number, which landed briefly at Gretna for re-fuelling ere its vapour trail vanished into the southern sky.

EPILOGUE

And now 'tis evenfall in the brave and beautiful Borderland, and long shadows fall across the smooth lawns and fragrant garden* of the hunting lodge which King James has booked for the weekend. Our principals are among those enjoying, more or less, the royal hospitality, but as Archie Noble paces the croquet lay-out in the twilight, cursing absently as he trips o'er a hoop, his normally serene brow is knit like a moody jersey, and he plucks distempered chin wi' disconsolate fingers. For alas! His Scottish Majesty, on hearing from our heroes' lips the mind-boggling tale of Operations Jimsnatch and Heretic, hasn't believed one stricken word of it—well, Gilderoy, knowing his monarch, never thought he would. For one thing, being of a

---

* Fragrant—in February? Certainly; spring came early in 159–.

timorous nature, James just *hates* to think he's been in mortal
danger, and for another, he wouldn't take Gilderoy's word for
the time of day, nor does he regard Archie, a confessed English
agent, as being any more reliable. Indeed, only with difficulty
has His shaken Majesty been restrained from consigning them
both to the coop for trying to spread alarm and despondency.

Fortunately for them, if not for Archie's amour propre, the
intercession of Lady Godiva Dacre, flower of the English
court, breath-taking dish, and confidante of the royal lady who
is James's chief hope for the future, has saved the day. He has
harkened to her, all right, with goggle right rapt and drools of
stricken wonder in both Scots and Latin, and believed her the
more readily because of all those fascinating details anent magic
wands and cauldrons—subjects dear to His Majesty's heart, not
least because they will give him an additional chapter for his
scholarly master-work, *Daemonologie*. Indeed, once he has
praised her courage and beauty, and ordered every comfort and
attention for her and Kylie, he has scampered off to start scrib-
bling, while couriers ride post haste to Edinburgh to hold the
presses for this sensational new material. Even the pressing
need to deal with Don Collapso, who has barricaded himself in
the toilet and is bawling diplomatic immunity, must wait as the
royal quill crackles o'er eager parchment.

But while King James is happily employed, what of our
four? Do they enjoy well-earned repose, hot baths, change of
underwear, well-cooked dinners, feet up wi' contented sighs,
etc., after all their shifts and stratagems, perils and onfalls and
escapes? Don't you believe it. They may have saved the old
country from the most fatal menace between the Armada and
the Maastricht Treaty, the strife and tumult may be happily
past—but what o' the romantic angle, eh? Who gets the girl(s)?

Or, for feminist readers, who gets the satisfaction of raising two fingers to our heroes with a resounding Bronx cheer and going on to career fulfilment? That's the question, gossips, and four young hearts are torn, and eight young feet are shuffling in passionate impatience . . . down there, in the dusky garden, for instance . . .

"Oh, come on, Noble, be a men end edmit defeat! Godaiva hes been maine from the furst—demmit, if Ai go wi'in three feet o' her she moans end gives et the knees!"

"Aye, o'erwhelmed by thy beastly after-shave, belike! Face up to it, Gilderoy, 'twixt thy cheap glamour and my solid worth, 'tis no contest! Anyway, I'm English, and she knows I won't rifle her handbag on the honeymoon—aye, think on that, jewel-thief!—or go hot-lipping after the likes of Busty Basset and La Infamosa—"

"Thet was in the laine of duty, you swaine!"

"Oh, yeah? She'll never be sure of that, though, will she?"

"Yur traying mai patience, Noble! Look, sirrah, put your pession where yur mouth is! Propose, end see what heppens!"

"For thy information, I already have, before dinner—"

"Wi' skent success, Ai warrant me! She gave ye the gate—"

"No such thing! She was choosing frocks, or something, and answered not 'Yea' nor 'Nay' but 'Anon, anon, sir, prithee come back later.' Which is more than you'll get, Jock!"

"Thet's where yur wrong, Sessenech! Know, thet Ai too hev pressed mai suit, end em confident o' success!"

"Why, what said she?"

"Turned pink end whaite, end fled to the bathroom wi' mingled craies of love end hate . . . just playing hurd to get, obviously . . ."

A long silence. Then:

"Oh, let's not kid ourselves. Her fond heart is riven betwixt us."

"Ai hate to edmit it, but yur probably raight. Ah, dear gurl, 'tis a cruel dilemma! Mai heart bleeds for her."

"Mine, too. So . . . there's only one answer. We must decide for her."

"Toss up, ye mean?"

"Faugh! Nay, we must leave her no choice. One of us twain . . . has got to go!"

"Where? Oh, ye mean purrmanently? Beyond recoll? Oll the way to the crematorium?"

"Precisely."

"Thet's ruther drestic, is't not? Ai mean, Erchie—may Ai coll you Erchie? . . . or Erchibald, that's a leff!—we've hed our differences, but Ai'd not laightly shed thy blood—"

"Don't worry, you won't . . . Ebeneezer . . ."

"Thet did it! Noble, you ret-ketcher, will you wock!"

"With thee, fellow, cheek by jowl!"

"Raight! Efter thee, caitiff!"

"After you, recreant!"

"Ai insist, reskal!"

"Don't you insist with me, mate . . ."

And in the silken comfort of the boudoir upstairs . . . "Ah, aid me, gentle Kylie! My fond heart is riven betwixt them! Oh, 'tis cruel dilemma . . . tell me, tell me, which am I to choose? Nay, answer me not, for well I know thou'lt give the nod to Noble, being thyself enamoured of that false lovely Scot, thou scheming, randy marplot! Not that I blame you, for when I think on him I moan and give at the knees—the two-timing, bijou-snaffling adorable wretch! Ah, how I yearn for him—and despise him . . . and, certes, Noble is a comely hunk of proven worth and stalwart inches, sexy, yet staunch and true, such as will stay home o' nights, nor hock the family silver . . . but don't start boosting him again, false friend, to serve thine own base ends—"

"Nay, Goddy, do me right! 'Tis true I fancy Gildy, but for a trip to Brighton only! Marriage is another ball o' wax, and frankly, who needs to buy a cow when you can knock a bottle of milk off any doorstep—"

"Oh, hard of heart, 'neath outward innocence! You speak of trips to Brighton, I of consuming love! The trouble is, I don't know for whom! Both? Neither? Half and half? Nay, I cannot . . . but stay! What is that noise I hear without? Clash o' steel, 'neath my window? At this time of night, for heaven's sake—does nobody in Scotland ever go to bed—?"

"Goddy, it's them! They're at it, foot and hand—for love o' thee, I'll bet! Haste, haste, you lucky girl! Gosh, look at that Gilderoy, his blade a flickering ubiquitous menace as he lunges low i' th'Italian style . . . mind you, Noble's jolly nimble, and plays wi' elbow close and beezer wrist-work . . . here, how about twelve to seven on who draws first blood?"

But even as Godiva swept distraught towards the window, pausing only to check that her complexion was suitably pale, select a stout kerchief for frantic finger-twisting, and snatch up some small change, a heavy knocking smote upon the chamber door. She stopped at once, and Kylie shot to her side, for both knew official knuckle-work when they heard it and were too well-schooled in courtly protocol to be caught hanging o'er window-sills giving the slow handclap and cries of "Quit waltzing, you bums!" Godiva seated herself with a look of queenly hauteur, slipping languid finger into a slim copy of Dr. Lopez's treatise on dieting, and Kylie stood by with hands demurely folded, as the door opened, a flunkey announced: "His Excellency the Russian Ambassador!," and in rolled Akim Tamiroff, beaming right smarmily, accompanied by a seven-foot Cossack of magnificent physique, rippling beard, hawk-like profile, and burning eye, clad in a fur hat and overcoat covered with those things that look like gold cigars. Kylie took one look at him and clung to a table for support, murmuring "Eureka!"

"L[e]dd[iz], I grit you!" said the ambassador, louting low. "End grittings also fram my impirrial master, Czar of all the Rooshas! Yar purdon a minnit," he added, drawing a miniature from his bosom, peering at it, then at Godiva, and bowing again. "Okeh! Y'are the Leddy Dykers, I theenk? Sure, jus' lak picksher, bot ivven byootifooler, eh, Count Alexis?" The Cossack stamped snowy boots and boomed like an organ. "Bolshoi barroom!" he agreed—yet his glowing gaze was fixed on fluttering Kylie, her heaving eyes and downcast bosom testimony to her agitation.

Tamiroff waved a plump hand. "Okeh. Enoff preleeminaries. To bizzness. You forgive, Leddy Dykers, my lousy Eenglish." He took a breath and announced: "My impirrial master, Czar of all the Rooshas, has sin your picksher. Teks wan look, says: 'Slava Bogu, that my Czarina, no argument. Spik with Tamiroff in Scotland, tell him this Leddy Dykers las' heard of north of Eengland, seek her out, mek proposal merridge. Okeh?' " He paused, snapping plump fingers, and the enormous Alexis whipped a huge valise from beneath his coat and upended it, pouring out a glittering cascade of jewellery on to the carpet. Before the startled eyes of our fair duo, it grew rapidly to a shimmering heap which swamped Tamiroff over the ankles. He gave Alexis a look, stepped out of the priceless pile, and continued.

"This my eentrodoction, lak colling card, okeh? My impirrial master ollso say, tell Leddy Dykers I geev her haff Siberia, ninety meelion serfs, an' as moch gold an' fur coats an' caviar as ten thousan' moujiks can carry—beeg moujiks, too, no leetle squeerts. Oll that," he shrugged, "is for engagement presen'. More later, efter married—palaces, provinces, mink hats, salt-mines, you name it." The ambassador paused, considering. "That oll, I theenk. I deescharge my embassy. I weary you wit' a lotta words, mebbe, bot my impirrial master say, 'Tell Tamiroff be deeplomatic, thiz Eenglish don' lak rosh theengs.' So, pardon my prolixitee, okeh?"

He assumed an expression of polite inquiry, while Godiva masked shattered amazement behind a beauteously blank countenance. Kylie, for her part, appeared to have heard not a word, so riveted were her baby-blues on the heroic figure of Count Alexis, who returned her regard with Rasputinish magnetism and a soft rumbling growl. With an effort, her ladyship recovered her inner composure, tried to think of something to say, decided it was beneath her dignity to vouchsafe any immediate reply, and resolved to stick to small talk for the moment.

"My thanks, good sir," said she, and inclined her splendid coiffure half a millimetre, "to you and your imperial master. Yet forgive me, for we didn't do Russia at school. Thy Czar—is he not known as Ivan the Terrible?"

Tamiroff did a doubtful scowl. "I don' theenk so. Not when we leave home. Hey, Alexis, which Czar we got now?"

"Who knows?" resounded the mighty count, stroking his beard ardently at Kylie. "Boris Godunov, mebbe."

Kylie tore her eyes from him to whisper a warning to her friend. "Watch it, Goddy," she cautioned. "Isn't he the noisy one?"

"Whoever," shrugged Tamiroff. "My impirrial master ollso say: 'Eef the Leddy Dykers don' say okeh right away, tell her I geev her the Caucasus as well. Bot after that, nawtheeng, no deal. Geev her two minnits, mebbe, then we try for thee Torkish dame, dotter of Sooblime Porte.'" He sighed. "Okeh, leddy, you got the Caucasus. Now you permeet I weethdraw, com' back two minnits. Okeh? Reverse grittings, leddies. Le's go, Alexis."

He bowed his tubby way out, and Alexis followed with a last suppressed growl in Kylie's direction. The door closed, and the dazed blonde turned bug-eyed to Godiva.

"Did . . . you . . . see . . . that? Was he real, or did I dream him? And did the small fatso say what I think he said?" She clutched astonished cheeks with trembling hands. "Gosh, Goddy—Czarina of all the doodahs! 'Tis fantasy stuff! And did ye clock that gorgeous giant i' the mink topee? Wow! Imagine sleigh-riding with that under a fur rug! And he's a Count . . . Countess Kylie of Slobovia or wherever . . . And thou the consort of Muscovy's top banana . . . Nay, but 'tis not on, is it? I mean, no more Benenden reunions or tea at 4 p.m., exile, nothing but snow and peasants . . . and groovy musclemen with beards . . ." She pouted, sighing, and marked her companion's abstracted state. "Hey, Goddy, wake up—I speak to thee, old thing! How are you going to give 'em the tactful brush, Goddy? What are you going to do?"

Lady Godiva stood in pensive silence, her lovely face serene, her dainty toe stirring, as in disdain, the priceless pile of loot at her feet. Then she turned, and as the distant clash of steel and cries of "Stend end faight!" and "Sa-ha to you, too!" floated through the open casement, a fond smile trembled her crimson lips, and a crystal tear blipped from her violet eye and bounced in spray from her soft cheek. She sighed, and shook her Titian head.

"Do?" she said dreamily, and then snapped out of it with decision. "Well, for a start ye can close that window!"

And now it's dawn, and as he swings rather awkwardly into the saddle of faithful Garscadden, and curses the scratches received in last night's duello, Bonny Gilderoy muses on the inconstancy of the fair sex, and decides that he'll get over it. He shakes his handsome head at the thought of Archie Noble, similarly scratched, whom he has left writing his report to Walsingham, describing how the devildoms of Spain have been frustrated, and delicately hinting—nay, pleading, beseeching, and finally demanding—that if Her Majesty wishes to requite him, will she please, please have him posted to the Moscow Embassy as military attaché, or cipher clerk, or boot-boy, even.

Well, good luck to him, thinks Gilderoy, and as he shades his eyes to gaze along the eastern road where the Russian Ambassador's retinue is setting forth for Leith with its precious double burden he smiles, and sighs, and reflects on his own future. His hand strays to the plump wallet inside his shirt, to reassure himself that the Dacre Diamonds are still there, as they have been through all his adventures and costume changes, including the tweed trunk hose. (Well, you never really believed he'd handed them in, did you?) On the whole, he decides, he'd be better out of Scotland for a while—England, too, for that matter . . . How about Ireland? Yes, under a false name . . . Protheroe? Capstick? Pym? No, something a shade more dashing, and slightly sinister . . . Brand, or Strang, perhaps, or Gaunt . . . no, he's got it—Blood. Yes, that has a nice picaresque ring to it.

Yet as he rides through the gate, he wonders if he has seen the last of those brief acquaintances . . . the lovely ivory face and parted crimson lips framed in the red-gold glory of her hair, the pert laughing blue eyes and golden curls, the reckless fighting smile of his rival-comrade . . . and all those others, friends and foes . . . Well, who knows? Perhaps, another day . . .

He puts his horse to the green slope at the gallop, and in a twinkling is over the crest and away, and the border hills lie silent and lonely under the darkling clouds. All in a moment, it's over and gone, so suddenly that you wonder if the mad rascals and fair ladies, the wily conspirators and eccentric adventurers, the anti-smoking monarch and tartan toper and morioned Spaniards and wizards and warlocks and hairy reivers and evil beauties and Amazon pygmies, were ever there at all.

Well, perhaps they weren't *there* . . . but they're *here*.

A NOTE ABOUT THE AUTHOR

George MacDonald Fraser was born in England and schooled in Scotland, served in a Highland regiment in India, Africa, and the Middle East, and died on the Isle of Man in 2008. In addition to twelve volumes of the *Flashman Papers* and several other novels, Fraser wrote screenplays, most notably for Richard Lester's *The Three Musketeers* and for the James Bond film *Octopussy.*

A NOTE ON THE TYPE

Pierre Simon Fournier *le jeune,* who designed the type used in this book, was both an originator and a collector of types. His services to the art of printing were his design of letters, his creation of ornaments and initials, and his standardization of type sizes. His types are old style in character and sharply cut. In 1764 and 1766 he published his *Manuel typographique,* a treatise on the history of French types and printing, on typefounding in all its details, and on what many consider his most important contribution to typography—the measurement of type by the point system.

Composed by Creative Graphics, Inc.,
Allentown, Pennsylvania

Printed and bound by R. R. Donnelley,
Harrisonburg, Virginia

Designed by Soonyoung Kwon